To Captain Janeway the creature resembled nothing so much as a dragon out of old Earth legends.

But what arms, strong and ending in sharp-clawed fingers, and what a head.

It was snakelike in form, a shapely diamond. Incongruously large, gentle eyes filled with concern graced a head that narrowed into a pointed muzzle. There were no teeth visible at the moment. The back of the head tapered into a long, sinuous neck that broadened at the base to very human-appearing shoulders. A heavy, multifaceted pendant, winking silvery in the light, hung about that throat. A white mane of hair decorated the head and continued down the length of the neck.

Its voice, as translated by the computer, was completely feminine.

"We have picked up your signal, Captain Janeway. Dare we hope that you have come to help us?"

Look for STAR TREK Fiction from Pocket Books

Star Trek: The Original Series

Star Trek: The Next Generation

Star Trek: Deep Space Nine

Star Trek: Voyager

STAR TREK VOYAGER™

THE MURDERED SUN

CHRISTIE GOLDEN

POCKET BOOKS

New York   London   Toronto   Sydney   Tokyo   Singapore

An *Original* Publication of POCKET BOOKS

POCKET BOOKS, a division of Simon & Schuster Inc.
1230 Avenue of the Americas, New York, NY 10020

Copyright © 1996 by Paramount Pictures. All Rights Reserved.

A VIACOM COMPANY

STAR TREK is a Registered Trademark of Paramount Pictures.

This book is published by Pocket Books, a division of Simon & Schuster Inc., under exclusive license from Paramount Pictures.

ISBN: 0-671-53783-0

First Pocket Books printing February 1996

10   9   8   7   6   5   4   3   2   1

Printed in the U.S.A.

This book,
my first flight among the stars,
is dedicated to my friend and colleague

Roger MacBride Allen,

who has, in the time that I have known him,
made me laugh, think, and dare to fly.

Thanks, Rog.

CHAPTER

1

IT WAS NEVER TRULY SILENT ABOARD THE *STARSHIP VOYAGER*. There was always far too much going on for that—the activities of the crew at all hours, whether on duty or off; the constant faint sounds of machinery operating smoothly and efficiently as it had been designed to do. These were all sounds that Kathryn Janeway had learned to know and love through years aboard starships, serving in one capacity or another as she forged a career that had earned her this command, this ship, this crew.

She shifted in the smooth, dark blue sheets, trying to mentally transform the faint, constant hum of her ship into the comforting white noise that had so often eased her insomnia into much-needed rest. But it did not seem that it was going to happen tonight. She buried her face against the pillow, trying to shut off her mind, which insisted on working busily even though the timecounter told her it was 02:32.

Her mind did not cooperate. It persisted in finding things to seize on and gnaw at worriedly. Janeway smiled a little at the image; it reminded her of Molly Malone, when that faithful dog had gotten hold of one of Mark's shoes and decided that it made the finest plaything in the world.

The smile faded. *Mark, I miss you.* Every night, as she prepared for sleep, Janeway promised herself sternly that she would not wear the smooth pink satin nightgown Mark had given her as a going-away present. She did not need the unnecessary physical token. It only sharply reminded her of all that she and her crew had been ripped away from. She told herself this quite brusquely. Yet every night, she disobeyed her own orders, donning the sleek garment and brushing out her long hair while staring at a picture of a smiling Mark and a grinning, tongue-lolling Irish setter.

By day, busy with either major or minor activities, Janeway could banish intrusive thoughts of her loved ones to the back of her mind. There was certainly an overabundance of things to do, plenty of problems to solve, more than enough people to worry about on this, perhaps the strangest mission upon which a Starfleet vessel had ever embarked. But at night . . . Ah, at night, alone in her too large bed in her too empty quarters, her own worries and needs crowded upon her and would not let her be.

Janeway grimaced at her own melancholia. *This is ridiculous. If I can't sleep, I might as well get up and do something.*

She sat up, reached for a brush, and began brushing her reddish brown mane into obedience.

"Computer," she called, "what is the status of holodeck one?"

"Holodeck one is not in use," replied the computer in its prim, crisp female voice.

"Then reserve it for my use," said Janeway. She swung her legs out of bed. Normally, she'd continue the conversation, asking the computer to replicate a specific costume. But in the months since the mysterious Caretaker had brought them to this quadrant, she had taken to keeping outfits rather than unduly taxing the replicator. It was an order she had issued almost at once. It was a good thing that the holodeck's energy did not have to be rationed, and she did not begrudge her strained, hard-working crew appropriate attire for the mental and physical exercises a jaunt on the holodeck provided, but for the foreseeable future they'd have to do as they did in "olden days" and take care of the clothing they did have.

Which suddenly makes closet space a premium, she mused wryly as she looked over her collection of costumes.

A ball gown from Earth's Regency period in England. A muslin dress from that same planet's western pioneer days. The sleek, inviting garb of a Marillian gem trader. The prim, proper garb of a British governess. She shook her head. None of these suited her present brooding state of mind.

"I want to fight something," she announced aloud. She had just found the perfect outfit—the garb of a twenty-second-century Orion pirate—when Tuvok's calm voice broke her mood.

"Tuvok to Janeway."

Instantly alert, Janeway absently rehung the forgotten garb. "Janeway here." Her voice was crisp, in control once again, her fleeting depression banished as always before the overwhelming need of performing her duty. "What is it, Mr. Tuvok?"

"I apologize for disturbing you during your off shift, Captain, but we have picked up some signals that are . . . most interesting. I suggest you come up to the bridge and examine them for yourself."

Before he had even finished speaking, Janeway had seized one of her uniforms. She laid it on the bed, her long fingers working nimbly to gather up her thick mass of hair, twist it, and pin it into place. There was no trace of self-pity on her features now. Her eyes snapped with excitement even as she tried to quell the hope that bubbled within her.

She had not served with the Vulcan this long without learning to decipher the subtle inflections of his almost purring voice. He had at least a dozen different ways of saying *interesting,* and by the way he'd pronounced it just now, there might be something to look forward to when she reached the bridge.

She forced the excitement out of her own voice as she replied, "I'm on my way."

A flash of amber eyes lit with warm amusement. A quick flick of gray tail, the smell of musk, the soft sound of wise feet on green grass.

She had come for him again tonight, and Chakotay, his lids tightly closed over his rapidly moving eyes, rose in his dream state and followed her silent call.

He rose without moving from the bed, his mind

following even as his body slept deeply, restfully. She seemed always to send revitalizing sleep when she came to visit.

He stood, his brown body fit and firm, clothed only in the loincloth of his ancestors, and smiled down with respect and love at the animal spirit who waited for him. Though it was dark in this dreamscape, a verdant forest illuminated only by a quarter moon, Chakotay knew the place well. He could come here by quiet meditation on his own, by day or night, in any season. For tonight's tryst, she had brought him a summer evening, and Chakotay closed his dark eyes and breathed deeply the heady scents of honeysuckle and cool moss, the furry musk of the unseen creatures who shared the realm of the subconscious with him.

It was real, yet it was only in his mind. Janeway had never said anything, but he suspected that she had problems understanding that the animal guides were very real and, at the same time, solely a product of one's inner consciousness. Most who were not of Chakotay's people had problems with that concept. Of all the crew, Chakotay suspected that only Tuvok, the Vulcan, whose own people had spent centuries unlocking the secret powers of the mind, could really understand that the two realities were not diametrically opposed. But then again, Tuvok would never admit to the powerful, primal joy that surged through one who was visited by an animal spirit.

Connections. It was all about connections, with oneself, one's totem, one's people, one's friends, one's world . . . one's universe.

But right now, with the cool night wind in his face, the wet grass beneath his feet, and his friend waiting for him with her lambent yellow eyes, Chakotay wasn't concerned with connections or concepts.

He just wanted to run. And so he did, his bare feet flying across the grass and stone and leaves without a care, for there was nothing here that would harm him and he knew it. Silent as a shadow, she moderated her swift lope to keep pace with him. Together, with stars he had seen in no sky outside of his own mind sparkling overhead, they ran. Chakotay's skin began to glisten with sweat and dew. His breathing came hard, but he kept moving, his strong limbs pumping. Laughing kindly, her tongue lolling from her own exertions, she ran with him until at last they came to an open meadow, and Chakotay, gasping for breath, staggered to a halt and collapsed in the welcoming, cooling grass.

He rolled over onto his back and she joined him, plopping herself down and rolling happily as if she were a mere newborn. He laughed and reached for her. Her gray fur almost glowing in the soft radiance of the moon, she snuggled into his loving embrace, placing her beautifully shaped head on his chest.

But she did not fully relax, and after a moment, he thought to her: *What is wrong, my friend?*

Nothing is wrong, she replied without a sound. *But there will not always be time for mirth and laughter, my playmate and friend.*

Tell me. Chakotay sat up, reaching to touch the animal spirit behind the ears in a gentle gesture.

She fixed him with her keen gaze. *You are a teacher. You are also a student. You teach the ways of your people. That is easy to do. What is harder to do is to be wise and teach the ways of people you do not know.*

Chakotay shook his head, not comprehending. *But how do I teach what I do not know?*

The amber eyes narrowed, and he knew she was laughing. *That is the challenge, is it not?*

He had just opened his mouth to reply when a sharp whistle sounded—in his real ears, not inside his head. The dreamscape vanished, dissipating like the sand paintings of the Navajo at the end of the Sing. Chakotay opened his eyes, calm, fully awake, in his own quarters.

"All senior officers, report to the bridge at once."

Janeway's voice. Tense. Hopeful? He wouldn't know till he reached the bridge. The dream and his friend's typically cryptic advice would have to wait.

By the time the complete senior staff had assembled on the bridge, which was still dimly lit in deference to the early hour, Janeway was experiencing a sinking feeling of déjà vu.

There it was on Tuvok's console, a subspace disturbance that was, as of yet, only registering on subspace bands. All the necessary ingredients for a typical wormhole seemed to be present: verteron emanations, tanali secondary particles. All the things that Ensign Harry Kim, fresh faced and hopeful, had found once before. That incident had led to an almost excruciating disappointment. As she met Tuvok's dark brown eyes, she read caution in their depths. She didn't need the warning. She'd once encouraged hope above all else. Hope did need to spring eternal aboard the *Voyager,* but it needed to be tempered by prudence.

"Full illumination," she told the computer, which

obliged by instantly raising the lights. There could be no true night on a starship, of course; the difference between "night" and "day" was purely artificial, but the regular cycles provided a sense of comfort and stability to a largely human crew used to normal planetary cycles. The crew on duty, other than the senior officers, were the third shift, but they would operate more efficiently in "daylight."

Chakotay and Paris entered the bridge together. Janeway allowed herself a slight spark of pleasure. They were getting along much better these days, the big Indian and the slim, cocky youth—just like two senior officers should. Curiosity burned in both blue and brown orbs as they glanced over at her. She waved them forward and let them see what she had seen, saw the glances that passed between them, knew that they were thinking exactly what she had thought.

Harry Kim had already examined the evidence and was at his station with it pulled up on his own screen. He looked as if he were trying to be stoic, and indeed a hint of remembered disappointment sat upon his open, friendly features.

Sensors also showed that the solar system in which it was located had a star and several planetary bodies, but those were of secondary importance to Janeway at the moment.

"As you can see, gentlemen," said Janeway, "it's got all the earmarks of a wormhole. This," she said, tapping a graphic, "is what worries me."

They could all see the analysis the computer had provided: an indication of heavy gamma and X-ray activity along with a great deal of degenerate matter. Chakotay's face, like Tuvok's, revealed little emotion, but Janeway saw the concern fall like a hawk's shadow across the dark Indian features.

Tom Paris, on the other hand, tried hard to look wise, but by the way he kept glancing back and forth at the others, Janeway knew that he wasn't quite putting two and two together. She suspected that Paris, capable and occasionally brilliant as he was, hadn't put studying first on his priority list at Starfleet Academy.

"This sort of activity generally indicates a black hole rather than a wormhole," she explained.

"Although the readings for the two phenomena are not entirely dissimilar," put in Tuvok. "For many decades it was widely believed that a wormhole could not exist outside of a black hole."

Paris snorted slightly. "A wormhole inside a black hole is about as helpful as no wormhole at all. We might get back to the Alpha Quadrant, but we'd be an awful mess by the time we got there."

Janeway strode down to her chair and seated herself, crossing her legs and settling in. "Lieutenant Paris does have a point. We've been closer than we'd like to singularities before," she said. "Mr. Kim, how far out of our way would following up on this take us?"

Kim glanced down. "Not far at all, Captain. We're almost heading directly for it as is."

Janeway made her decision. "Then let's go check it out. Mr. Paris, make adjustments to our course and take us to it."

Paris was already in his seat, his knowledgeable fingers flying with practiced ease over the controls. "Course adjusted, Captain."

Janeway stifled a yawn. "Let's go slowly. Drop to warp two. Mr. Kim, keep your eyes glued to your controls. I want to be able to see that thing coming long before we get anywhere near it, is that understood?"

"Yes, ma'am—Captain," Kim hastily corrected. Janeway didn't glance back at her Operations officer; she didn't need to see him to know that he'd be blushing at his slip of the tongue. Janeway always preferred "Captain" to "ma'am."

She settled down to wait. After a while, Janeway fought back another yawn. Now that the initial excitement was fading, she realized just how tired she was from a long night of . . . well, of not sleeping. She had just risen, about to give Chakotay the bridge and head into her ready room for an increasingly rare cup of hot black coffee, when Kim's voice halted her.

"Captain . . . I'm picking up readings of debris ahead."

"Slow to impulse. Put it on screen." At first glance, there appeared to be nothing other than the comforting, familiar starfield. "Magnify."

Now Janeway and the others could see them—the blasted, broken remains of what had once been vessels of some sort. Engrossed, Janeway leaned forward in her chair.

"I don't like the look of this. Not one bit." She hit her comm badge. "Janeway to Neelix." There was a long pause. "Neelix, come in please."

"Captain," came the Talaxian's normally chipper voice, thick and slurry with sleep, "do you have any idea what time it is?"

She heard a chuckle from Tom Paris, but she wasn't amused at all. "It's *time* for you to come up to the bridge and answer some questions for me," she retorted, an irritated edge creeping into her voice.

There was a soft, female murmur—Kes's quiet voice, doubtless urging him to comply—and finally Neelix growled, "Very well. On my way."

Janeway stood and planted her hands on her hips, her chin tilted up in an unconscious gesture of defiance. She strode toward the screen, her gaze roving over the corpses of ships whose pilots and crew had long since disappeared. They whirled past the *Voyager* in the cold silence of space, drifting close to the ship's shields before being gently repelled.

"Mr. Tuvok, analysis." She did not take her eyes from the screen.

"Some of this debris has been floating here for a very long time," replied the Vulcan, his alert mind working and analyzing almost as swiftly as the computer. "The further we go toward this disturbance, the newer the debris becomes. Judging from the rate of drift, I would estimate that all of these ships met their fate in Section 4039."

"Directly where we're heading," said Chakotay softly.

"Precisely." Tuvok's smooth, dark face was as tranquil as if he had just emerged from a deep meditation.

Janeway envied him his composure. She took a deep breath. "How technologically advanced are these ships? Any theories as to what destroyed them?"

"If you are asking if our vessel is technologically

superior, the answer is yes. I am unable to determine the method of their destruction at the present time. I do not have enough information to extrapolate."

"Captain," interrupted Kim, "we're being hailed. There's some sort of vessel up ahead—about twenty thousand kilometers away."

"On screen." There it was, a knobby, diamond-shaped buoy made of a dull gray material. "Where the hell is Neelix when you need—*there* you are!"

Neelix still looked as if he had just woken up. His horsetail hair was unbrushed and stuck out wildly, and the side whiskers that were his pride and joy had not been combed. He blinked sleepily, but he was, fortunately, adequately dressed.

"Yes, yes," he grumbled, padding down to join Janeway in front of the screen, "here I am, at your beck and—oh, my."

He froze as he glanced casually up at the screen. His small, yellow eyes grew enormous, and his mouth dropped.

"Open a hailing frequency, Mr. Kim," said Janeway, her mental warning alarms going off like mad. "Let's see what this buoy has to say to us."

Kim obliged. There was a few seconds' silence while the translator speedily dealt with deciphering a completely unknown language by cross-referencing and adjusting faster than any human mind could calculate. The quiet pause seemed unduly long to Janeway, but finally the computer was able to play the message in English.

Words emerged, the computer rendering them neutral against the hostile sound of the speaker's natural voice—a voice that was closer to an animal's bellow than to what issued from a human throat. The sound rumbled, still audible beneath the message, deep and gravelly, as if the communication had been torn from a throat that was more accustomed to roaring in wordless fury than in rasping out a coherent message.

"Attention, alien vessel. You have violated Akerian space. Retreat immediately. We will not tolerate trespassers. You will be destroyed. Attention, alien vessel. You have violated Akerian space. Retreat—"

"Turn it off, Mr. Kim," snapped the captain. "I've heard enough." The unpleasant voice stilled at once. Janeway leveled her piercing gaze upon the Talaxian, who almost literally shrank away from it. "Neelix, I take it you know these . . . people."

Beneath his spots, the little alien grew pale. "Um, well, I've never had the dubious pleasure of actually *meeting* an Akerian, if that's what you mean."

A vein pulsed in Janeway's temple, prompted by a dull pain. She really ought to have had a cup of coffee if she expected to be fully awake at this hour. Knowing how clipped her voice sounded, she nevertheless continued. "What do you know about them? You recognized this buoy." She pointed at the lumpy metal object, still twirling in the silent darkness of space, presumably continuing to emit its obstreperous message.

"Um . . . yes, yes, I do. They post these warning buoys at each quarter of their space. The Akerian Empire is to be respected, Captain. I suggest you show some respect and vacate this sector." He paused. "Immediately would be good."

"Neelix, we think there's a wormhole in this sector," Chakotay put in. "We'll need to know more about them before we go anywhere." He glanced over at Janeway—*Did I overstep?*—and she gave him a slight gesture of approval.

"Commander Chakotay is correct."

Neelix sighed and plopped himself down in the chair to Janeway's left. His feet didn't even reach the floor. "Well, as I said, they're an empire. Their technology is about the level of ours, though as I've often said, the *Voyager* is the finest vessel in a hundred light-years."

"Go ahead," said Janeway coolly. She was not about to be swayed by flattery.

He opened his mouth, closed it, thought, then resumed. "Let me put it to you this way. They are *not* people one wants to cross. The threat from that buoy was not idle. They would have no compunctions about murdering everyone on board to protect their interests—and their interests just might include taking over this ship."

CHAPTER
2

JANEWAY BARELY HAD TO CALL FOR A MEETING BEFORE everyone hastened to the conference room. Chakotay eased himself into a seat and sat silently while everyone filed in.

He watched their faces, as he knew Janeway was doing, as any captain worth his or her salt learned quickly to do. Both he and Janeway were well-respected leaders of a largely contented crew. He knew his own methods of dealing with his crew, and he'd had enough time to watch Janeway—even as he knew she was watching him as well.

Some wore their emotions on their sleeves, like Ensign Kim and, on occasion, Tom Paris. Others, like Tuvok and Chakotay himself, had learned to hood their feelings, though Chakotay was adept enough at expressing himself should the occasion arise.

The windows were large in the conference room, and Chakotay turned his gaze momentarily upon the starfield. Unbidden, her image rose in his mind. He could not help but wonder if her puzzling advice was related to the new and apparently aggressive race whose warning buoy they had just encountered. As he watched, his eyes not really focused on the stars, a huge chunk of a spaceship went slowly past the window, turning end over end in a disturbing ballet.

The door hissed open one final time and B'Elanna Torres entered. As usual, Torres was the last to arrive, having to come all the way from Engineering. She caught Chakotay's gaze, but her own face was inscrutable. Graceful and slim despite the physical power granted by her Klingon mother's blood, she slipped easily into a seat, folded her hands on the desk, and looked toward Janeway expectantly.

"Here's the situation," said Janeway without preamble. "We've got indications that there might be a wormhole in this sector. We just encountered a warning buoy placed by a race calling themselves the Akerians, warning us not to trespass. Mr. Neelix, please continue telling us what you know of the Akerians."

Neelix looked very uncomfortable. In his limited contact with the pudgy little alien, Chakotay had found him extremely anxious to please. The self-appointed "morale officer," the Talaxian liked nothing better than to cheer people up. Neelix dreaded being the bearer of bad tidings, and now he fumbled for words.

"Well, as I told you on the bridge, they are an advanced culture. They have formed the Akerian

Empire, which consists of various planets they've conquered and, well, shall we say . . . plundered, I suppose, is the term. Nobody knows for sure where their home planet is—they are very territorial, hence the warning buoys."

"What do they look like?" asked Kim.

Neelix hesitated, then replied, "Well, I know they're bipedal. Strong. And very tall."

"Humanoid?" queried Paris.

Neelix shrugged his shoulders. "Can't say for sure. Nobody knows much about them—only about the damage they leave in their wake. They always wear masks—don't want their faces to be seen, apparently. Possibly humanoid, yes."

"Level of technological development?" put in Torres.

Chakotay felt a brief twinge of sympathy at Neelix's obvious discomfort. He'd been on the receiving end of Torres's grilling style himself.

"Warp and shield capabilities. They have a unique sort of weaponry that seems to impact unshielded ships and planets very harshly. And no, I don't know what type," he added, preempting Torres's next question. The chief engineer glowered at him.

Neelix turned pleadingly toward the captain. "I strongly urge you to respect their boundaries, Captain," he said. "I'm not sure how badly they could hurt us, but I know that they can. Can't we get what information we need from here about the wormhole?"

Janeway glanced over at Kim, who shook his head. "Impossible," said the ensign. "We'll need to be much closer in order to get any readings that would be worthwhile—even to determine if the wormhole is inside the black hole or not."

"I would like to reemphasize that all the spaceship debris we have encountered up to this point has been from vessels inferior in construction to the *Voyager*," said Tuvok, his dark face as calm as if he had been making idle conversation. He tilted his head, his eyes scanning the rest of them. "While this is far from being a definite assessment of their power, it is certainly an indication of the type of vessels they have encountered and subsequently been able to defeat."

Janeway leaned back in her chair, her eyes on the table. Chakotay watched her intently, wondering if her mind, like his, was racing with a hundred thousand scenarios of eventual encounter with this mysterious race that had gotten Neelix so agitated.

"Mr. Chakotay?"

Her sudden turn of attention to him forced the first officer to refocus his thoughts, but he recovered at once. "It's a calculated risk," he said. "But then, so is every single move we make out here in the Delta Quadrant. We're constantly facing the unknown. There's nothing to count on out here but ourselves and our ship."

He leaned forward, his gaze locked with Janeway, but his words addressed to them all. "I say we proceed but with caution. The wormhole—or black hole, whichever it turns out to be—is located in a solar system with eight planets. Neelix doesn't know where the Akerians' home world is. I think there's a good chance that the Akerian home world is one of these planets. Perhaps we should travel slowly, constantly sending out a greeting. If the Akerians think we're looking for them in a peaceful fashion, perhaps they will behave in the same manner. Let's give them no cause to perceive us as a threat."

He'd been watching Neelix out the corner of his eye as the Talaxian grew more and more agitated. Now Neelix exploded with, "It doesn't matter to the empire if you're a Bekovian toth-eater with six-centimeter fangs or a little bug on their nose, they're going to perceive you as a threat and deal with you accordingly!"

"And just how is that, Neelix?" Tom Paris's face was all guileless innocence, save for the crafty smile that quirked his lips and spoiled the illusion.

"I'm not the one who wants to find out, am I?"

Janeway sighed. "What I'm hearing from Mr. Kim is, we can't determine if that wormhole is or isn't a way home by sitting here, correct?"

Kim nodded. "Yes, Captain."

"And Tuvok thinks that we'd be fairly safe if our unpleasant neighbors do show up."

"Correction," said Tuvok. "We have no specific reason to think we would not. However, there is always the risk of danger in encountering a new race."

Chakotay smothered a smile. He had learned to respect Tuvok when the Vulcan had worked undercover on Chakotay's Maquis vessel. The respect continued, even when Tuvok had revealed the true nature of his mission.

"Well, it sounds to me like we should go ahead—cautiously. Any objections? Besides you, of course, Neelix."

Chakotay glanced around the table. Nobody seemed inclined to disagree.

"Then let's do it." Janeway's cool expression

melted into a warm smile that lit up her features. "It's the best possibility to come our way in a long time. If there's a wormhole in that system, we're going to find it, Akerians or no Akerians. Stations, everyone. Yellow alert."

It was always easy to sound brave, Janeway had found. Almost always easy to appear brave. Snap out the words, hold your head just so, force your body language into communicating what you wanted your crew to "hear." But making yourself feel brave? That was another matter entirely. As she walked with her senior staff back onto the bridge and slid into her chair, she said a silent prayer to anyone or anything that might heed such missives: *Please, let this be the right thing.*

She'd been doing that a lot since this mission began. And thus far, she'd made the right choices more often than not.

"Ahead warp two, Mr. Paris," she ordered. "Mr. Kim, prepare to record a message."

"Aye, Captain," came the two youthful male voices, almost in chorus, as they set about following her orders. "Ready, Captain," said Kim an instant later.

Janeway did not rise, but she did sit up straighter. "This is Captain Kathryn Janeway of the Federation *Starship Voyager* to any Akerian vessel in the area of this transmission. We come in peace"—*for all mankind,* she thought, feeling a surge of pride at the remembrance of those powerful words that, even today, still graced the surface of Earth's moon—"and have no conflict with anyone in this sector. Please respond. Let us open a dialogue." She nodded to Kim, who nodded his own dark head in acknowledgment.

"Message recorded, Captain."

"Broadcast every two minutes on all frequencies." She rose, sighed softly, and turned to Chakotay. "Commander, you have the bridge. Call me when we're within visual range of the wormhole. I'll be in my ready room," she said, smiling slightly, "with a hot pot of coffee."

She wanted a Danish, too, very badly, but contented herself with a strong cup of hot black java. She inhaled the scent, sighed, and smiled. One needed the little luxuries every now and then, she had found.

Janeway took a sip of the hot brew and sat down at her desk. She recorded a brief log of the situation, citing their heading and incorporating images of each piece of debris that floated within visual range. Later analysis might prove useful.

She had finished the first cup and was debating splurging on a second when there came a beep at her door. "Come," she called.

The door hissed open, and Tuvok stood in the entrance, his hands folded behind his back, his impassive face betraying nothing. Only the slight hesitation in his wording alerted Janeway to possible problems.

"We have reached the vicinity of the . . . concavity, Captain."

Concavity? thought Janeway. *Nothing more specific? Not wormhole nor black hole?* No time for a second cup now. Adrenaline would provide any energy she needed. Janeway hit her comm badge.

"Janeway to Neelix. Meet me on the bridge at once."

The first thing she perceived was that her crew was, to a man, still and silent, staring at the screen—even Chakotay and Tuvok, who had, like her, seen many wondrous and fascinating sights. Almost at once she froze in midstride as well, riveted by the awesome sight that greeted her.

The spatial distortion—to use Tuvok's carefully neutral and scientifically accurate term, the concavity—was enormous. It did indeed look like a black hole, but far and away the biggest one she'd ever heard of. It devoured almost half of the screen space—a huge pit of eternal, starless night, haloed by a gorgeous display of purple, red, blue, and yellow dust and matter that formed the swirling accretion disk. Every few seconds, there would be a bright eruption from the inside, a brief fountain of gaseous matter spewed out into space like a geyser.

A lively imagination might have anthropomorphized the concavity into a celestial monster, feeding on a flow of bright energy that it seemed to be sucking from the system's sun. The sun itself appeared to be in the later stages of its starry life. It was enormous, swollen, emanating an angry, orange-red hue—almost at the stage known as a red giant. The eight planets that ringed it seemed pitifully small and vulnerable in comparison to the turgid, dying star.

Beautiful and awe inspiring, certainly, but Janeway quickly redirected her attention to more practical matters. "Distance from the accretion disk?" asked the captain, never taking her eyes from the screen.

"We are presently 0.8 light-years away from the

concavity," replied Tuvok, his head bent over his console.

"Then I hope that I'm seeing a magnification here."

"Aye, Captain, four-db magnification."

"What kind of pull is its gravity exerting on us?"

"Unusually minimal, considering its size." Tuvok answered the question she had not asked, anticipating her. "We could venture closer without undue risk."

His brow furrowed in concentration. Something about the situation was bothering him, Janeway realized. She waited an instant, but no further information was forthcoming. Tuvok was never one to speak before the facts were in if he could possibly avoid it, and Janeway knew that behind that slightly troubled countenance his brilliant Vulcan brain was busy sorting out information that would enable him to reach a conclusion.

She didn't push him. He'd tell her what he knew when he knew it. She sat down in her chair and turned her attention back to the screen.

"Then let's move closer, Mr. Paris. Keep to warp two until we've entered the system, then drop to half-impulse. Ensign Kim, keep monitoring the gravitational pull. I don't want to get mired in this thing."

The big ship moved forward, the celestial images on the screen gradually growing larger as a result. There was a soft whisper of a door opening, and Janeway glanced up to see Neelix entering. He looked slightly better groomed than he had earlier but no happier with the situation. Silently, she nodded toward the chair next to her. Just as silently, he sat down.

"Recognize any of this space?"

"Nope. Grand spectacle, though, I must say."

Janeway found her attention turning to the little planets, not so little, truth be told; any one of them was the size of Earth if not larger. But against that menacing blackness slowly destroying the red giant, "little" seemed to be an accurate description.

"Any sign of the Akerians around here yet, Mr. Kim?"

"Negative, Captain. Sensors are not picking up any ships in this system at present. We're still seeing a lot of debris, though."

"Scan the planets. Could one of them possibly be the Akerian home world?" She found herself hoping that there would be no developed life-forms on those doomed orbs. Admittedly, though, the Akerians did sound like prime candidates for a comeuppance, and they had the technological capability to move their people to a more hospitable system if this was indeed the home world of the masked, mysterious beings.

Kim glanced at his controls. "Negative, Captain. I'm picking up signs of advanced societies but nothing to indicate development on the level that Neelix attributes to them."

Compassion washed over Janeway. "Damn." She hated scenarios like this one. Even with their technologies and knowledge of the vagaries of the universe, *Voyager* and every other ship that trolled the stars was completely at the mercy of natural catastrophes on this scale. She grieved for the innocent people whose sun was dying.

A thought cheered her briefly. As such things went, suns took a while before they laid down and died— or, more accurately, went out in a blaze of glory. "Mr. Kim, extrapolate for me. Judging by the present level of technology on this planet, will these civilizations obtain the capability of warp drive before the world becomes uninhabitable?"

Kim's face grew thoughtful. He hit a few controls quickly, lightly, and examined what the computer told him. "Well, the sun won't die for another few million years, but life on the planets will die out long before that. Their technology is somewhat beyond what Earth's was at the end of the twentieth century. They've already got a complex satellite communication system, which could indicate that they're aware of extraterrestrial life."

He raised his face and met Janeway's questioning glance with an unhappy expression. "If they're sharing information with another society about improving their technology, they might be able to get out of this system before it's too late. On their own . . . I'm sorry, Captain, I don't think they'll make it. They've only got about a century or so left."

"Captain," said Tuvok, "I would disagree."

Hope sprang in Janeway's heart. "They've got more than a century?"

"Unfortunately, no." No hint of disappointment or compassion in the statement—just the cold, logical facts. "I have been continuing to gather information from the sensors, and I believe there is enough evidence here for me to state that this star is not what it appears to be."

"Explain." She was pleased that her voice did not betray the disappointment she felt.

"The star appears to be a red giant. In fact, by almost all accounts, it *is* a red giant. The size is correct, it is clearly beginning to burn the helium at its core. Nearly all the criteria that we would use to judge it a red giant are evident."

"Get to the point, please, Mr. Tuvok," came Chakotay's voice laced with tension. Janeway glanced over at her first officer. Of course, he would be even more profoundly affected by the situation than she. Chakotay had a deep respect for life—all life—that approached reverence. His people, Janeway recalled, had been taught to honor the life-force in all things. The deaths of four planets, teeming with living beings, must hurt him terribly for him to have snapped at Tuvok that way.

"I am attempting to do so, Commander," the Vulcan rebuked mildly. "But the true and final definition of a red giant must be that it is a star of a certain age. This star is clearly at the end of its life, but sensors have confirmed that it is only 4.2 billion years old—younger than Earth's own sun. By all accounts, this star should be less than halfway through its natural life."

Chakotay frowned. "I don't understand."

"The concavity is artificially aging this star," said Tuvok. "It should not be a red giant, according to its years. Yet it is a red giant. Therefore, there is an external force at work aging the star and causing it to age prematurely. It would be comparable to our own youthful Mr. Kim dying of old age."

Janeway tore her eyes from Tuvok's dark face to gaze at the screen. Suddenly, the thought of the concavity as an evil monster didn't seem quite as ludicrous as it had just a few moments earlier.

"I know that sometimes black holes drain hydrogen from nearby stars," said Tom Paris, his normally lively voice gone soft and somber. "But I've always seen just a thin spiral of hydrogen going into the hole. This isn't a trickle . . . It's a damn *river.*"

And he was right. The flood of hydrogen into the maw of the concavity was fully as wide as the sun itself. The thing wasn't just feeding on this solar system's central star; it was gorging on it.

"You said the planets have less than a century left," said Chakotay. "How long?"

"If the sun continues to age at this accelerated rate," replied the Vulcan, "and if there is no technological assistance involved, all life in this system will cease to exist within 24.3 years."

"A quarter of a century, and then that's all she wrote." The sentence was flippant, but Paris's voice remained somber. Janeway closed her eyes briefly. Tuvok had, to all intents and purposes, just pronounced an irrevocable death sentence. The only hope these people had now was if they could evacuate the planet.

"Ensign Kim, just how many people are we talking about?" Janeway asked.

"Over two billion, Captain," the young man replied, his voice low.

Unbidden, the thought arose. *We could do it.* Physically, yes, but as soon as the thought came, Janeway dismissed it. *No, we cannot. That's interference on a major scale.* This system was naturally destroying itself. To intervene in a prewarp society's natural development so drastically would be not only violating the Prime Directive, but positively thumbing her nose at the Federation's highest ideal. She'd have to hope that the inhabitants of this system had powerful friends with warp-speed ships to spirit them away from their unnaturally dying star.

Janeway took a deep breath. "Let's concentrate on that concavity. Are we still picking up verteron emanations?"

"Yes, Captain," Kim confirmed. "Everything still points to there being a wormhole in there. But if it's *inside* the black hole, there's no way we could get to it. The gravitational gradients would be too strong."

"Oh, too bad," said Neelix happily. "Guess we should turn around and vacate this space, right, Captain?"

"Neelix," sighed Janeway, "if you don't mind." Neelix resettled himself in the chair without looking the least bit hurt or embarrassed. "Mr. Tuvok, you said something about the gravitational pull being strangely low. Please elaborate."

"There is a bit of a mystery here, Captain. The gravitational pull the concavity is exerting on our ship at the present moment is approximately one-seventh of what it ought to be. Since that is an accurate way of estimating the amount of gravitational force within the concavity, I would say that, theoretically, our shields would hold if we decide to venture into it."

Amid the feeling of renewed excitement Janeway could sense rising on the bridge, the captain locked onto the key thing that her security officer had said.

"It's one-seventh what it ought to be," she repeated, "far less than is necessary for its size. Just like this sun is far older than it ought to be. I wonder if there's any kind of connection?"

"Curiouser and curiouser," said Paris, "as Alice said when she fell down the rabbit hole."

Paris's quip had an unforseen effect on his captain. Janeway felt her body tense. "Something is very wrong here, isn't it, Mr. Tuvok? There's too many things happening in this system that just aren't making any sense."

Neelix opened his mouth as if to further his attempts to get them to leave, but a cold glance from Chakotay caused him to close it again.

"Correct, Captain." Janeway knew that, though he would never admit it, such illogical occurrences were frustrating the hell out of the Vulcan. "The distance between the sun and the concavity is three trillion miles. The gravitational pull exerted by the concavity is insufficient to siphon off the star's hydrogen at all, certainly not to the extreme extent that it is doing so."

"Let me get this straight," said Janeway. She was starting to become a bit frustrated herself. "We've got a red giant that's too young to be a red giant. We've got a concavity whose gravitational power is too weak for it to be the size that it is. And we've got hydrogen being pulled across an impossible distance at an impossible rate. Have I got all this right, Tuvok?"

"That is essentially correct, Captain."

Janeway wished she'd gone ahead and had that second cup of coffee.

"Captain!" Kim's voice was urgent. "I'm picking up a hail from the planet farthest from the sun."

Janeway rose, planting her hands on her hips. "Maybe they've got some answers for us. Put it on screen, Mr. Kim."

The figure that appeared on the screen was one of the most fascinating combinations of creatures Janeway had ever seen, and she'd met over a hundred different races in her time in Starfleet. At first glance, the creature resembled nothing so much as a dragon out of old Earth legends. But that first superficial comparison did not hold up to closer examination.

Janeway could not get a proper size estimate nor a complete view of the being as it was seated in a chair that seemed fashioned of equal parts stone and plastic. The pose in itself bespoke a bipedal creature, and from the waist up there was a certain resemblance to a humanoid: a torso, two arms, and a head.

But what arms, strong and ending in sharp-clawed fingers, and what a head.

It was snakelike in form, a shapely diamond. Incongruously large, gentle eyes filled with concern graced a head that narrowed into a pointed muzzle. There were no teeth visible at the moment. The back of the head tapered into a long, sinuous neck that broadened at the base to very human-appearing shoulders. A heavy, multifaceted pendant, winking silvery in the light, hung about that throat. A white mane of hair decorated the head and continued down the length of the neck. Soft, mottled, pale fur covered all, though the creature wore comfortable drapelike garments that modestly covered its body.

The voice, as translated by the computer, was completely feminine.

"We have picked up your signal, Captain Janeway. From what you say and from what we know, you are not known to the Akerians. Dare we hope that you have come to help us?"

CHAPTER

3

CHAKOTAY STARED. IT WAS IMPOLITE, AND HIS FATHER would have been disappointed in his behavior, but the first officer couldn't help himself. In his mind, the animal spirit's message thundered, and his skin crawled with gooseflesh.

Others might stare at this creature—no, this *person*—because of her curious appearance, her unusual combination of reptile and mammal into one being that seemed, to human eyes, bizarre yet not unappealing. Chakotay stared for another reason entirely. He stared at the female alien's white mane of hair . . . hair that was braided with feathers and beads. Ornamentations that were uncannily familiar to Chakotay. He stared at the patterns on her garb, at the easy and comfortable union of natural and artificial in her surroundings.

Had it been a human on that video screen, he might have addressed her as Grandmother. *Don't go attributing human characteristics to aliens,* he chided himself. *That's led to some of the worst incidents in Federation history. Learn about them and take them on their own terms. Just because she's got the dignity and bearing of Grandmother doesn't mean she's old and wise.*

But now Janeway was speaking, and Chakotay quickly recovered himself.

"As you must know from our message, we have no quarrel with anyone in this sector. We are not friends of the Akerians, but neither, we hope, are we their enemies. Who are your people? How may I address you?"

"I am called Nata. I am a *Viha,* one of the elders of my people."

So much for incorrect assumptions, thought Chakotay with a trace of annoyed exasperation.

"We are the Verunans," continued *Viha* Nata. "This planet is Veruna Four." The great, lambent eyes narrowed and the snakelike head cocked to one side. The gesture sent the soft white hair flowing. The beads and feathers in its length danced. "Do I have your word, Captain Janeway of the Federation, that you have not come here on behalf of the Akerian Empire to continue their attacks on my people?"

"You do indeed, *Viha* Nata."

Some of the tension left the Verunan's stance. "We are a people of honor despite some of the actions to which our present situation has driven us. We take you at your word and trust that you, too, are a people of honor."

Chakotay tensed even further. He was usually good at not telegraphing his emotions, but he saw Janeway glance at him quickly, then back at the screen again. Chakotay resigned himself to talking with her soon and explaining his reactions. He should have known better than to think he could get anything past the captain. She was too shrewd and was learning to know him too well.

"Your trust means a great deal to us," replied Janeway. "I must emphasize, in the interest of being open with you and your people, that we have not come here to assist you. We've come to explore the spatial concavity in your system. Are you aware of it? Can you tell us more about its nature?"

Viha Nata closed her eyes, as if in pain, then opened them slowly. "How can we not be aware of the great Sun-Eater? We see it in our sky every day, a brown-purple bruise against our violated stars. Your ship boasts technology far beyond anything we have ever encountered, and we have seen many a ship in this system. You probably already know more about its scientific nature than we do."

Janeway was standing, her eyes meeting the great orbs of *Viha* Nata steadily. "We have seen the debris of other star-faring vessels in this area. From what I am hearing of the nature of the Verunans, you are not the ones responsible for their destruction."

And then something totally unexpected happened. The huge eyes of the *Viha* filled with liquid. *Tears,* Chakotay marveled. *They can weep!*

"We did not fire upon the vessels," said Nata. "Yet in a way, we are partially responsible for their destruction. Some merely came to this area, as you did, for reasons that had nothing to do with our conflict. Others came, thinking to fight the Akerians—most for their own purposes but a few on our behalf. Their deaths are partially on our heads. We mourn them." She wiped her face with the back of a clawed hand and composed herself. "Every moment you linger here, within the space that the evil Akerians claim as theirs, you risk yourself and your crew."

"We are travelers from a far part of this galaxy," said Janeway. "We were brought here against our will, and we're trying to find a way home. We have reason to believe that there is a wormhole in the concavity that might allow us to travel back to our home area of space."

Viha Nata's eyes widened. "Wormhole?" she repeated, clearly confused. "Captain, worms cannot live in space."

Chakotay smiled a little at the miscommunication. The universal translator was clearly functioning perfectly—too perfectly, perhaps, translating the literal meaning of the word rather than the technical meaning it held for speakers of English.

"I apologize for our incorrect translation," said Janeway. "We use the term to describe a sort of tunnel in space, a corridor from one part of the galaxy to the other."

"Ah!" exclaimed *Viha* Nata, nodding her comprehension. "I understand now. I am familiar with the phenomenon, though I cannot say if there is one within Sun-Eater."

"Please," said Janeway, stepping closer to the screen. "Tell us what your scientists have been able to learn about the con—about Sun-Eater. Anything would be helpful."

Viha Nata looked slightly uncomfortable. "Captain, I repeat, I do not think you realize the danger you are in every moment you tarry here. Nor do I think you appreciate the dreadful danger we Verunans are in." She paused, then continued. "Time is precious here on Veruna. We do not have much of it left. Yet perhaps if I answer your questions and inform you of the situation, you can be convinced to lend your help."

Chakotay glanced at Janeway, who flinched ever so slightly. "I can promise you nothing," said Janeway, "but I will listen. Please continue."

By now, everyone on the bridge had turned their attention to the Verunan *Viha*. She and her lyrical words were far more interesting than the computer's graphics and strange, contradictory conclusions. Everyone, Chakotay mentally amended, except for Tuvok. Yet even the dark-skinned Vulcan could not help glancing up from his station now and then to examine Nata. And Chakotay knew that Tuvok was hearing and analyzing every word the reptilian mammal—mammalian reptile?—uttered.

"Sun-Eater appeared several millennia ago. Then, it was a harmless aberration, according to the tales. The Akeriansss"—*Viha* Nata hissed the word with obvious loathing—"came very soon afterward, as the shadow follows the body. They were more advanced than we, then and now, and we were helpless to resist when they came and stole our people right in front of our eyes. They simply . . . disappeared, fading as we watched!"

"Transporter technology," said Paris. Janeway nodded acknowledgment and agreement but kept her attention upon the alien.

"Why did they steal your people? How many were abducted?" asked the captain, compassion in her voice.

"They took five, six each time they came. As to why, we do not know." Again tears filled the limpid eyes. Clearly, Verunan emotions were close to the surface. Nata lowered her head, fingered her bulky pendant as if seeking comfort.

"We never saw any of them again. They continue to do this to this very day. When we started to fight back several turns ago, they began attacking our planet. They are able to inflict damage upon our poor world that resembles earthquakes, which have had some dreadful consequences. A few months ago, an avalanche destroyed one of our hatching pits. Can you imagine an enemy so callous, so cruel, that they would destroy *hatching pits?*"

Viha Nata shook her head in disbelief and sorrow, then continued. "Time came and went. We grew used to seeing the Akerian violators in our skies. Our telescopes revealed that there was a harmony between the Akerians and the hole in the heavens. They flew in and out and seemed to make it a sort of home."

Her manner of speaking was rhythmic, almost a chant. Chakotay knew at once that these were people with a strong oral tradition. Perhaps there were written records, but history was clearly kept alive by verbal communication. He was so lulled by the power of her cadence that he almost missed the most vital statement of Nata's speech: that the Akerians flew in and out of "the hole in the heavens." He turned to Janeway and saw her own face alight with eagerness. But her diplomacy won out; Janeway permitted the alien to continue at her own speed.

"Three hundred turns ago, the hole in the heavens grew cruel and became Sun-Eater. Now, we do not know how much time is left to us. Our days on Veruna have numbers, and we believe that the Akerians have done something to make that so."

"Have you tried negotiating with the Akerians?" the captain asked, putting her hands behind her back and pacing back and forth.

Nata's reply was vicious, blistering, and apparently untranslatable. "They would not understand the meaning of the word!" she spat. The *Viha*'s visage changed with her quick anger, and she snarled. Chakotay caught a glimpse of powerful yellow-white teeth. "How can one negotiate with a race who hides their faces? Who comes and takes our people and murders our children?

"No, Captain, we came to the reluctant conclusion twenty turns ago that our only chance is to fight back. We had some knowledge and technology, our inheritance from the Ancestors. To that we have knowledge gleaned from Akerian debris. We have learned now how to build vessels that soar in the darkness of space. We have stolen their knowledge as they have stolen our future. Our weapons and ships are no match for theirs, but we will not let them despoil our planet and take our people anymore."

She was standing now, her hands flat on what was clearly a desk. Chakotay saw that her body was mostly humanoid, widening at the hips to flare into what he suspected were powerful thighs and legs. He mentally added a long, reptilian tail to his image of the Verunan. He was almost immediately corrected. A full sweep of a tail similar to that of a horse flicked quickly into his vision, then out again. *Viha* Nata snorted, then forced herself to sit down.

"Forgive my outburst. But you see, I am one of the leaders of this planet, the keeper of the knowledge granted to us by the Ancestors. I am a *Viha,* a protector of my people. You cannot imagine how it feels to watch the fertile land being scorched by a sun who no longer cares, to see plants and animals dying by the thousands. To know that your people have only a few generations at most before they are . . . forever gone."

Her words cut Chakotay's heart to the quick. The Verunans, physically so different from him, had a closer grasp of the Indian's relationship to his world than most of his fellow humans. Every fiber of his being cried out to help these people. They were not only dying, but their whole *world* was dying. And if, as he suspected, these people believed that everything— earth, sky, star, plant, cloud—had a "spirit," then they were constantly being surrounded by needless, senseless, incomprehensible death.

The thought was nearly intolerable.

He turned in his chair to Janeway, the words, *Let us help them!* on his lips. But he did not, could not, speak them. The Prime Directive forbade it. And for better or worse, he had agreed to uphold Starfleet regulations. He wished, at this moment, that he had not.

On Janeway's face was empathy and the evidence of her own internal struggle. Chakotay knew her to be a person of great depth and wisdom and passionate caring. But her hands were tied even more so than his.

Nata spoke again, breaking the silence. "Can you not find it in your heart, Captain Janeway of the *Starship Voyager,* to help us stop these abominations? Your ship could do things that ours could not, could help us fight back with at least a chance of success!"

Janeway's voice when she spoke was heavy with regret. "Your plight does not leave me unmoved, *Viha* Nata, believe me. But we cannot embroil ourselves in your fight. When we leave our space, we have rules about interference in other cultures. In attempting to help, we might make things unspeakably worse."

Viha Nata looked unconvinced. "Tell me, how can things possibly get any worse for us?" A hint of sarcasm soured her voice.

They can't, thought Chakotay, the knowledge sitting like a lump of lead in the pit of his stomach. *But there's not a damn thing we can do about it.*

Janeway was spared the painful necessity of a bleak reply when the Operations station began to light up and beep like crazy. Before Kim or Tuvok could even get words out, *Viha* Nata sprang up from her chair crying, "They have returned!" pausing only to hit a control. Her image blipped out.

Simultaneously Kim yelped, "Captain, a ship has just emerged from the concavity!"

"On screen," snapped Janeway.

The small ship, an unattractive, gawky little vessel that made early Earth attempts at spaceflight look sleek and elegant, exploded out of the concavity. It was a pathetic hodgepodge of styles and materials, and Chakotay realized almost at once that it had been cobbled together by those who didn't have access to materials on their own but had to find them where they could. He was achingly familiar with the scenario. One thing the small craft had in its favor: it was fast.

Apparently, though, not fast enough. Right on its tail came another vessel, dwarfing the first. It was big, although not as big as the *Voyager,* and every line of its bulky form spoke menace. It did not move with the quick urgency of the first; it did not need to. It was already gaining.

"That," said Neelix somberly, "is an Akerian ship."

"Shields up, red alert," ordered Janeway. Immediately, the bridge lighting darkened. Red lights began to pulse.

Chakotay stared at the big vessel, taking in its blunt and angled sides, its gleaming gun metal blue hull. Red glimmered from its four cylindrical engines, which seemed to comprise more than half its weight and bulk. The ship moved purposefully, turning to follow its quarry and allowing Chakotay a good look at it straight on. At its front was the ship's most curious feature: six circular units that clustered about the face of the vessel. They were gleaming black, chitinous in appearance, and reminded Chakotay of nothing so much as shiny black insects. In their center, encased by a semitransparent dome, throbbed four red units of energy. The first officer couldn't even guess at their purpose.

In front of this threatening apparition, like a rabbit in front of a mining machine, the little scout ship— Chakotay presumed it was Verunan—dipped and dodged frantically. Suddenly, the space in the front of the Akerian ship shivered and twisted ever so slightly. The smaller ship went reeling from an invisible impact.

"What the hell was that?" demanded Janeway.

Tuvok, whose eyes had been glued to his console, had an answer ready. "The Akerian vessel has just generated an intense wave of gravitons, which resulted in a spatial distortion. The distortion emitted a focused gravity wave of considerable force. The impact on the smaller ship was tremendous. Its shields have been reduced twenty-seven percent by the attack."

Neelix snapped his fingers excitedly. "That's the weapon I was telling you about! All I knew from what I'd heard was that it was a forceful blow of some sort."

"Estimated effect of this weapon on our shields?" asked Janeway.

The Vulcan's dark fingers moved confidently on the pad. He shook his head. "Impossible to compute. It appears that the spatial distortion engendered by the weapon is confusing the sensors."

"Captain." Chakotay's voice caused Janeway to turn around. "We've got more trouble."

A second ship, malevolent sister to the one now firing upon the little vessel, emerged from the concavity. It hastened to catch up with its twin. The two ships moved with grim determination, the second one curving around in a clear attempt to corner the scout between them.

Chakotay now spoke up, directing his query to Kim. "Ensign, how many life-forms aboard the smaller vessel?"

The young man shook his head in frustration. "Hard to tell, sir. As Tuvok said, all this intense graviton activity is wreaking havoc with our sensors. Attempting to compensate." His golden fingers flew over the controls. "Best estimate is six, sir. But that's just a guess. There could be more."

Chakotay was flooded with empathy. Not so very long ago, he was in that same position—in a vastly inferior ship fleeing from a dreadful enemy that had every possible advantage. And for the smaller vessel, there was no Badlands in which it could hope to seek refuge.

"The engines of the smaller ship are overheating, Captain," reported Kim, anxiety creeping into his voice. "They're not going to last much long—"

The second big ship fired. Again the space between the Akerian vessel and the Verunan scout ship shuddered. This time, though, the scout's quickness saved it. It whirled to port, turning wildly but evading the damaging wave.

"It may be primitive," said Paris, admiration creeping into his voice, "but whoever's flying that thing is one hell of a good pilot."

"Captain." Kim's voice was tense. "I'm picking up a message from the smaller ship directed toward the planet."

"Let's hear it," replied Janeway. "On speakers."

A taut, frightened male voice blared through the bridge. "—was successful, *Viha.* I'm going ahead and transmitting information about the Akerian base to you now. I don't—I don't think we'll be able to deliver it to you personally."

"Base?" said Paris. "They've got a base in that thing?"

"Ensign, are you getting this information?" demanded Janeway, her body stiff and tense.

"Already on it, Captain," Kim answered.

The first Akerian vessel fired again. The little scout managed to dodge a direct shot but clearly took some damage.

"The scout vessel's shields are down thirty-two percent," reported Tuvok.

"This has gone far enough. Ensign," ordered Janeway, "open a hailing frequency to the Akerian ships." She waited for his nod, then proceeded. "Attention, Akerian vessels. We do not wish to interfere in your politics, but we cannot tolerate this sort of violence. Break off your attack. Repeat, break off your attack."

A tense few seconds ticked by. "No response, Captain," said Kim.

"Damn it," said Janeway softly.

The first Akerian ship fired again, this time landing a square shot.

"Shields on the Verunan scout vessel down seventy-two percent," intoned Tuvok.

Chakotay couldn't take it any longer. He slapped his comm badge. "Chakotay to transporter room. Lock onto the life-forms aboard the smaller ship and prepare to—"

"Belay that order, transporter room," interrupted Janeway. Her eyes narrowed.

"Captain," exploded Chakotay, "the Akerians clearly don't give a damn about our request, and if we don't do something, those people are going to die! They won't be able to take another hit!" He was aware how angry and tense his voice sounded, but he couldn't help it. He *was* angry and tense, damn it.

Janeway hesitated, then nodded ever so slightly. "Bridge to transporter room. Beam those people aboard *now.*"

"I'm having problems locking onto them," came the disembodied voice of the transporter operator. "The spatial distortion around the vessel—"

The Akerians, ignoring the *Voyager* completely, had been steadily maneuvering into a perfect position. The scout ship was positioned directly between them. Frantically, it tried to pull up. At that moment, both Akerian ships fired again.

It was a square hit; it could have been nothing less. The Verunans aboard the little scout ship, still speaking frantically to their *Viha,* didn't even have time to scream. For that one small mercy, the first officer was grateful.

The ship exploded into fragments, no longer truly a ship but merely debris, rushing to join the dozens of other chunks of vessels that fairly littered the orbit of Veruna Four. Chakotay had perhaps felt as helpless at other times in his life but certainly never more than he felt at this moment. Six people were gone, blown to bits.

It now had become chillingly clear why there was so much wreckage about a planet of peaceful inhabitants. The Akerian Empire's arm was long indeed. And as he watched, both ships turned, slowly, languorously, to face the *Voyager.*

CHAPTER
4

THERE WAS A HORRIBLE, SICK FEELING IN THE PIT OF Janeway's stomach. She knew what it was, recognized it from many times before when it had made its nauseating presence known. She had, once again, been forced to witness the destruction of life. Once or twice, she'd even looked into the face of the dying as she'd fired the weapon that had ended the life. More often, she'd watched a ship blow up, just as this small Verunan scout had, from a distance. Familiarity made it no easier, especially when it was coupled with the dreadful thought, *Was this my fault? Would this have happened had I acted faster or differently?*

She could not indulge in the luxury of guilt, not now, not when the Akerian ships had trained their terrible attention upon her ship and her crew.

"Open a hailing frequen—" she started to say, but

the Akerian commander beat her to it. Without warning, a helmeted face appeared on the screen. A large, blocky shape that sat atop a pair of broad shoulders, it gave little clue as to the nature of the creature whose face it shielded. Metal horns affixed to the top of the mask curved into sharp points, giving the utilitarian helmet the grace note of a ceremonial mask. The horns looked scarred; something had made deep notches in them. Janeway was briefly reminded of the old Earth tradition of armoring for battle. The Akerians wore metal body protection as well as helmets, undecorated for the most part save for swooping winglike tips that extended off the shoulders. The mask, vague and featureless except for horizontal slits at the areas where she presumed the eyes and mouth were located, faced her directly.

"Attention, *Viha* Nata, the inhabitants of Veruna Four, and the alien vessel who has trespassed into our space." The voice provided by the translator was masculine. The background against which the words sounded was harsh, rough, and snarling in a sharp contrast to the rather purring, soft sounds of *Viha* Nata's voice.

"This is Linneas, first warrior of the Empirical Exploratory Unit, commander of the Akerian vessel *Victory*. Verunans, your continuous rebellion against the might of the Akerian Empire grows troublesome. We have been lenient, even merciful, but we will no longer tolerate your interference. Make peace with what gods you have, and prepare to suffer the same fate as your scout ship. You have gone too far. Your populace will be destroyed.

"Alien vessel, you have ignored our warning. You

sought to interfere between us and those who bla-
tantly defied our rule. You have engaged in open
dialogue with our enemies. I offer you one last chance
to turn and vacate our space. If you do not, you, too,
shall be destroyed."

"Silence audio," said Janeway. Kim obliged. Safe in
the knowledge that Commander Linneas could not
hear, she asked with a grim smile, "If anyone has
anything to say, speak up now."

"Captain," said Neelix anxiously, "maybe our
shields will protect us. Maybe not. I suggest we take
advantage of the opportunity Commander Linneas
has given us to retreat."

Janeway shook her head. "Unacceptable. We've
come this far to investigate that concavity, and I'm
not going to turn and run at the first sign of trouble.
Not when we know that the Akerians can get inside
and out of it safely. Mr. Tuvok, what's the real risk to
that planet? Can that arrogant devil actually do what
he says he'll do?"

"Perhaps not on the sweeping scale that he boasts,
but he certainly can do damage," Tuvok answered.
"*Viha* Nata spoke of the Akerian ability to inflict
damage that resembled earthquakes. Given what we
have seen of Akerian technology, that is entirely
feasible. She also spoke of these earthquakes destroying 'hatching pits.' If the Verunans are, as I suspect,
egg-laying creatures, targeting the hatching pits—the
eggs—could indeed drastically reduce the popula-
tion."

Thoughts raced through Janeway's mind. She could
feel the eyes of her senior officers upon her, knew
what they wanted her to do. Neelix certainly wanted

to retreat. Others wanted to defend the gentle-seeming Verunans against this violent enemy. Still others saw in the huge "Sun-Eater" a way home. In her mind's eye, she saw again the little scout ship being blown apart by the force of the Akerian's gravity-based weapon. She hadn't acted in time to save those six lives. Maybe she could act in time now to save the lives of those who remained.

"Restore audio," she said. She squared her shoulders and faced the Akerian. "Commander Linneas, I am Captain Kathryn Janeway, of the Federation Starship *Voyager*. You must understand that, though I do not wish to involve myself and my ship in your affairs, compassion forbids me standing by and being a silent partner to certain genocide. I offer myself as a mediator. I have no political ties with either you or the Verunans. Perhaps we can come to some sort of—"

"Captain Janeway, you and your *Voyager* are in a war zone where the only victor can be the Akerian Empire." Linneas's voice was as cold and expressionless as the mask he wore. "I offered you the opportunity to retreat. You have refused it. You must now consider yourself an enemy of the empress Riva and the Akerian Empire. We declare war on *you* as well. Surrender at once."

Linneas's gall, especially in the face of the brutal action he'd just ordered against the planet, angered Janeway. She kept her voice calm, though, as she replied, "So you can take our ship? I don't think so."

"Then face the consequences." Abruptly, Linneas's masked visage disappeared.

Almost at once, the attacks came. Linneas's vessel,

the *Victory*, launched a gravity wave on *Voyager*. Simultaneously, the second ship, which the computer had translated as the *Conquest*, fired on the planet.

"Brace for impact," commanded Janeway. She didn't know how badly the spatial distortion would damage *Voyager*. She gritted her teeth and dug her fingers into her chair, awaiting the blow.

The *Voyager* rocked slightly. That was all. Janeway closed her eyes in relief. "Lieutenant Paris, keep an eye on the planet. Mr. Tuvok, analysis."

Tuvok told her what she wanted to hear. "The Akerian weapon is kinetic and gravimetric in nature. Our shields operate under the same gravimetric principles as the Akerian weapons system. Both utilize highly focused spatial distortions in combination with localized graviton energy. The kinetic energy produced by the directed wave was effectively dispersed. It simply washed over our shields—similar to the action of water over an eggshell."

"Who says you can't fight fire with fire, eh, Mr. Tuvok?" smiled Janeway. "Any chance that an increase in power could damage the shields?"

"Highly doubtful. The shields would continue to compensate. We are in no real danger from the Akerians—unless of course they have other weapons systems, such as directed energy." He addressed the statement to Neelix, lifting one slanted eyebrow.

"I've never heard of anything other than this," said Neelix. "This 'gravity wave,' as you call it, has always been enough for them."

"All right then," said Janeway, leaning forward in her chair. *Victory* was no longer a threat, but *Conquest* was still firing on the planet. She could see the shuddering of space as the *Conquest* fired. Her ship safe, she could now get on with the job of helping those people down there. "Mr. Paris, report."

Tom Paris's face wore an unusually sober expression. "They're taking massive hits, Captain. There are at least three areas that have taken impacts equivalent to 4.2 on the Richter scale."

"Veruna Four is sending out a distress call," chimed in Kim. "Shall I open a frequency?"

Janeway shook her head. "I know what they're saying," she replied. "And I'm doing what I can. Open a hailing frequency to the *Conquest.*"

Kim hit a few controls, then shook his head. *"Conquest* not responding."

Janeway rose and walked toward the view screen. "Mr. Chakotay, fire a warning shot across their bow. Let's see if that will get their attention."

"Aye, Captain," replied the first officer. Red phaser energy exploded in a sword of light in front of the *Conquest.*

"Again," commanded Janeway. "Closer this time."

Chakotay obliged. The second phaser blast sliced very near the strange, circular units affixed to its front, like insectoid eyes.

"The *Conquest* has temporarily ceased firing on Veruna Four," announced Tuvok.

"Try to raise them again, Ensign," said the captain, folding her arms across her chest.

"No reply," came Kim's frustrated voice.

"Damn it," hissed Janeway under her breath. "What kind of game are they playing?"

"They might not think we're serious," suggested

Paris. "We haven't attacked them directly yet. Sometimes bullies only understand force."

"An insightful comment, Mr. Paris, but I'm not about to fire on a ship that can't hurt us. I'm ready for a fair fight any day, but so far all the Akerians have done is to manage to get my Irish up. Try it again, Mr. Kim."

She had just started to turn around, intending to head back to her chair, when the *Victory* began to move closer. She paused in midstride and returned to her position in front of the viewscreen.

"What are you up to, Linneas?" asked Janeway softly.

As if in direct reply to her rhetorical question, the six circles affixed to the *Victory*'s face suddenly launched themselves in *Voyager*'s direction. Janeway now saw clearly that they were small pod ships. She didn't know why, but suddenly the chilling image of a shark moving languidly through cold blue depths, remora fish affixed to its body swimming in silent attendance, flashed into her mind.

"Captain, the *Victory* has just launched six small pods—" began Tuvok.

"I see them, Mr. Tuvok. Any life-forms on board?" She wondered if the Akerian culture was the sort to embrace the concept of suicide runs.

"Impossible to tell. The graviton activity—"

"Is interfering with the sensors, I know." Janeway slapped at her comm badge. "Janeway to Engineering."

"Torres here," came the chief engineer's voice.

"I want all possible power to the shields, Torres.

And I want you to get someone on recalibrating the sensors to operate through all this gravity confusion. Without our sensors we're blind. Understood?"

"Shields are at full power, Captain, and I'll put someone on the sensors immediately."

"Sooner, Torres. Janeway out."

The little pods were approaching steadily. "Fire a warning shot, Commander."

A phaser blast screamed across the path of the six approaching pods. There was no reaction from either the pods or from the Akerian ships. Janeway did notice with grim satisfaction that the *Conquest* had, for the moment, ceased firing on the planet. It was clearly waiting to see the outcome of the latest . . . attack? Probe?

She didn't want to fire on the pods without making sure there was no one inside. They were so small that one phaser blast would probably destroy them. She'd have to wait, see what Linnea's objective was in launching the glistening black globes.

Janeway hated waiting.

The spheres came closer. "Five hundred kilometers and closing," said Tuvok.

"That's more than close enough, whatever they are. Paris, move us away from them."

Swiftly Paris obliged. The ship eased to port, out of the path of the incoming pod ships. "I don't get it," said Paris. "They know how powerful our shields are. Those things are going to bounce right off them."

"Let's hope you're right, Lieutenant. Ensign, any luck on clarifying those sensors?"

"Not yet, Captain."

Slowly, continuing their inexorable approach, the

six pods moved to form a hexagon. The space between them began to distort. They were linking themselves together by means of graviton beams, Janeway realized. *To what end?*

"Captain, the pods are sending out a sort of tractor beam. Unable to assess strength." The voice was Tuvok's. "It is aimed at our shields, in the aft section of our saucer."

"Let's keep them in sight," ordered Janeway. The video angle shifted, providing her and the rest of the bridge with a clear picture of the area in question. There was a slight flash of blue, then nothing.

"Shake them, Lieutenant," she commanded. Obediently, the helmsman took the ship down. The pods followed as if their tractor beam were a tether. Paris saw what she saw and instituted a more vigorous attempt to break free. It did not work. Indeed, as Janeway watched, her concern growing, the hexagon formed by the linked pods moved rapidly closer to the shields. There was a second flash of blue as the hexagon fastened itself to *Voyager*'s shields, apparently with no ill effects.

This is not good, thought Janeway with just a hint of apprehension. "Ensign Kim, I want to know if there are any life signs aboard those things *now.*"

The young man was keeping admirably cool, sounding only a little flustered as he replied. "Whoever's in Engineering working on this is doing a good job. It's starting to clear up. I don't think— *Captain!*" All trace of coolness vanished. "They're— they're *eating* our shields!"

Tuvok added his voice. "Ensign Kim's assessment, while unduly colorful, is essentially correct, Captain.

They are managing to penetrate the shields and open up a small gap by forcing the graviton field away from the point of entry."

Janeway listened, staring at the image of the six little pods. Their action was invisible, but she had no doubt that what Kim and Tuvok were reporting was the truth.

"How big a hole?"

"Twelve meters—eighteen meters—twenty-four," counted Kim, fighting to keep his traitorous voice under control.

"Get phasers on line," ordered the captain. "I don't know what—"

At that moment, the *Victory* released a gravity wave. Janeway saw the space distort around the vessel, suddenly knew just why the pods had been sent to perform their odd little task, and cried out, "Brace for impa—"

A blow of enormous force buffeted the *Voyager*. Janeway was hurtled sideways. She forced herself to relax, to absorb the inevitable shock of striking the floor of the bridge rather than fight it, just as she had been trained to do since her Academy days. Even so, her right shoulder hit the floor hard, and she felt something tear. White-hot pain raced down her arm. The bridge lights flickered, then returned.

Getting to her feet, she glanced around. Tuvok's nostrils trickled green blood from where his head had slammed up against his console. Others had bruises or cuts as well and were clearly shaken, but no one seemed seriously injured.

"Damage reports coming in," managed Kim, gulping. "Two dozen are reporting minor injuries, six serious injuries. Damage to decks four through six in sections ten through thirteen. Reading structural integrity field generator failure on deck eleven. Switching to backup systems on deck thirty-two. The warp engines are off-line."

"The hole in the shields is widening, Captain." Tuvok's voice was slightly thick due to his injury, but he appeared as calm as ever. His steadiness was a rock, Janeway thought.

"The *Conquest* has resumed its attack on the planet," said Paris, "and the *Victory* is gearing up to fire again."

"Hard to port," commanded Janeway, clutching her injured shoulder for one brief, blessed second before she removed her left hand. She gritted her teeth against the pain. It would be easily treated once she could get to sickbay. In the meantime, it was demoralizing for any crew to see their captain in pain. She could bluff it out.

She sank back in her chair and braced herself for the fresh wave of agony as Tom Paris expertly pulled the big ship, as she had commanded, very hard to port. The second Akerian attack thudded harmlessly against *Voyager*'s shields, and the ship trembled only slightly from the impact.

"Captain, sensors have been able to ascertain that there is no life on any of the six pods," Kim announced with a hint of relieved triumph.

"Excellent." Janeway leaned forward, her eyes snapping. "Then let's blow those things to kingdom come."

She allowed herself a brief, ignoble flush of pleasure as she anticipated the small, empty pods responsible for the damage to her ship exploding with a single phaser blast. The first one burst asunder, sending fragments flying, just as she had envisioned, but then something terrible and unexpected happened.

The one immediately beside the first destroyed pod self-destructed. It blew up with considerably more force, sending shards of slick black metal flying. The space around it shuddered, and Janeway realized with a sinking feeling what kind of trap they'd walked into by firing on the first pod. The third followed suit immediately, then the fourth, fifth, and sixth. Each destructing pod emitted its own wave of gravitons, forcing the shield open even further. By now, the hole in the shields was enormous—a clear and easy target for the *Victory,* who even now was hastening to maneuver its bulk into position to fire.

"They were booby-trapped," she cried. "They were set to self-destruct and take more of our shields with them! Mr. Paris, evasive action. I give you a free hand, just keep us out of *Victory*'s sights. That ship's too fast, and it knows just where to hit us."

"Aye, Captain," responded the helmsman. *Voyager* immediately dove. Paris had read her urgent tone of voice correctly. There was little smoothness to his maneuvers, but they did the job better than any sleek, level movements would have. "The *Conquest* is continuing to fire on the planet."

Another surge of pain hit Janeway as she moved. She fought it back. There was no place for personal physical pain aboard a starship bridge in battle, and like it or not, the Akerians had embroiled them in one.

"We're going in. Fire at both ships at your best opportunity," she commanded. Paris's fingers flew over the consoles. *Voyager,* with the speed of a predator, lined up *Conquest* in perfect range. Silently, Janeway commended Paris. Again, he anticipated her wishes. Either ship would have been a prime, and indeed necessary, target, but the one that was actively attacking innocent civilians got just a little higher priority than the one that had attacked them personally.

Tuvok fired. Red screamed across the space and hit the *Conquest* solidly, connecting directly behind where the now-infamous black pods were situated. Its shields held.

"Again," commanded Janeway. Tuvok obliged. This time, *Conquest* took damage. There was an explosion, and the ship veered off at a crazy angle.

At the same moment *Voyager* rocked from yet another attack from the *Victory,* which was even now racing around from their starboard side, trying to position itself for an attack on the unprotected area of the saucer.

Automatically Janeway reached to slap her comm badge, wincing as the gesture sent red-hot torment up and down her arm. Instead, she used her left hand. "Bridge to Engineering. How long till we can repair that hole?" She didn't ask the real question that raced through her mind: *Can the shield even be repaired.*

To her surprise, it was Lieutenant Carey's deep voice that answered. "Not any time soon, Captain.

The graviton polarity source generators have been damaged. That attack knocked out one of the millicochrane subspace field distortion amplifiers. Torres is leading a crew and working on it now. Even if she can repair it immediately, it'll be at least another hour before—"

The menacing form of *Victory* swung into view. "Fire phasers," snapped Janeway. Again, the phasers screamed, doing no damage. Janeway didn't need to repeat the order; Tuvok fired again. This time, as with the *Conquest,* the ship took a hit. It tumbled to port, temporarily out of control. Janeway resisted the urge to order another attack. Her job was to disable the vessel, not destroy it.

"Captain, the *Conquest* has resumed its attack on Veruna Four," came Paris's voice.

"Carey, tell B'Elanna to work at warp speed on getting those shields back up. Tuvok, fire again. These people just won't quit, will they?"

"No," said Neelix, although the question was rhetorical. "Those who've run afoul of them say they never surrender and never flee."

How reassuring, thought Janeway sarcastically, but she said nothing. The pain in her shoulder was screaming now. She'd need to get it looked at soon, or else she wouldn't be able to concentrate. She forced back the torment. Tuvok fired yet again, directing the phasers at the already damaged area. This time, the damage was far greater. *Conquest* jagged to port, spinning slowly, at last coming to a stop. It hung at an odd angle, and any movement was clearly drift. It was obviously now dead in space.

Janeway swore softly. "Number of life-forms aboard the *Conquest?*"

"Can't get an exact number, but there are quite a— Captain!" Kim glanced up. "The *Victory*'s shields just went down. I'm reading a transporter carrier wave. My guess is they're beaming their comrades from *Conquest* aboard." A heartbeat later, he reported, "*Victory*'s shields are back up."

"Let's hail them, Mr. Kim." She leaned back in her chair, eyes still locked on the image of the ship on the screen. "Maybe they're willing to talk to us now."

But the Akerians, just as Neelix had said, were not about to surrender. They responded to the hail by firing another wave. Janeway saw the twisting, invisible shimmer and cried, "Evasive action!"

Paris had beaten her to it, and the *Voyager* slammed hard to starboard before the words had left her lips. But fast as Paris was, he was not fast enough. The tail of the wave hit the vast, open area engendered by the pods, and another powerful blow slammed into the ship. Janeway's vision grew dim as the impact jarred her wounded shoulder, and she fought like a tigress to hang on to consciousness.

"Damage reports coming in from all over the ship," said Kim. "Engineering reports a coolant leak in the primary warp core. We're venting plasma from the port nacelle. Engineering is responding."

On the view screen, their enemy appeared to be using this final volley as a distraction. It veered off speedily but not going immediately into warp. For a moment Janeway wondered if it would seek refuge in Sun-Eater. Instead the vessel peeled off in another direction entirely.

"Of course," she said, continuing her train of thought aloud, "it can't go into Sun-Eater, not now. We damaged its shields. Until they repair them, the gravity well would crush them." She took a deep breath. She'd have to go to sickbay soon, but she couldn't leave the bridge just yet.

"Cancel red alert." At once the bridge's lights brightened and the pulsing crimson beat ceased. "Try to raise the planet, Mr. Kim."

A pause as Kim attempted to hail. "Not responding, Captain."

Damn, Janeway thought. "Keep at it."

"Torres to bridge."

"Janeway here. What's going on down there, B'Elanna?"

"The coolant leak has been locked down, but the warp engines are going to be off-line for a few more hours." The disgust was evident in her voice. Janeway smiled slightly. B'Elanna Torres took any fault in her engines personally. "Lieutenant Carey's taking care of that. My crew and I are making good progress on the field distortion amplifiers, though. We should be able to have full shielding capability back within eighty minutes."

"Excellent, Torres. Good work. Janeway to sickbay."

"Sickbay," came the doctor's annoyed voice. "Captain, I've got twenty-seven people in here, some with severe injuries. Kes has her hands full and so do I. May I ask what—?"

"I'll tell you myself in a few moments when I'm down in sickbay," Janeway soothed. "No casualties?"

"Only my nerves," replied the hologram.

Janeway smiled. "I promise, Doctor, I—"

"Captain," interrupted Kim, pleasure on his golden face, "Veruna Four is hailing us!"

Relief vied with apprehension as Janeway replied, "On screen."

The graceful, composed visage of *Viha* Nata again appeared on the screen. This time, though, she was surrounded by rubble and scenes of wreckage. Her own face was bruised and cut, her clothing stained and torn. Behind her, her people bustled with activity. Janeway saw many limp, torn bodies being carried off to sounds of mourning and cries of fear. She'd known to expect this scene, but it moved her deeply nonetheless.

"Captain Janeway," said the Verunan, her voice deep and laden with grief. "Thank you. We know that you tried to defend us, indeed succeeded. Had the Akerians been permitted to continue bombarding our poor planet, they would have left nothing behind. We are grateful."

"I'm pleased to see you well, *Viha* Nata," said Janeway sincerely. "Can you tell us"—*What?* Janeway thought, with an uncharacteristic flash of bitterness, *How many of your people died? How much of your civilization lies in ruins?*—"the extent of the damage to Veruna Four?"

"We cannot yet know for certain, but the casualties number in the thousands," replied the *Viha* soberly. "And that is not counting the two hatching pits, filled with dozens of our unhatched younglings, that have been obliterated." She paused, fighting for composure and losing it. Great tears welled in her eyes, made wet furrows down the fine fur of her face. "Three of the dead are two of my daughters and my mate of twenty turns."

"*Viha,* I am sorry," breathed Janeway. The words sounded so useless, but she hoped the Verunan elder knew she meant them. "We can best help you if we understand the situation with the Akerian ships. We rendered one dead in space. The second one fled, but not into Sun-Eater, as we expected. Do you have any idea where it has gone?"

Viha Nata looked so lost and forlorn, Janeway ached to comfort her. The captain didn't even want to think how she'd hold together had she undergone what Nata had just suffered—her people slain by the thousands, her husband and children lying dead somewhere, and she, because of her duties, unable to go and properly mourn their loss. With the strength that had made her the leader of her kind, Nata composed herself and answered.

"This star system is not their home. They are strangers here. They have a base inside Sun-Eater, but their home planet lies in another system a few light-years from here. Where, we do not know; we cannot travel at the speed of the light. I suspect that Linneas has taken the *Victory* there for repairs."

"And from what we've been able to determine about Sun-Eater, Linneas would not have been able to communicate with the base inside."

Hope flickered on Nata's exhausted face. "They will not return for hours, certainly, perhaps not even for days. Thank you again, Captain Janeway. You have bought us time—the most precious thing in the world to us now."

Janeway conjured a mental picture of the system's sun being drained of its hydrogen as if by some celestial vampire and knew that despite the Verunan's kind words, time was running out.

CHAPTER

5

JANEWAY DISCOVERED, AS SHE ENTERED SICKBAY, THAT the doctor had not exaggerated. The place was crammed with patients. The most seriously wounded occupied the three beds and the biobed, and a few others sat on the chairs in the doctor's office. Even so, many who were bleeding or who clearly had injuries that were far from trivial had to sit on the floor or even stand. The captain's first instinct was to let others proceed ahead of her. Had the crisis truly been over, she probably would have followed that instinct. But the ship was still in danger, even though that danger was not immediate, and she would better serve her crew if she didn't feel as though any sudden movement would cause her to pass out.

"Captain!" Kes's soft, lyrical voice was filled with concern. The slim young Ocampa female approached

Janeway quickly. There was blood on her leaf green outfit and slender hands, Janeway noticed. But the girl's large blue eyes were strong and steady. None of this had shaken her. "What happened?"

"I took a tumble on the bridge," Janeway explained. "I know something tore, but I'm not sure just how bad it is." Gently, the nurse laid cool fingers along Janeway's arm, probing. Despite herself, Janeway hissed in pain. Kes grimaced in apologetic sympathy and indicated a bed that was still occupied.

The holographic doctor was just finishing up. He ran the scanner up and down the patient's leg, his eyes fastened on the readings given by his medical tricorder. He did not look up, but he was aware of his captain's presence.

"And here she is in the flesh, Captain Rough and Ready herself," he snapped. "And what new, exciting adventure have you embroiled us in this time, Captain?"

After the tense battle on the bridge, the doctor's sarcasm was a refreshing breath of normalcy. Others might find his taut, strident attitude irritating, but at this moment it was music to Janeway's ears. She could feel the knot in her belly, that cold hardness that had been there since the little Verunan vessel had hurtled out of the concavity, starting to untie.

She rejoined in kind. "Defending gentle dinosaurs against faceless aliens who live in a giant black hole." Close enough.

His dark eyes met hers for just a moment, then lowered again to the tricorder. "My fault for asking," he sighed. Addressing the young man on the table, he announced brusquely, "You're fine. You may return to duty now." The man hurriedly vacated the bed, seemingly relieved at the thought of returning to perhaps a second battle rather than remaining under the good doctor's scrutiny for a moment longer.

With a smile and whisper of soft fabric, Kes had gone, leaving the captain to the doctor. There were other patients she needed to help. Janeway eased herself onto the bed. "During the battle I took a spill. I tore something in my right shoulder, maybe did something else to it as well."

The doctor nodded absently. His instruments whirred softly as he ran the scanner down her arm. "Torn ligaments and a hairline fracture of the humerus. Nothing serious." He reached for an instrument, activated it, and shone the warm red light on the injured area. At once Janeway felt the pain begin to recede.

"I've noticed some other injuries that are harder to explain. Two people," he nodded over at the other beds, "suffered internal injuries. They bled from all orifices, but there was nothing to indicate a direct blow. Just what kind of battle were we in?"

"We were struck by a very powerful gravity wave. Your patients suffered from a brief intensification of the gravity surrounding their bodies—from one *g* to, I'd guess, maybe three. There were no casualties, were there?"

"Negative. They were in a lot of pain, and there was some damage, but they'll be fine."

"I wasn't kidding about the dinosaurs," she continued, watching him work. "Well, at least not much. We've encountered a bipedal sauroid race that's presently under attack. We were defending them when we were attacked by the gravity wave weapon." Her face sobered as she recalled *Viha* Nata's plight. "They've suffered terrible tragedy. I'd like to do what we can to aid them. I know our supplies aren't unlimited, but when the dust settles with the Akerians, perhaps we could assist them in tending to their wounded."

The doctor snorted. "So now I'm to play nursemaid to dragons, hmm? Well, it will be an interesting challenge, if nothing else." The pain had completely vanished. Janeway reached to rub her shoulder, flexed it experimentally.

"Good as new. Thank you, Doctor."

She slipped off the bed, yielding it to a pretty, pale young ensign who had a vicious rip down her face. Janeway took comfort in the knowledge that even in the crowded sickbay, everyone would receive attention and recover completely. There would be no such luck for the unfortunate inhabitants of Veruna Four, Janeway thought as she stepped into the turbolift.

Tom Paris's eyes were red and full of grit. He was exhausted, just like everyone else present. He sighed and rubbed at his itchy eyes, trying to get them to clear.

I know this conference room better than I do my own quarters, he mused without humor. Stifling a yawn, he forced himself to sit forward on his chair rather than slumping back. It was easier to stay awake that way.

"Status reports, everyone," requested Janeway. She looked alert and on top of things as usual. Idly, Paris wondered how she managed it. "B'Elanna, how's Engineering coping with everything?"

The half-Klingon grimaced, the gesture making her

face look more Klingon and less human than it normally appeared. "Not as well as I'd like, but frankly as well as can be expected. The good news is, we've managed to repair the graviton polarity source generators. The shields should be up to full strength within the hour. The bad news is, we won't be going anywhere fast anytime soon. We'll need at least six more hours to repair the warp engines. As for the structural damage to decks eleven through fourteen, I've got crews working on it."

Janeway looked relieved and waved a hand reassuringly. "The shields are the most important thing. We don't need warp drive at the moment. Six hours will do. I've just been down to sickbay myself, so I can report on that situation. I saw nothing that the good doctor won't be able to handle. We got off damn lucky." Her face hardened. "We'll have to see to it that this doesn't happen again. Now," she said, leaning forward and lacing her fingers together on the table, "I would like to bring *Viha* Nata in on the rest of this conversation. She might be able to tell us more about the concavity they call Sun-Eater and about the Akerians. Any objections?"

She glanced around the room, catching and holding every officer's eyes. Paris thought she held his gaze unusually long, and he was glad there wasn't a telepath in the room. He felt sorry for *Viha* Nata and her people, naturally. Who wouldn't? But there was something about that serpentine head, the elongated muzzle, that . . . well, that gave him the creeps. He'd never liked reptiles, whether they walked, crawled, slithered on their stomachs, or stood upright wearing clothes and talking. He held his tongue nonetheless. If the captain wanted to talk to these . . . could one really call them "people"? . . . then it wasn't his place to nay-say her as long as they didn't pose a threat.

"Captain, are you proposing beaming her on board?" Tuvok's question held a slight—oh, so very slight—trace of disapproval.

"Certainly not. I don't want to contaminate this culture any further than we have already. But she can be privy to this meeting via viewscreen. She's seen our bridge. I doubt there's anything in this conference room more revealing."

Tuvok dipped his head in graceful concession. "With that stipulation, I see no reason not to have her input on this situation."

Nobody else voiced any problem. Paris noted that Chakotay even looked eager to have the *Viha* as a participant. Janeway reached forward and activated the viewscreen on the table.

The alien visage flashed on the screen—huge yellow eyes, pointy muzzle, strange shock of white hair. Paris thought he did an admirable job of hiding his dislike. He forced his face to remain neutral as the creature started speaking.

"Thank you, Captain, for agreeing to this audience. I will do whatever I can to assist you and your crew."

"Are you certain this isn't keeping you from more pressing duties, *Viha?*" asked Janeway.

Viha Nata shook her head. "I am but one individual. The need here on Veruna Four now is for many helping hands. I can best serve my people by sharing the knowledge housed in this old head with those who have so valiantly fought the Akerians on our behalf."

The captain opened her mouth as if to contest the

Verunan's last statement, then apparently decided to let it slide. "Let me briefly introduce my officers. This is my first officer, Commander Chakotay; Chief Engineer B'Elanna Torres; Security Officer Lieutenant Tuvok; Chief of Operations Ensign Harry Kim; and here on my left is Lieutenant Tom Paris." The introductions over, she leaned toward the *Viha,* all business now. "You say the Akerians have a base in Sun-Eater. Do you know if it takes them anywhere? Is it a tunnel of sorts?"

Again, the *Viha* shook her head. "We know they go in and they go out. Our five scouts who died so bravely apparently discovered much on their fatal mission. Unfortunately, the transmission was lost to us shortly after reception. We did not have time to interpret the data for which they gave their lives."

"Well, then, *Viha,* I've got a surprise for you," said Janeway. "We *did* get the data. We'll be more than happy to transmit it to you after the meeting. For now, Mr. Kim, can you summarize?"

Beaming, Kim sat up straighter, occasionally consulting the PADD in front of him. "We got both visual and audio from the scout ship but not very much of either. There was a lot of interference." He reached forward and activated the program on the viewscreen. *Viha* Nata's face blipped out to be replaced by a strange oblong shape that resembled a planet—provided it was viewed inside a fun house mirror.

"We have no records of the ship's entrance into the concavity. I'd guess sensors, maybe even visual, were too confused to record any useful information. This . . . hole, for want of a better term, is enormous.

That's not just a base in there, Captain—that's a whole *planet.*"

Paris whistled softly.

"The hole's gravitational pressure is strong enough to distort light, as you can see here, making all the images themselves appear contorted. That's what makes me think the concavity is not simply a worm-hole, but something more complicated. Normal space would not be distorted, and a true black hole wouldn't permit any light at all. What we can see here and what the audio confirms is that there are the ruins of some sort of ancient civilization on this planet."

Kim enlarged the picture, leaned forward, and pointed a finger at some puckers and shapes on the distorted planet face. "These," and he indicated a couple of dome-shaped objects, "are constructs that have been erected by the Akerians—for the purpose of housing Verunan slaves." His face was somber.

"Slaves? For what?" demanded B'Elanna. "What could they possibly want on a destroyed planet?"

"Information," said Janeway. "Under that kind of gravitational pressure, excavation of the planet would be a long, difficult, dangerous job. Am I right, Mr. Kim?"

Kim nodded. "That is what the three rescued Verunans said."

"How many more remain?" asked Chakotay.

Kim shrugged. "The ones the scout crew managed to rescue had no idea how many others were left. Shortly after the rescue, the scout ship apparently tripped some sort of sensor alarm. The *Victory* and the *Conquest* appeared shortly afterward. The scout ship fled—and the rest we know." He deactivated the program, and the *Viha*'s face returned to the screen.

"This still doesn't tell us if there's a wormhole in there or not," said Chakotay.

Tuvok cocked an eyebrow. "The fact that it was not mentioned would appear to indicate that there was not one present within the concavity."

"Not necessarily," commented Paris, leaning forward. "We already know that the graviton activity this far away from the concavity is interfering with our sensors. We can only imagine how bad it would be in the heart of the thing. Maybe the scouts didn't report it because they weren't able to determine that it was there."

"Or it wasn't important to them," put in Chakotay.

"That is correct, Commander," the *Viha* confirmed. "Our people went in to discover information about the base and the Akerians with an eye to fighting them—and, now that we know they exist, to freeing our enslaved brethren. We care nothing for wormholes—only our own survival."

Mentally, Paris shrugged. It was unfortunate from *Voyager*'s standpoint, but it made sense.

Janeway sighed and drummed her fingers lightly on the table for a moment. "Ordinarily, I'd send in a probe. But its sensors would be just as confused as the ship's sensors are."

"Plus the sheer gravimetric force would crush it," added Torres.

The captain nodded her agreement.

Kim spoke up. "According to the transmission, neither the *Victory* nor the *Conquest* fired on the scout ship. It was only after it entered normal space that the Akerians mounted an attack."

"*Viha* Nata," said the Vulcan, leaning forward to address the viewscreen, "was your scout ship equipped with weapons of any sort?"

"Yes," answered the *Viha*. "Poor things in comparison to your weaponry, of course, but we, too, know how to harness the red lightning."

"You have directed energy technology?" asked Paris, the question bursting out before he could censor it.

"Yes, indeed, Lieutenant Par-is." Beneath the artificial voice created by the computer, Tom could hear the real sounds of *Viha* Nata's voice stumbling over the pronunciation of his name. "It is part of the gift of knowledge granted by the Ancestors. We have forgotten much of what they left for us. We had no need of so much of it, you see. At least," she amended sadly, "until the coming of the Akerians and the growth of Sun-Eater."

"The Akerians clearly have a very effective weapon in their gravity wave," said Tuvok. "And apparently, the small scout ship was not weaponless either. Yet neither antagonist fired a weapon while inside Sun-Eater. This would seem to indicate that it would be unsafe to engage in any sort of energy manipulation while inside Sun-Eater, be it firing weapons or even attempting to use the transporter."

Janeway nodded. "What we've heard from Mr. Kim appears to substantiate your hypothesis, Mr. Tuvok."

"We know something else," said Chakotay. "Both the Akerian vessels and the small Verunan scout had sufficient shield strength to protect them from the gravity inside Sun-Eater. *Viha* Nata," he said, turning toward the viewscreen, "you have expressed interest in rescuing your people."

"Indeed, Commander. That is a top priority." *Viha* Nata's voice was crisp and hard. The large eyes narrowed with determination.

"Captain, may I make a suggestion?" asked the first officer. Janeway nodded that he might proceed. "*Viha,* your people would be safe from attack while inside Sun-Eater, wouldn't you agree?"

"Yes," said the *Viha* cautiously. She, like everyone else, was clearly wondering what Chakotay was getting at.

"It's when you leave Sun-Eater, when the Akerian ships are free to attack, that your ships would be in danger."

"I see," said Janeway. "You're suggesting that we provide cover for them while they go in and rescue their people."

"And," finished Chakotay, "while one of us goes in with them to see if the verteron emanations really do indicate a wormhole."

Paris felt hope stir within him. He saw it reflected in the tired faces that encircled the table, in the sudden tautness with which the officers sat a little straighter. And he wondered if he really wanted to go home after all, home to prison, albeit a scenic one in New Zealand.

But *Viha* Nata was shaking her head. "It would be a fine plan, but unfortunately the only ship with enough shield strength to withstand the jaws of Sun-Eater was the scout vessel."

"You don't have any other ships with shields?" Kim's disappointment made the question sound like an accusation.

"We learned the shielding technique from a disabled Akerian vessel only recently," the *Viha* explained. "There was no time to implement it in other vessels. We were uncertain even if it would work."

"There goes that idea," said Paris glumly.

Janeway looked thoughtful. "Not necessarily. *We* could go into Sun-Eater and find out for ourselves."

"I do not think it would be prudent," Tuvok advised. "There can be no doubt that, if there are more Akerian vessels at this base, and we must assume that there are, they would perceive it as an attack."

"My thoughts exactly, Vulcan!" piped up Neelix. "We should not put this vessel directly at risk. I don't think anyway."

"I seem to recall a certain Talaxian saying that the Akerians never surrender and never flee," said Paris archly.

Neelix didn't miss a beat. "And delighted I am to be wrong. Absolutely delighted."

"But would it even matter?" chimed in Kim. "I mean, if there is a wormhole in there, and all the evidence we've gathered seems to indicate that there is, then we'd simply go through it."

"Mr. Kim," replied Tuvok, "I did not think I needed to remind you that there is only a one in four chance that this wormhole will lead to the Alpha Quadrant."

Kim ducked his head, blushing. Paris felt a wave of sympathy. Harry was a good kid. A little overeager, perhaps, but his enthusiasm had made Paris's day more than once. He didn't like to see Harry getting slapped down, even if it was by a Vulcan who certainly didn't mean it as a personal attack.

"But even the Beta Quadrant would cut down our time immensely," said Paris, defending his friend. "That means it's a fifty–fifty shot."

"And even if there is no wormhole," said Chakotay, "we know that we are more than able to defend ourselves against the Akerians as long as we don't let those pods attach themselves to our shields a second time. I say we go in."

Everyone else seemed in agreement, and Tuvok raised an eyebrow and nodded, yielding to the will of the majority. Neelix alone looked thoroughly unhappy with the decision.

"Captain," came the *Viha*'s voice. "If you have decided to enter Sun-Eater, may we ask that you attempt to rescue our people?"

Janeway looked apologetic. "*Viha*, much as we sympathize with your cause, such direct involvement would have to be looked on by the Akerians as an act of war. And that, we're not prepared to do. I'm sorry."

Viha Nata lowered her head. Even Paris felt a twinge of sympathy for the strange-looking creature.

Chakotay spoke up. "Captain, we could take a few of them in under our shields. That way, we'd be providing protection from the gravimetric force without openly engaging in the rescue mission."

Janeway considered this. "B'Elanna, would extending our shields to cover the Verunan ships put an undue strain on them?"

The half-Klingon engineer shook her dark head. "Negative, Captain. Not once they're up to full strength."

Janeway straightened in her chair, fixing her officers with a hawk's gaze. "I'd like to help these people where we can," she announced. "Passive shielding could help them transport innocent people to safety without jeopardizing our ship or our own mission to explore the concavity. Your opinions?"

"Captain, if we are successful, we would not be returning," Tuvok pointed out.

The captain's face hardened. "It would cost us nothing but a little time to escort them back out, see them safely to Veruna Four, and reenter Sun-Eater. I'm willing to give them that time."

"Captain," and Chakotay's smooth voice was somber, "we will be abandoning them to the wrath of the Akerians. Do you wish to rescue them, then leave them to their fate?"

Viha Nata spoke up before Janeway could reply. "Commander Chakotay, we do not expect you to fight our battles for us—even though you could win them and we cannot. It is not your sun that is dying by the day. It is not your children who die huddled in their shells. It is not your planet that now reeks of decay as the temperature warms by the hour. You have already frightened our enemies away, something that even the most idealistic of us never dreamed possible. Certainly, they will return. Certainly, they will destroy us, and even if they do not, only a few more generations of Verunans will survive on this besieged planet of ours.

"The question is not if we will die. It is when and

how. We ask that you help us to die with honor, die resisting to the last, with our stolen people brought home to be reunited, however briefly, with their loved ones. It is better to die free than to die a slave. That will be enough. We cannot and will not ask you for more."

Paris wasn't sure if the words were meant to cause guilt or to alleviate it, but he knew that he sure as hell felt guilty. Then again, it was a feeling that was no stranger to him. He'd endured that emotion often throughout his checkered career. He glanced furtively around to gauge the reaction of his fellows. Kim looked miserable. Everyone else, with the expected exception of Tuvok, also looked uncomfortable to various degrees.

Janeway broke the awkward silence. "Then we're agreed. Very well, *Viha* Nata, we'll escort your ships into Sun-Eater. Now, on to other matters. First of all, I plan to transport over to the damaged Akerian vessel and see what we can glean from their computer that might help us. Mr. Kim, I'd like you to accompany me."

"Request permission to also be part of the away team," said Torres. Her dark eyes were snapping with enthusiasm. She was never happier than when she was with her beloved engines, mused Paris; she seemed more at home with them than with people. He couldn't think of anything that would interest her more than getting her hands on a totally alien engineering system.

"Request granted," said Janeway, "but you're to report back to the *Voyager* as soon as you can. I need you to get everything back on-line. And when that's done, I'm going to send you down to the planet to look at the Verunan vessels. We'll see if we can't beef them up a little bit, get them operating at peak efficiency when we go into that concavity."

Both B'Elanna and Nata expressed pleased surprise. "Captain, thank you! We would welcome Torres's expertise more than you can know."

"Lieutenant, I'd like you to go with her."

It took Paris a full five seconds to realize that she was talking to him. His gut clenched. "Me, Captain?"

A peculiar smile curved Janeway's lips. *"You,* Lieutenant. I want you to take a look at the ships, see what they're capable of doing. Talk to the pilots. Get to know them. When we go into Sun-Eater, I want you in the shuttlecraft leading them."

Talk to the pilots. Get to know them. Great, just great.

He didn't hide his expression as clearly as he'd hoped. A furrow creased his captain's forehead. "Do you have a problem with that, Lieutenant?"

"No, no," he hastened to reply. "No problem whatsoever."

"Good. Now, I think—"

"Captain," interrupted Chakotay, "request permission to accompany Torres and Paris."

She looked at him searchingly. "I need you here, Mr. Chakotay."

"I think . . ." The big man glanced over at the image of the reptilian alien on the viewscreen. "There are many things about the Verunan culture that intrigue me. I'd like to learn more about it."

Janeway sighed. "Commander, we are in a rather difficult position, not to mention dangerous. I understand that the Verunan culture must be fascinating, but—"

"Captain, there are many aspects of it that are similar to my own. I might know how to ask questions that generate clearer answers than ones anyone else might suggest." He paused, gathering his words. *"Viha* Nata, correct me if I'm wrong, but your people have a strong oral tradition, don't they? The past is preserved, passed along from person to person through tales and stories."

Viha Nata nodded. "Quite correct, Commander. There are other means of recording events, but we have found this most suitable for us."

He glanced triumphantly over at Janeway, then took another leap. "You personify the concavity—call it Sun-Eater. But you know it's not alive, correct?"

"Of course not. But even things that are not alive have spirits that should be honored."

"Captain, many Native American tribes share that sentiment. I understand that a sun can be a huge ball of burning hydrogen, yet have a spirit. I *think* like the Verunans. That can only be an asset. If we analyze their tales, their mythos—"

"—We might find some cold, hard realities that could help us," finished Janeway, her face beginning to share some of the excitement of Chakotay's. "Very well, Commander. You may join them. Now, let's start putting these plans into action. Mr. Tuvok, the bridge is yours. Ensign Kim, prepare to send *Viha* Nata the communication from the downed ship. Everyone else, to your stations."

Viha Nata's image disappeared. Everyone rose at

once, chattering among themselves. Paris lingered behind, gathering his thoughts and not wishing to talk with anyone else.

But it was not to be. Janeway waited for him outside, walked with him across the bridge, and accompanied him into the elevator. "Transporter room two," she instructed.

Paris stood quietly, his hands behind his back. "Something's bothering you about this, Tom. What is it? Do you find their appearance repugnant?"

"Is it that obvious?"

Janeway smiled kindly. "If you know what to look for," she answered gently.

Paris shrugged, feeling awkward and defensive. "I won't let it interfere with my duties if that's what you're worried about."

"Of course you won't. You're a good officer. It's natural to be uncomfortable around races that we're not familiar with, especially ones that appear unattractive to our human aesthetics. You'll get used to it over time."

"It's foolish. I just . . . they're like overgrown lizards or something."

Janeway smiled a small, secret smile. "I happen to like lizards myself."

CHAPTER
6

HARRY KIM HATED HIS ENVIROSUIT.

Intellectually, he understood and appreciated its many protective functions. He was aware of how much lighter, efficient, and maneuverable it was compared to the bulky "space suits" of the early spaceflight era. And he knew that it was without question a necessity; his examination of conditions aboard the *Conquest* had established that beyond doubt.

But all that didn't mean he had to like it. It made him feel confined, trapped in its head-to-toe swath of protective material. The gravity boots on his feet, here in the one *g* gravity of *Voyager,* felt unbelievably awkward. A quick glance over at B'Elanna Torres showed that the chief engineer, too, disliked the necessity of the suit. But it was the only way they would be able to survive on the Akerian vessel.

He was nowhere near as wide-eyed, as fragile and green, as he had been when he first boarded *Voyager*. But he couldn't even fake the calm, steady movements of his captain and the security guard, both of whom were old hats at this sort of thing. They were about to board a hostile alien vessel that had no life-support on it for the purpose of obtaining information they didn't have from computers they'd never seen.

Harry Kim couldn't *not* be at least a little bit excited.

Moving slowly and awkwardly, the four crew members positioned themselves on the transporter pads. The security guard checked his phaser and held it at the ready. Janeway, Torres, and, belatedly, Kim turned on their wristlights.

Kim's heart began to pound hard as Janeway ordered, "Energize."

An instant later, they stood on an alien bridge. They had been right to come fully prepared, Kim thought to himself as he glanced around. This place was a wreck. Lights flickered on and off in a disconcerting, random pattern. Kim moved his wristlight about, revealing an enormous room filled with hard, black, practical-looking furnishings and consoles. There was little of *Voyager*'s sleek grace apparent here. Like the outside, the bridge of the *Conquest* bespoke brutal efficiency.

Right now, though, that brutal efficiency had been broken by *Voyager*'s attack. Smoke obscured Kim's vision, wafting past in a thick, slow cloud. The ends of wires bobbed, floating like tendrils of sea anemones. The one thing of surprising, powerful beauty was the enormous panorama of space that greeted them when they turned around. The entire bow section of the bridge faced a sheer wall of stars. Kim guessed it was about four stories high and comprised the wall. The beautiful sight of open space it afforded was little short of stunning and strangely incongruous with the sinister feel of the rest of the bridge.

Janeway hit her comm badge. "Janeway to *Voyager*. Transportation was successful. We're on the bridge right now."

"We will continue to monitor you from here, Captain," came Tuvok's reassuring voice.

Kim's eyes narrowed. In front of him was a large globule of liquid. It appeared very dark in this erratic, subdued lighting. Frowning curiously, he automatically reached to touch it with a gloved hand. It burst into several smaller globes, each of which floated off.

"Captain, there appears to be some kind of leak," he said. *Leak from what?*

At the sound of his voice, Janeway turned to regard him. Behind the clear plastic of her face mask, he saw her eyes focus on something slightly above and behind him. She opened her mouth to speak, raised her hand to point.

At that moment, something bumped into his left shoulder. Startled, he whirled around, the movement initiating as swift and sure and degenerating to slow and clumsy in the zero *g*.

He came face-to-face with a floating corpse. The mask covering the dead features hovered mere inches from his own. Kim gasped and instinctively jerked backward. The movement set him off balance, and for what felt like an eternity, he flailed. Then Janeway's hand was there on his elbow, steadying him. Her face was compassionate, and Kim knew that his own radiated his shocked surprise and horror. He'd seen and examined bodies before, but the whole situation here was so surreal, like something right out of a nightmare. He realized with a second jolt of sick dismay that the floating globule he'd put his hand through was no "leak"—at least, not one from the ship. That and the other many balls of dark liquid currently twirling lazily through the zero *g* atmosphere had been the blood of the dead Akerians.

For just a second, Kim hyperventilated. His captain's hand was strong. He caught his breath, calmed himself, and nodded to her. "I'm okay."

She nodded her own head in acknowledgment. "I'm glad you're here to see this, Harry." Her voice was soft, laden with accepted regret. "This," and she gestured to the dead, floating in their damaged vessel, "is the real aftermath of battle."

Torres, who had been examining equipment, turned to regard Janeway.

"They fired on us first, Captain. You were down in sickbay, you saw the sort of damage they could have inflicted if we'd let them."

"I'm not saying we didn't do the right thing." Janeway paused, her blue eyes taking in the scene. "We had no choice. I'm only saying that every action has a result. We made this. We must not *ever* forget how devastating the consequences of our behavior can be. Carry on."

Kim swallowed hard. He was able to look squarely at the corpse now, still shamefully glad that its face, whatever it may have looked like, was covered by the warrior's helmet. Kim didn't feel up to gazing into dead, accusing eyes at the moment. From what he could tell of the Akerian encased in the armor in which he had died, their race was bipedal, vaguely human shaped with regard to the proportion and placement of arms and legs. The head, though, if the helmet was an accurate indication, was enormous. When he was a child, he had adored tales of the Greek gods. The dead being floating in front of him reminded him of the story of the Minotaur—a misconceived creature with the body of a man and the head of a bull. Perhaps it was simply the size of the head and the placement of the ornamental horns that decorated the metal helmet, but once the idea had occurred to Kim, he couldn't shake it.

"I'm picking up energy sources, Captain." B'Elanna was all cool efficiency. Kim admired her calm detachment even as he knew he'd never be able to fathom it. "The readings seem to be emanating from below and behind the bridge area. Permission to locate them?"

"Granted. Take Lieutenant Frazier with you, and report back immediately upon arrival. Watch your step. This ship wasn't designed for humanoids." Torres nodded her understanding. She and the big security guard moved off slowly toward the stern of the bridge, toward what appeared at first glance to be a steep dropoff but proved to have rungs and bars for gripping.

Kim flipped open his own tricorder and regarded it. Its readings indicated, thankfully, that the computer system was still up and running, at least partially. He didn't relish the thought of trying to reboot an entire alien computer system. The console ahead and to his right seemed to be the least damaged. Lights blinked on and off. The general lighting still blitzed in and out, though, and it was rapidly giving Kim a headache.

Time enough to see the doctor when you get back. Right now, focus on the job, Harry.

He stepped forward, glancing from tricorder reading to console, and felt fairly sure that this was his best bet. He sat down in a seat that was clearly not designed for the comparatively narrow breadth of human buttocks and examined the console.

At Starfleet Academy, Kim had been a superior student. He loved the whole theory behind Operations, the linking together of every system, the symmetry of diverse parts working together to create a harmonious whole. He viewed his role as that of a technical diplomat of sorts. His job was to placate all parties, integrate all their strengths, and smooth out or eliminate any discord, all the while working toward a goal that would benefit everyone.

Kim seemed to have a real gift for it. Part of his training had been with a large variety of alien computer systems, and after his seventh or so encounter, he'd begun to realize that some things really were universal. Sentient beings, whatever their culture, tended to have certain needs. Given enough knowledge about the culture itself, Kim found he could walk in cold, analyze a system, and figure it out in record time.

He concentrated on what he knew about the Akerians, what they would hold of value, where they might place what. Deep in thought, he was startled to hear Torres's voice.

"Torres to Janeway. I'm in their Engineering section."

"Go ahead," said Janeway.

"Most of this vessel seems to be given over to their engines," said Torres. "I'm looking at four enormous engines centered around a central core. Everything appears to be off-line."

The unasked question was in the engineer's voice. Kim heard it, and so did Janeway, who replied, "Do not attempt to operate them, Torres. Your job here is as an observer. Make visual and sensor records, then you and Frazier beam directly back over to *Voyager*. Is that understood?"

"Yes, Captain." Acceptance but reluctance. "We should have our analysis complete in about five minutes. I'll get back on board *Voyager* and finish getting her back up to speed. Torres out."

It was time. Kim took a deep, steadying breath, then hit his comm badge. "Kim to *Voyager*."

"Tuvok here."

"I'm sitting in front of the computer console right now," Kim continued. "Prepare to activate the secure partition." Before he had left *Voyager*, Kim had installed a secure partition—a buffer that could easily shut down any dangerous overload should the two computer systems not mesh. Though he would have to instigate the transfer of data here on the *Conquest*, he'd have to trust Tuvok back on *Voyager* with monitoring the influx of information.

"Secure partition activated," came Tuvok's voice.

"Beginning hookup to tricorder now." Kim felt

sweat gathering at his hairline, automatically reached up to wipe it away, and frowned in annoyance as his hand bumped up against the faceplate. He'd just have to endure the tickle. His protected fingers moved over the console, activating it. There was a faint clicking sound, then a steady low whir.

Steadying the tricorder on the console, his fingers found the comm transmission area. With a silent prayer, he pressed the intership key. It worked: the tricorder began to blink, signaling that the subspace transceiver assembly was activated. Hope rose within Kim. It hadn't shorted out so far.

"Link successfully established with the Akerian computer," he informed Tuvok. Out of the corner of his eye he noticed that Janeway had stopped recording on her own tricorder and had turned to watch him. *Nothing like the captain herself watching you to turn the pressure on,* he thought.

"Attempting to transfer data to the *Voyager.* Watch that secure partition, Mr. Tuvok." He licked suddenly dry lips and pressed the pool key.

"Receiving information, Ensign Kim. There appears to be no difficulty in the transfer," said Tuvok's voice.

Kim sagged slightly with relief. "That's music to my ears, Lieutenant."

"That is an inaccurate statement." Tuvok sounded completely unperturbed. "I did not sing the words. Therefore, they could not be interpreted as music."

A grin spread across Kim's face as he caught Janeway's eye. She returned his smile. "Transfer of information should take about ten minutes," said Kim. "Let me know if there's any glitches."

Janeway stepped over to him and placed a gloved hand on his padded shoulder. *Well done,* said the strong grip. Harry smiled with pride, shifted his weight, and waited for the transfer to finish.

While Torres was busy examining the alien's engines and Kim sat engrossed in attempting to set up the transfer, Janeway kept busy herself. She set her tricorder to record images and slowly walked around the *Conquest*'s bridge.

The captain of the *Voyager* was a woman of tolerance and compassion but also of strong opinions. And her opinion of the aesthetics of this Akerian design was extremely low. She liked the elegant, graceful lines of starships, their ergonomic chairs, their egalitarian marriage of beauty, comfort, and efficiency. Even Klingon vessels had more to offer their crew than this chock-a-block construction.

She glanced up at the two bodies floating around her, wondering if she ought to try to take hold of one and attempt to remove its mask. She wanted to know what these creatures looked like, wanted to see what kind of face sat in front of a brain that had no remorse in destroying an entire planet of gentle beings.

She decided against it. *We've dishonored the dead quite enough by killing them in the first place,* she thought. *Leave their corpses to the stars. We'll find out enough about them when we analyze the data from this computer.*

The bridge was enormous, at least four times that of the *Voyager*'s bridge. The Akerians were clearly a strong, agile people, judging from the fact that there were no steps or ramps, only rungs and protruding cylinders that served as footholds. There was a second level above Janeway, and she directed the tricorder at that for a while.

But what drew her attention the most and what she had kept for the last was the almost overwhelming panorama of stars at the bridge's bow. Finally, almost as if she were giving herself a reward, Janeway walked toward the railing and peered down.

Indications of graviton activity suddenly shot up on her tricorder. Below and slightly in front of her, its sphere cut cleanly in half by the windowlike shield, sat what the tricorder reported as a graviton generator. It was not alone. There was a total of four round generators, spaced out evenly on the top, bottom, left, and right of the viewing window. Two of them, the one above and to Janeway's left, were dark. The other two, the one below her and the one to her right, blinked on and off like the lights. When active, the circular generators were a dark orange-red hue. Janeway cast her mind back to the recent conflict, remembering the four red dots—and one in the center.

The lights and the generators went off. She waited, her eyes fastened on the two that had been active. Sure enough, a few seconds later there came another surge. The two generators reddened. Between them stretched a red beam of energy, which vanished as the generators again went dormant.

She was willing to bet that when all four were active they were connected by beams that served to focus power toward the center, and that was what created the powerful force of the gravity wave. Again, Janeway recalled the six small pods, performing a similar dance of destruction. She pointed her tricorder at the graviton generators, recording an active cycle, then turned her gaze toward the third level, situated directly below where she stood.

There, she caught glimpses of more levitating corpses. She steeled herself to look beyond them, but a cursory visual examination yielded little of value. None of the strange equipment would make any sense without detailed examination. They were here to get the information from the computer, and that was whence their knowledge of this culture would finally come.

Her tricorder sensors, like those aboard *Voyager,* were not up to one hundred percent accuracy, but Janeway trusted them when they revealed that a force field was in place about five meters directly in front of her. It would make sense. If the *Conquest* were to receive a direct hit on this clear shield, the consequences would be devastating if there was no backup protection system in place. She suspected that, like the light that flickered on and off and the computer that was still operational, this field had been programmed to withstand an inordinate amount of damage to the ship.

The vista of stars moved slowly as the ship turned in space. Now *Voyager* came into view. Janeway's heart quickened at the sight of her vessel. She didn't often get to see her ship like this. She knew *Voyager* from the inside out, mostly. Certainly, she'd studied her construction, knew her functions almost better than the specific chiefs did. But it was a rare treat, this view from the bridge of an alien ship. She admired her sleek, clean lines, the softness of her curving saucer section, the simple elegance of her.

She spoke often of the "return home," back to the Alpha Quadrant. For her, that meant Mark and Molly Malone. But home, in a sense, would always be the ship. Some people had adventure and traveling in their blood. Much as she loved Mark and the laughing-eyed Irish setter, *Voyager* was as much home to her as any building could be.

Kim's voice cut into her thoughts. "Transmission complete, Captain."

Reluctantly, Janeway turned from the railing and the spectacular view of stars and ship it afforded.

"Then let's get back to our own ship and leave *Conquest* to her dead." She tapped her comm badge. "Janeway to *Voyager*. Two to beam over."

Second Warrior Garai studied his commander without appearing to. He had learned, after many cycles of working closely with the first warrior of the Empirical Exploratory Unit, to read Linneas accurately, despite the lack of facial expression or hand or tail gestures. The commander's voice often gave him away. The way he held his body, suited thought it might be in armor and topped with the all-concealing mask that none of them ever removed save in private, also revealed more than it hid.

Because they were away from family and home so often, the warriors tended to form their own close-knit units. Second Warrior Garai looked upon First Warrior Commander Linneas as kin. Which was why the recent behavior of the first warrior was so disturbing.

Now, as he sat in front of the curving console of *Victory* and stared through the huge window as the stars went streaking by, Linneas drummed his gloved fingers on the smooth, black surface. The click of claws came, even through the gloves. His body was rigid with tension, and the sharp ears of Garai could hear him snorting a little from time to time—a sure sign of distress.

Casually, Garai inclined his head, feigning a stretch. He tilted his helmet, allowing his gaze to fall upon the disgraced Nelek, former first warrior commander of the *Conquest*. No enemy had ever disabled an Akerian explorership—warship, Garai thought to himself—before. Some had tried and failed. For each ship the powerful empire's graviweapon had destroyed, Linneas had proudly carved a notch into the horns atop his helmet. They bore many such scores.

But they did not bear one for the strange alien vessel called the *Voyager*. That failure, plus the hitherto inconceivable dishonor of actually *losing* a ship to the foe, had put Linneas in a bad temper—and had spelled the end of Nelek's formerly illustrious career.

Linneas, outraged and humiliated, had wanted to leave Nelek and his shameful crew to their fate, which would almost certainly have been a brutal death at the hands of the ugly, deformed aliens. Nelek had begged, not so much for his own life as for those of his crew, to be teleported back to safety.

Garai had urged Linneas to mercy, and nearly a hundred Akerian lives had been saved by his pleas. Glancing now at Nelek, Garai wondered if he'd done the right thing. Nelek would go home to Akeras now not in honor, but in disrepute, as would all of his crew. Linneas, bitter and needing someone to blame for the unpredictable catastrophe of defeat, had selected the crew of the ill-named *Conquest*.

The commander had, with his own powerful hands, himself ripped off Nelek's horns. He had ordered him demasked, but the helmets could not be removed by anyone other than their wearers, and Nelek had been so distraught he had been unable to comply with the orders. Now the former commander sat in a huddle on the floor of the bridge, shaking and whimpering. He had practically become a Verunan himself, Garai thought.

It was a dark hour for the empire.

"There is no honor in fighting a losing battle," Garai said, keeping his voice firm and strong. It was an age-old motto, exemplifying the warrior mentality: winning at any cost.

But the phrase brought no comfort to First Warrior, who growled warningly. "We have never had to flee before," snarled Linneas. "The flavor of cowardice sits ill upon my tongue."

"The empress will commend your wisdom, First Warrior, and your courage in returning to continue the attack for the glory of the empire. Surely it is better to bow out of conflict, go home, repair our ship, and return with greater numbers than to fight and not win."

It was what Linneas wanted to hear, what was expected of Garai, the good second warrior, Linneas's first hand. Yet Garai wondered if Linneas's decision to return to challenge the *Voyager* was indeed wise. They hadn't reached Akeras yet, did not know how badly *Victory* was damaged. Too, perhaps Linneas had misjudged the aliens. Perhaps they did not care at all about what lay at the heart of what the Verunans so naively called the Sun-Eater.

Linneas's body relaxed ever so slightly. "Perchance you are right," the commander allowed. "Yes, possibly our eventual victory will be the more honorable because it was so heatedly contested. And when we have won, we shall blow *Voyager* out of the skies and destroy every last one of the Verunans." His big, powerful hands clenched and unclenched. "And I want to take at least one life with these."

This was most disturbing to Garai, but he gave no sign of disapproval. He wondered if he was, as Linneas teased, too soft. Surely no true son of the empire would feel for the Verunans, would question the right of the Akerians to use them for the glory of the empire.

He wondered just what Linneas would tell the empress. More lies or the truth? Probably the former. Only a few emperors had been let into the secret. He didn't think Riva would be one. He wondered how willing the other commanders would be to follow the commander of *Victory* into a battle that some, quietly and anonymously, were already beginning to question.

Garai, good, loyal second warrior of the Empirical Exploratory Unit, first hand to Commander Linneas, looked out at the streaking stars, recalled the face of the beautiful empress, relived the brutalities he had been part of over past few months, and thought extremely disloyal thoughts.

CHAPTER

7

THE FIRST THING THAT FLASHED INTO TOM PARIS'S MIND as he, Chakotay, and Torres materialized on Veruna Four was the title of an old Earth poem: *Paradise Lost*. He'd never read the piece, knew nothing of what it was about, but the two words seemed to sum up the dreadful enormity of the catastrophe that was occurring, both in the space above the planet and on the surface itself.

The moist heat of the place and the glimpses of once-lush vegetation called to mind images of curvaceous females, rum punches, and, well, moments where a wonderful time was had by all parties concerned. But this heat was cloying and uncomfortable, with no ocean readily available to cool the skin. The sun, far redder than it had any real right to be, beat down through a hazy gray cloud layer that, Paris knew, was all but permanent now. It was a direct result of the atmospheric evaporation caused by the growing red giant.

These tropical trees were shriveling up, their formerly luxuriant foliage brown and decaying. Fruit that had never been permitted to ripen now rotted on the trees. The nearly overpowering stench of decomposition of plants and, Paris realized, animals—everything probably from fish to fowl to the Verunan dead themselves—dispelled any image of paradise with an evil laugh.

He felt his gorge rise at the smell and swallowed hard. It wouldn't do, he mused darkly, to throw up upon immediate sight of the planet. The Verunans just might take that as an insult.

He felt a gentle pressure on his back. "It makes the heart and body sick, I know. I have seen this destruction every waking hour, scented it in my dreams, and it affects me thus as well."

Startled, Paris jerked away, glancing over at the speaker . . . and up . . . and *up*. He hadn't realized just how tall these creatures were. The sharp, reptilian face grimacing (*smiling, Tom, smiling!*) down at him was attached to a sinuous neck that was fully two-thirds of a meter long if it was a centimeter. The enormous shoulders to which the neck attached were broader than even Chakotay's. And the hand that rested so softly on his shoulder had sharp, wicked-looking claws that were as long as human fingers.

He forced himself to smile in return, recognizing the figure as *Viha* Nata and telling himself that she meant to comfort him.

"My apologies, *Viha*," he managed, straightening. "I was not prepared for the full extent of the devastation of your planet. It is . . ." Words failed him, but apparently *Viha* Nata understood, for she nodded, sighing and shaking her head in sorrow. She composed herself and turned to face the others, straightening to her full height of perhaps two and a half meters.

Paris realized that Nata was not alone. Two others stood with her, slightly behind, as befitted her position. Both of them wore not the flowing, simple garb of the *Viha*, but something that resembled uniforms—close-fitting, padded, single-colored fabric that covered them from head to, well, ankle. Their feet, large, splayed, and lizardlike, were hard enough so that the Verunans didn't seem to need shoes. There were holes cut into the garments that permitted the thick white tails to come through.

One, who stood with its arms crossed and snakelike head cocked in a rather pugilistic attitude, met Paris's eyes evenly. Its tail swished restlessly back and forth. The second stood as if at attention, its arms folded behind its back and its amber eyes trained on *Viha* Nata. Other than their poses and attitudes, they looked exactly alike to Paris's eyes, unused as of yet to the subtle differences between individuals.

"Please allow me to introduce my compatriots. This is Kaavi, our top remaining pilot. Lieutenant Paris, she will be your liaison here on Veruna."

Kaavi's eyes narrowed, and she ducked her head in a quick bow of courtesy. Paris did likewise. *She's got a chip on her shoulder a kilometer wide,* he thought sourly. *Wonder if it's about us?*

"And Chief Engineer Torres, this is *our* chief engineer, Anahu."

In contrast to Kaavi's brusque, almost rude acknowledgment, Anahu dipped his long neck in a graceful gesture of welcome. "Your presence here gives us new hope, Chief Engineer Torres." The comm badges translated the voice as masculine.

"Commander Chakotay, your captain told us that you were interested in our culture. Such interest honors our people. I myself will do my best to familiarize you with our ways."

Chakotay bowed, almost as graceful as Anahu. "I hope by learning about your people to learn how best to help you."

While the introductions were going on, Paris felt Kaavi's eyes drilling into him, as if she thought she could read his soul if she looked at him hard enough. It was very uncomfortable. He feigned unawareness of her perusal and glanced about the beamdown site, trying to ignore the trickle of wetness already starting to form beneath his armpits in response to the almost overwhelming heat and humidity of the place. He activated his tricorder and began to take readings.

At first glance, the Verunans were an extremely simple—one might say "primitive"—race. Nothing about *Viha* Nata's garb or ordinary manner of speaking displayed any knowledge about faster-than-light spaceship travel, electronic communication, or anything beyond the knowledge of a simple village elder. The little area to which they had beamed down also gave that impression. In the immediate vicinity at least, nothing other than organic materials registered on the tricorder.

They stood in a large, flat area. A few meters to their right was an open, bubbling pit of hot mud. This seemed important to the Verunans, for they had erected some sort of shelter over the pit. Smooth-surfaced and curving, displaying no harsh edges, it resembled a canopy made out of shiny brown stone. The heat emanating from that area was almost intolerable.

Leading off from the pit, in four regimented lines, were smaller huts apparently constructed of the same glossy stone. They were little more than token protection against the elements. Through the open doors, Paris could see flat, woven mats; a few bowls and pitchers of the ubiquitous brown stone; and small, shadowy shapes—their young, perhaps?—moving back and forth. These individual huts stretched off several more meters, each line ending in a larger, closed hut.

There was a movement, and a miniature version of the adult Verunans poked its head out. He'd been right; the shapes he'd glimpsed in the shadows had been children. The young Verunan was only about two feet tall, and it stared at Paris, wide-eyed, for a second or two before ducking back into the shadows. Like all young things, it was more appealing than the adults.

Paris turned his eyes back to the churning, foul-smelling mud. He wondered why in the world the Verunans would choose to set their camp around such a, well, unpleasant natural formation. Casually, he glanced down at the tricorder, and his pulse suddenly jumped.

"Commander, something alive is trapped in there!" he cried, already moving toward the pit.

The harsh rasping that he was learning to recognize as Verunan laughter stopped him. Puzzled, still tense, he glanced questioningly at *Viha* Nata.

"Of course there is something alive in the pit," chuckled the elder. "The day that there is not will be a day of great mourning. That is one of our hatching pits."

Paris stared. "Hatching pit?" he repeated stupidly.

"You . . . you put your eggs in that?" asked Torres, a trifle indelicately.

The *Viha* nodded. "The heat incubates our eggs. Whenever a female is with child, she enters the hatching pit and deposits her eggs there. And whenever a mated pair is desirous of a child, they come to the pit and wait for a hatchling to choose them."

"So, there is no way of determining actual parentage?" asked Chakotay.

Paris stared at the steaming pit of hot mud, slightly incredulous.

Viha Nata seemed puzzled. "All are parents to the child. Every child is wanted. No child will lack for a loving family. Does it matter whose body lays the egg?"

The adrenaline that had been surging through Paris's body abated, leaving him feeling slightly weakened. He breathed deeply to steady himself, trying not to gag at the stench. Kaavi's serpentine head drooped slightly, and she looked unhappy. Duty rather than real concern prodded Paris to ask, "Is something wrong?"

The top Verunan pilot shook her head. "No. Not really. I—I have refused to take a mate, to have a child, until we have banished the Akerians from our skies, until we have somehow managed to wrest a future for ourselves on this dying planet." She smiled, a hard smile that even Chakotay would have called a grimace. "And that day seems to be longer and longer in coming."

"That's why we're here," said Chakotay, reaching to touch Kaavi's arm.

She did not jerk away from the touch but fixed him with an appraising stare. "You are here to learn what you can about Sun-Eater, not to help us win this battle."

"Kaavi!" snapped *Viha* Nata, her normally pleasant voice harsh with rebuke.

The younger female raised her head, tossed her white locks defiantly. The beads braided in them clattered at the motion. "I have listened to everything they have told us, *Viha*. I have no doubt but that they mean well, but let us not fool ourselves into thinking that they are here as our saviors."

Paris kept his face neutral, but his mind went over what he had seen thus far of Verunan culture. They'd need saviors indeed to fight the Akerians on any kind of level other than verbal. Nothing he saw indicated an advanced civilization. But there *had* to be something. They'd managed to communicate with the *Voyager* via viewscreen, and Paris himself had observed the complex satellite system in place above the planet's surface. What was going on?

"Kaavi is right. We'll do what we can, but I'm not

sure how much help we'll be. But I think, Kaavi, that that is how you would wish it. For your victory to be a true one, you must be the ones to fight the battle," said Chakotay.

Kaavi's hard face softened a little. "Then . . . you do understand us, how we think."

Laughing, Chakotay held up a warning hand. "I have some ideas, Kaavi, but I must learn much as well before I can presume that I know how your people think."

"Then let us go and show you the implements with which we plan to win this difficult victory." *Viha* Nata gestured, and they followed.

Out of the corner of his eye, Paris watched Kaavi walk. Her legs were long, humanoid in shape and bone structure, but with powerfully muscled thighs and buttocks. Her stride was smooth and even, almost feline in its contained grace. The long, clawed feet— the Verunans had five toes and five fingers with opposable thumbs, Paris noted—would be formidable weapons in a one-on-one attack, as would the strong white teeth he'd glimpsed. There was no doubt in Paris's mind that if Kaavi took it into her head to attack one of the *Voyager* crew, she'd be able to rip out the throat and lay open the belly before the hapless crew member could even reach for a phaser.

It was not a pleasant thought, and he forced it aside. He was annoyed with himself. The Verunans had displayed nothing but benign intentions toward the *Voyager* crew. And if they wanted to "banish the Akerians from the skies," well, after what he'd seen of the Akerians, he couldn't blame them. This prejudice he bore them simply because of their appearances was offensive, inappropriate, and stupid, and he knew it.

He only wished he could overcome it by sheer willpower alone.

The walk was not a short one, as *Viha* Nata led them through the jungle of rotting foliage up and down small hills. The heat began to get to Paris, and he saw that his fellow shipmates were also reacting to the harsh environment as they followed the leader of the Verunans. The air seemed inadequate, and no matter how deeply he breathed, he couldn't seem to get enough of it. He'd give a lot for a tall, cool glass of iced tea right now. The skies grew grayer, and he heard thunder rumble in the distance.

"We have lived in the open for thousands of years," the *Viha* was saying. "There was no reason not to. The shelters that you saw, we built from the mud pits. Our bodies can withstand the heat sufficiently for us to hand-make any structures, even purely decorative ones, from the mud."

So, the canopies and the huts were mud, not stone. "How do you get the mud to harden?" asked Paris, wiping the sweat from his forehead.

Nata shrugged and brushed aside a huge branch with little visible effort. Courteously, she held it and permitted the others to walk through before she let it spring back with a *whoosh* and a tremor of foul scent. "We treat it with various oils from the plants. It hardens in the sunlight." A few more steps, then she brightened. "Ah, here we are."

They emerged from the jungle into a flat, open space. Paris blinked in slight surprise. Here in the middle of nowhere, seemingly growing from the soil as the vines grew on the trees, was a small island of gleaming metal. It, too, was protected from the elements by an overarching building of the hardened mud. But inside, Paris glimpsed colored lights blinking on and off, heard the familiar sounds of electronic equipment hard at work. Withdrawing his tricorder, he began to take readings.

This is more like it, he thought to himself as he heard thunder rumbling again, closer this time. Even as he opened his mouth to ask the question, Anahu answered it for him.

"This is not our technology. This was put here many turns ago by the Akerians." The engineer's usually pleasantly modulated voice grew hard. "They wished to be able to communicate to us, keep us firmly under their command by knowing exactly what was transpiring here on Veruna Four. This is where *Viha* Nata first contacted you."

Paris's mind flashed back to the next to last contact they had had with the *Viha.* He remembered screams of pain, images of blood and agony and carnage. Glancing around quickly, he saw that blood still stained the hard-packed earth around the site.

Chakotay beat him to it by asking, "Where are your injured, *Viha?* Perhaps we can help them."

Nata straightened slightly, and her eyes narrowed. But her voice when she spoke was not unfriendly, merely firm. "Our dead and our injured are our business, Commander. Your desire to help shows you to be a compassionate person. But our pain, our suffering—that is not for the eyes of strangers, however well-meaning they may be." She cocked her head to one side in an almost birdlike gesture. "I hope you do not take offense?"

The first officer shook his head. "Of course not. We are not familiar with your people, as I have said. You must forgive us if we do anything that seems rude or offensive. I assure you, our only desire is to help." He caught Kaavi's eye and grinned a slow, understanding grin. "And learn," he added.

Paris hit his comm badge. "Paris to Kim."

"Kim here."

"Hey, pal, you sound beat." Kim's voice was heavy, and Paris had no doubt but that the young ensign was exhausted, physically and mentally.

"I've been better. What's up, Tom?"

Paris blinked, trying to clear his vision. Breathing the heavy, hot, moist air was tiring. "There's a structure here that *Viha* Nata tells us was erected by the Akerians, not the Verunans. I thought you might be interested."

"You bet I am!" Paris smothered a grin at how the simple statement had perked Kim up so completely. "Record everything you can. I'll factor it into what we're already learning about them."

"Any answers yet?" Paris asked.

"Well . . . nothing concrete. I'm still trying to make heads or tails of a lot of it."

Sweat dribbled into Paris's eye. It stung, and he wiped at it, succeeding only in getting more sweat and dust from his fingers into his eye. He blinked, trying to clear it, aware that he was attracting concerned looks from Chakotay and Torres. He took a deep breath.

"I'm sure you'll do just fine, Kim. Matter of

fact . . ." The words suddenly dissolved into gibberish as his tongue ceased to function properly. The dimness that had been coyly playing about the corners of his vision now descended full force. His firmly muscled legs gave a damn good impression of rubber as they suddenly refused to support him.

The last thing that Paris was aware of as he sped toward unconsciousness was how swiftly Kaavi could move when she wanted to and how firm a support her strong arms were as they caught him before he hit the ground.

Paris started to regain consciousness the minute the medication from the hypo hit his system. He blinked fuzzily, trying to manage a sardonic grin for the benefit of Chakotay, who stared intently into his face. From the first officer's expression, though, Paris knew the grin was feeble.

"How do you feel?" asked Chakotay, concerned.

"Did you get the number of that transport that ran me over?" quipped Paris weakly.

Chakotay's full lips quirked in a slight smile of his own. "That's the Tom Paris we know and love." He gestured with the empty hypo. "I've given one to myself and Torres as well. It was the heat and the humidity. Plus, the air is extremely thick. If you'd checked your tricorder, you'd find that the heat is somewhere around forty-nine degrees centigrade on the planet surface. Of the three of us, you're the one least used to that kind of temperature. I grew up in a hot climate, and Torres's chemistry is different from ours. You should be fine now."

And to his surprise, Paris found he was feeling

better. Even the headache that beat an angry tattoo inside his temples was starting to fade.

With his recovery came a new awareness of his surroundings. He felt a lot cooler now than he had before, that much was certain. They were all apparently underground now, and the light seemed to be emanating from the rocks themselves.

He was in a sitting position. The rocks beneath him were cold, but something warm and soft supported his back. He turned around and was startled and embarrassed to see that he owed his comfort to Kaavi, who held him cradled against her long, muscular body. She smiled and for the first time seemed genuinely pleased. He could tell by the way her large amber eyes crinkled happily at the corners.

"I was worried about you, Par-is. I am glad that you have recovered so quickly."

"Kaavi caught you before you fell and insisted on carrying you down here personally," said Chakotay in a tone of voice that sounded slightly like a teacher's rebuke. Paris wondered if Janeway had briefed her first officer on his initial dislike of the Verunans. It would be just like her and Chakotay to sneak in a lecture even when it didn't sound like one.

"Um, thanks, thanks a lot, Kaavi," he said as he edged away from her. "That was . . . kind of you."

The Verunan shrugged. "You are my charge while you are here. I didn't want anything happening to you." She rose to her feet with far more dexterity than he would have guessed from the sheer bulk of her body. Moving slowly, still not certain of his own body's response, Paris followed suit.

And received still more surprises.

If the area on the surface indicated a primitive culture, the chambers below ground were so advanced as to astonish Paris. The cooling stone arched over a startlingly complex array of computers and equipment. Dozens of Verunans, wearing clothing identical to that worn by Anahu and Kaavi, moved about purposefully. From what he could glean, the Verunans' technology wasn't that much far behind the Federation's.

"What . . . ?" he began.

"Tom," said Torres, her hands on her hips and a smug grin on her face, "shut up and turn around."

Thoroughly surrendering to the situation, the lieutenant did so. "Oh, my God," he breathed softly, "she's gorgeous."

Not eight meters away, raised on a platform so that the uniformed engineers could reach her underbelly, was one of the sleekest, prettiest little ships it had ever been Tom Paris's good fortune to see. She glistened and gleamed. Unlike the only other Verunan ship he'd seen, there was no hint of helter-skelter construction about this beauty. She had not only been lovingly built, it was clear that she'd been lovingly designed. A little bit larger than a standard Starfleet shuttlecraft, the ship reminded Paris of a small hawk, with angled wings that swept forward rather than back and a foresection that mimicked the sleek Verunan necks. Three mechanics worked on her at the present time, grasping strange-shaped equipment in their clever, dangerous-looking hands and wielding them with the languid grace of surgeons.

He ached to climb aboard and get his hands on her,

see what she could do in open space. As he walked slowly up to her, his blue eyes hungrily taking in every curve and arc of the alien vessel, he began to think that the beleaguered Verunans might just have a chance after all.

"I will take you aboard *Conviction* in a moment. Be patient!" Kaavi's voice held a chuckle, and when Paris tore his eyes off *Conviction,* he saw that the Verunan pilot held her head at an angle and her eyes crinkled. She was amused at his reaction. "Let us briefly explain some other things first, yes?"

"All right," he replied, knowing that his voice gave away his reluctance. The three Verunans exchanged glances with the *Voyager* crew, and Tom knew they were sharing a joke at his enthusiasm. He didn't mind.

He and the others accompanied Anahu, who briskly stepped into the position of leader with an easy confidence Paris hadn't suspected, given his subservient demeanor on the planet's surface.

"For many thousands of years," Anahu began, "all this technology, given to us by the Ancestors, lay all but forgotten. We simply didn't need it. Veruna Four provided shelter, sustenance, beauty, and a chance to create art. But when we realized we had to defend ourselves against the Akerians, the elders remembered these places."

"What do you mean, remembered?" queried Chakotay.

"By and large, we are a verbal people," explained Nata. "We have a written language, but most of our histories are kept in the form of stories—memorized verbatim and kept intact through hundreds of years. We went back over those tales to find the truths clothed in legend."

"Nata, I'm going to want to hear more of these tales," said Chakotay.

She smiled. "As many as your ears will bear, my friend."

"I've been taking some readings," said Torres. "There are trace materials in the stone of Veruna Four that effectively block sensors, which explains why we detected no trace of advanced technology."

"And more importantly," said *Viha* Nata, "the Akerians do not know we have these capabilities. They see only what we wish them to see: the simple life of a simple people. Even today, they saw a ship that was a combination of many different technologies. We do not yet have the Guardian ships"—she gestured to *Conviction*—"fully functional."

"Anahu, you and Kaavi seem to be more comfortable here than above ground," said Chakotay. "Do you reject the simpler life that exists on the surface?"

"Not at all," replied Anahu, stepping up to a huge, complicated machine that took up several meters of the cavern's wall space. "We stay below, rediscovering what we can, in order to attempt to save that lifestyle. Kaavi and I had parents who researched this; they trained us to love the feel of metal and understand technology, much the way *Viha* Nata trained her children to love the smell of the *ichaki* flower and understand the turning of the seasons. But I fear that time may be running out."

His long, clawed fingers moved rapidly over the computer. An image sprang to life on the meterwide screen that was located at eye level for the Verunans. Paris tilted his head back and took a step away so he could see it better.

A complicated array of figures and graphs filled the screen. "We have been analyzing the effects of Sun-Eater on our planet," explained Anahu, pointing here and there with a long claw. "I could take a full turn explaining to you the formulas we use, but let me sum up. We have charted lightning activity through many turns, using it as a basis by which to calculate the rise in temperature over the entire planet."

"Lightning?" asked Torres, who up until that statement had been following Anahu perfectly.

Paris was glad she'd brought it up, not him. He'd embarrassed himself sufficiently for one day.

"Lightning resonates at a consistent frequency of eight cycles per minute," Anahu explained. "If you take enough readings, you can, as I said, calculate the overall temperature." He dropped his head slightly as if suddenly bent by the weight of the knowledge itself. "The temperature has risen steadily over the last hundred and fifty turns, which is how long we have been monitoring it. You have scented the death such an unnatural rise has left in its wake. Soon, nothing will be able to live on Veruna Four."

"The oceans have risen to devour the land," said *Viha* Nata, her voice falling into the singsong chant she had used a few times before. "Birds fall from the skies. Fruit rots on the vine. Children die in the pits, slain before they take their first breaths. Clouds obscure the dying sun, and lightning and thunder are our constant companions. And all this," she said, her voice rising into anger, "we owe to the Akerianssss."

"You can't be certain of that," said Chakotay.

Viha Nata whirled on him, pain and impotent rage in her great yellow eyes. Her voice was thick.

"There was no distress in our peaceful skies until three hundred turns ago. I do not know what they did—perhaps no one will never know—but they have done something incomprehensibly terrible. Can you not understand the depth of the atrocity they have committed, Commander? They have *murdered* our sun!"

CHAPTER
8

FOR THE SECOND TIME IN AS MANY DAYS, JANEWAY LAY awake in her quarters. This time, though, her mind was not filled with thoughts of loved ones seventy thousand light-years distant. She lay thinking of the Akerian ship and its quiet dead, of *Viha* Nata's tears, of the concavity known as Sun-Eater.

When Harry Kim's voice interrupted her musing, her own voice was wide awake as she replied, "Janeway here."

"Captain, I think I may have some important information for you."

"Haven't you been to bed yet, Mr. Kim?"

"Um . . . no, sir. Ma'am. Captain." An awkward pause, then "I was just too curious."

"I understand." She smiled. "What do you have for me?"

Another pause. "Well, I kind of need to show you as well as tell you."

"Very well. Wake Lieutenant Tuvok, and I'll meet you both in my ready room in about ten minutes."

"Aye, Captain." The young man's voice was filled with barely restrained glee. He'd found out something big, that was for sure.

Seven minutes later Janeway entered her ready room and found Kim and Tuvok already there. Kim, of course, had admitted not sleeping, and she had a sneaking suspicion the Vulcan hadn't seen his bed either.

"Don't you ever sleep?" she asked with a tinge of amused exasperation.

A lift of his black eyebrow was all the Vulcan granted her by way of an answer.

Kim couldn't keep quiet anymore. "I've spent the last several hours sifting through every record they had—histories, personal logs, everything," he said, his body taut and his handsome, open face alight with excitement. "And, Captain, what they've learned, what they've done . . ."

Janeway raised a calming hand. "Compose yourself, Mr. Kim."

He blushed. "Sorry. I tried to put everything in some kind of order to present it to you. May I proceed?"

"By all means, go ahead." His youthful enthusiasm was contagious, and she sat down and leaned forward for a better view as he activated the viewscreen.

What appeared was a graphic depiction of two solar systems. Kim served as narrator, occasionally bending over Janeway to point things out as he talked.

"This," he said, indicating a system in the left-hand corner, "is the Verunan system. There's their sun, right here. And over here"—his finger moved to the upper right-hand corner—"is the Akerian system. That's their star, and their home world is the only class-M planet in the system. It's called Akeras."

He zoomed in on the system and pointed to a planet. "Right here. From what I've been able to determine, the planet is not overly fertile, to say the least. It's a harsh, desertlike environment for the most part, and the Akerians adapted to that. About two thousand years ago, they developed faster-than-light travel and basic shielding capabilities, and that's when they began forming the Akerian Empire. They expanded out in this direction"—Kim indicated the system directly below the Akerian system—"and all of these six worlds are subject to their rule. The Akerians were not all that technologically advanced, but the other planets were extremely primitive. It was apparently an easy conquest."

Kim straightened and continued. "The logical development of all this was that the military grew more powerful. It's pretty much the dominant influence in the Akerian culture."

"Which ought to indicate that you may not be able to trust their records implicitly," warned Tuvok. "Isn't there a human quote to the effect that the winners write the history?"

"Yes, indeed, Mr. Tuvok," said Janeway. "And if those winners are the military, the editing is sometimes done with a very heavy hand indeed. Keep this in mind, Mr. Kim."

Kim nodded quickly, sending his jet-black bangs

falling over his face. He brushed them aside absently and continued. Hitting a touch pad, he brought up another depiction on the screen.

"This I got directly from their system," he explained. "It's a map of Akerian space. And here we are, right there—right next to Sun-Eater. And *this* is where it gets exciting.

"Up till now, Akerian development was nothing unusual. We've cataloged thousands of similar empirical societies before. But when the Akerians entered the Verunan system, they found the concavity. And they decided to investigate, eventually even going inside to see what was there."

"A wormhole?" asked Janeway, her voice catching in her throat.

Kim sobered slightly, his enthusiasm dampened, and shook his head. "Sorry, Captain. Just like before, we don't know if there was one or there wasn't one. They may not have had the technology to recognize it. Or they may have traveled through it without knowing what happened at the time. Remember, this is a pretty unsophisticated level of technology we're talking about here."

"But by now, wouldn't they know?" Janeway was starting to become very frustrated by the maybe-it's-there, maybe-it's-not turns their investigation was starting to take.

"Probably. But they're not interested. They have everything they need, Captain. They found something that was the lost continent of Atlantis, the ruins of ancient Egypt, and the forgotten civilization of Namaris Two all rolled into one glorious package. Look at *this*."

Triumphantly, he called up another image. Janeway recognized it as the distorted image of the planet she'd glimpsed in the briefing room when Kim had delivered his last report. "Yes, we've seen this already. I don't . . ."

Kim quickly ran his fingers over the control pads. "I've asked the computer to eliminate the distortion and hypothesize from the information I've given it so far. Here's what it looks like now."

The graphic straightened itself out, and Janeway glimpsed bits and pieces of a dark, destroyed civilization. She was no archaeologist, but even she could tell that some of the buildings were unique designs of extraordinary beauty. The image of the planet turned, and now Janeway could see the ruined hulls of vessels of some sort.

"And here is what I think it might have looked like in its heyday."

Suddenly the dead planet sprang to life. Huge, complicated, gleaming cities thrust toward the skies. Ornate ships hovered about, and a race of bipedal, humanoid creatures interacted with one another on what seemed to be a pleasant level.

"Estimated technological level?" asked Janeway.

"Higher than our own in some areas," replied Kim. "They were an extremely advanced race."

"But . . . what is their planet doing in Sun-Eater? What happened to them?" Janeway leaned forward, fully aware that the image in front of her eyes was wholly the result of Harry Kim's best guess but caught up in the beauty of it nonetheless.

"The Akerians didn't know. In fact, I was able to make more sense out of the information the Akerians recorded about this civilization than they themselves were. But, Captain, can you imagine what it would be like if we were the ones who stumbled across this when we had just discovered faster-than-light travel?"

Slowly, the captain nodded her auburn head. Kim had been right. "They would hardly have known what to make of it," she said. "Like . . . like a medieval serf finding a starship. The possibilities . . ."

"Especially to a military organization," interrupted Tuvok. His face was impassive, but Janeway detected just a slight note of excitement in his voice.

"Exactly!" crowed Kim. "The military concentrated all their efforts on learning about this devastated civilization. The concavity became the heart of their empire. I can't go into everything they learned— we'd be here till we got home—but the main information they gleaned by studying this civilization's ruins was a profound understanding of gravity."

"Hence, their preferred choice of weaponry," deduced Tuvok.

"It makes perfect sense," said Janeway. Her own eyes flashed in excited comprehension. "They're operating in a gravity well. The more they learn how to manipulate it, control it, the more they can learn from the civilization. It's a positive cycle."

"Most of the technology we saw on that Akerian ship was stolen directly from that ruined planet. Look." His fingers flying almost as fast as his sharp brain, Kim called up blueprints of a ship. "This was gathered from the planet. Now, watch." As Janeway sat glued to the screen, Kim superimposed the image of the Akerian vessel over it. It was almost exact.

"The only difference is the position of the weapons array, although the weaponry itself is virtually identical. The Akerians chose to lay it out in this sort of pattern." He pointed to the graviton generators that Janeway had noticed while on the bridge of the *Conquest*. "While the original inhabitants of the planet laid their weapons out in a semicircle, the Akerians preferred this pattern—four generators arranged at the compass points, like so."

"Fascinating," commented Tuvok.

Kim allowed himself a pleased grin. He didn't often get a chance to so impress his superiors. Janeway smiled her approval and nodded for him to continue.

"Of course, trying to perform excavations in a space that has such intense gravity is slow and dangerous. After they decided to investigate this system, they discovered that Veruna Four had inhabitants—inhabitants that were intelligent, bipedal, as they were, and extremely strong."

He hit another keypad and displayed the corrected image of the planet. Zooming in, Kim focused on one of the structures he had earlier identified as slave quarters. Janeway could now see Verunans, clad in what was clearly the Akerian version of envirosuits, working slowly and painfully with special equipment.

"The slaves," she said softly. Kim nodded.

"They were perfect." His face hardened, and his voice was angry. "In one of his personal logs, the captain raves about how long they lasted—a few months to a year, at most. They were utterly and completely expendable."

Janeway sighed. "It would be nice if such attitudes

were confined to our species alone. But I'm afraid that it's a more common view than the idealist in me would like to think."

"Now, about three hundred years ago," Kim continued, "something horrible began to happen." The image of the enslaved Verunans disappeared to be replaced by a scene depicting the concavity. "I've put together a series of pictures gleaned from the Akerian computers. I'm going to time-lapse them. Watch this."

Janeway obeyed, gazing intently at the image of the concavity the Verunans called Sun-Eater. It shifted, becoming longer, then broader, in a series of fluctuations that would not be abnormal for such a spatial aberration. She leaned her head on her hand, then suddenly her eyes widened. She sat up straighter.

"Good lord," she said softly, "it's . . . it's shrinking."

"Exactly." He ran a few more images, and it became obvious that it was rapidly growing smaller and smaller. "The concavity existed for thousands of years, doing no harm to anyone in this system. Then it began to close." He straightened up, locked Janeway's eyes with his own dark, almond-shaped ones. "The Akerians could not permit that to happen. The planet had become their cornerstone, the greatest source of information they could hope for. They couldn't let it just vanish."

"So they found a way to keep it open." Janeway's body was taut as a whippet's. She couldn't sit still any longer. Rising, she began to pace, her mind racing at a light-year a minute. "I didn't notice it before, but you're right, Ensign. The draining of hydrogen from the sun *has* to be artificial. There was no damage until about three centuries ago, when the concavity turned *into* Sun-Eater. Go back to the earlier images."

Kim obliged. Triumphantly, Janeway banged her fist on the table. "Look at the concavity in relation to the sun. There is absolutely no indication of a hydrogen drain."

"This new information does a great deal to help explain some of the mysteries of this sytem, Captain," said Tuvok. "As you will recall, when we first entered this system, there were several things that were not possible, yet the irrefutable proof lay directly in front of us."

Janeway nodded. "So *that* explains how we got a red giant out of a sun that's only four billion years old."

"Four point two," Tuvok corrected gently. "It also answers the question of how the sun's hydrogen managed to leap across a gap of three trillion miles into the concavity."

Janeway recalled her frustrated summation upon first encountering the mysteries of the Verunan system. *We've got a red giant that's too young to be a red giant. We've got a concavity whose gravitational power is too weak for it to be the size that it is. And we've got hydrogen being pulled across an impossible distance at an impossible rate. Have I got all this right, Tuvok?*

Answers. That was what it all came down to. And they'd gotten two of the three mysteries solved. "Do you know how they went about performing this task, Mr. Kim?" she asked.

The young ensign nodded. "Not only do I know, they recorded the event for posterity. I found something that they put together to show the people of Akeras."

His voice and posture were censorious, and Janeway couldn't blame him. The Akerians had viewed killing the Verunan sun as a great achievement for the glory of the Akerian Empire and had wanted to preserve this finest hour. The fact that two billion innocents along with countless plants and animals were going to die for it seemed to have bothered the Akerians not at all. She was reminded of the old Earth films of Hitler, of the biorecords of the death camps on the twin moons of Kamarica. Some things didn't change.

She shook off her melancholia. "Let's see it, Mr. Kim."

Janeway knew that, unlike the dreadful footage of the death camps of Earth and other planets, what she was about to see would contain no dreadful image of the dying or the dead. This would be only cold space shots; the devastation would come afterward. Nonetheless, she braced herself. Knowing what she did, she could never watch something like this with detachment.

A face appeared on the viewscreen—or rather, a helmeted head. It appeared virtually identical to the visage of Linneas. Apparently, the helmet and the armor were indeed ritual garb that hadn't changed over the passage of three centuries.

"Greetings, Most Honored Emperor Iphus, and to the people of Akeras. I am Telarac, first warrior of the Empirical Exploratory Unit and first warrior commander of the proud vessel *Dominion*. As many of you know, much of the peace and harmony we have striven to bring to our beloved home world stems from the rich knowledge we have gained from the planet we call Blessing. Our entryway threatened to close, but our brilliant Akerian scientists have learned a way to keep Blessing and all its gifts available to us. What you are about to see is a visual record of one of the proudest moments in Akerian history."

Proudest moment, my foot, Janeway thought but kept her silence.

Telarac kept narrating, but for the most part Janeway tuned out the Akerian propagandist. She didn't need to know the names of the ships involved in this "historical triumph" or the captains who piloted them. She'd learn what she needed to just by watching.

It was so simple, so logical, that Janeway knew they ought to have guessed what had transpired the minute they had been attacked by the *Victory*'s pod ships. Four Akerian ships flew in perfect formation toward the Verunan sun. As Janeway watched the centuries-old footage, the four ships began to execute an uncannily familiar maneuver. Each one powered up its individual generators, and she saw the four generators on each ship light up and link as the ships moved toward their fellows.

"Graviton beams," she breathed. "They're making a gravition beam link!"

One by one, the ships joined their gravity waves just as the six little pods had done when they had attacked *Voyager.* Then together, as graceful as dancers in a painstakingly choreographed ballet, the ships moved closer to the sun. In the background, the concavity yawned, a spatter of nothingness against a star-crowded sky.

Then it happened.

The massive wave created by the four ships was far in excess of what any one ship could produce. The ships fired it at the Verunan sun—not at its center, but across its photosphere. Janeway was reminded incongruously of skipping stones across a brook. The gravity wave skimmed across the top, forcing the energy in front of it like a sheepdog herding its charges. It was an awesome spectacle, and Janeway forgot to breathe as she watched the stream of burning hydrogen hurtle toward the mouth of the concavity.

"It's siphoning the energy," she managed. "Like sucking liquid through a hose."

"And it's been doing that extremely effectively for the last three hundred years," finished Kim.

"It is utterly brilliant," announced Tuvok, approval creeping into his voice. Janeway knew the Vulcan better than to think that he endorsed the action; he was merely giving credit where credit was due. Kim, however, turned a shocked gaze upon the security officer.

"Lieutenant Tuvok, with respect, I'd like to remind you that billions of people are going to die because of that brilliance!"

Tuvok regarded him mildly and opened his mouth to reply when Janeway interrupted him. "Mr. Kim, you've done a marvelous job. I'll be sure to mention your extraordinary efforts in the ship's log. I suggest you download all the information on the Akerian weapons system—including this little demonstration of their power—and make sure everyone in Tactical sees it. Is there anything else that you need to tell me about at the moment?"

"Well," said Kim, "I don't know about you, but I got very curious about what they looked like. Apparently, the warriors never remove their helmets except in private, and there was little or no information about nonwarrior individuals. But I did catch one captain in an unguarded moment before he switched off his personal log. I think you'll find this *very* interesting."

He quickly pulled up the log in question. It was Nelek, summing up a rather uneventful day. The commander sat for a moment, sighing, then reached for a small, handheld instrument. He placed it to his throat, and it glowed. Something went *click*. Tilting his head to the left, Nelek reached up, unfastened his helmet, and removed it.

"Well, I'll be damned," said Janeway softly in utter amazement.

CHAPTER
9

CHAKOTAY LIKED IT HERE IN THE COOL CAVERNS BELOW
the rapidly perishing surface of the condemned planet. Here, there was no unpleasant foretaste of death
haunting the soul. The lichen that covered the rocks
glowed, providing a natural radiance that supple-
mented the artificial lighting given off by the equipment. The Verunans who worked here were alert,
attentive, excited. The three dozen or so technicians
who scurried back and forth moved with purpose
and enthusiasm. They had something that Chakotay
suspected the surface dwellers did not: hope. What
they were doing down here just might make a difference.

Just might. The key words, weren't they? Despair
was not truly conquered here, merely kept at bay by
productive activity. Anahu seemed to be able to put

the knowledge that the planet had a quarter of a century or so left aside. Kaavi was noticeably bitter and hostile. And *Viha* Nata herself? Where did she fit in here? He'd have to talk with her at length soon.

But first had come enforced sleep. The *Voyager* crew had been exhausted, and the heat had wiped them out. Chakotay had ordered a rest period of five hours, and not surprisingly he, Torres, and Paris had all managed to get a bit of shut-eye in spite of the exciting new situation in which they found themselves. Nata had led them to a quiet alcove, and they had nodded off.

Now, it was back to work. He walked up the ramp that led into *Conviction*'s interior. It was small inside what served as the operational area. Over toward the back, Tom Paris examined the structure of the vessel with hungry eyes, while Kaavi, her own eyes bright with excitement, pointed various things out to him. Chakotay turned his attention to Torres, who was at the present moment lying on her back to get a better view of the underside of *Conviction*'s console.

"You look like a twentieth-century Earth mechanic," he quipped, smiling.

She eased herself out and grinned back up at him, waving one of the tools Anahu had given her. "Well, I'll tell you, I almost feel like one."

Chakotay felt his smile falter. "Are the ships that primitive?" he asked, disappointment seeping into his bones. *Conviction* was so pretty, so elegant in her lines, that he assumed what was inside her was just as advanced.

Torres shook her head. "No, it's not that. It's just— Chakotay, these things are old. *Ancient.* We're talking millennia here, not just centuries." Her voice was hushed, almost reverent, and Chakotay understood why. He glanced about with renewed respect. "Anahu tells me that there are five other ships just like *Conviction,* all hidden in caves like this. Other crews are working on getting them in spaceworthy shape, but it's been slow going. And time—"

"—Is the one thing they don't have."

She nodded, her face intense. Sweat trickled along the ridges of her brow despite the cool temperature. "The Verunans are basically relearning how to operate these things."

The first officer squatted down beside her to keep the conversation a bit more private. Part of him wondered why he even bothered; it was clear that Paris and Kaavi were totally engrossed in admiring the ship.

"And how does it look to you?" he asked quietly.

Torres glanced away, then met Chakotay's brown eyes with a level stare that he recognized—and didn't like. She was going to tell him something he didn't really want to hear.

"Frankly, it looks very good." Chakotay narrowed his eyes, waiting for the other shoe to drop. "Once you've figured out the basic structure, nearly everything else falls right into place. There are a few things that are a total mystery to me, though—things I've never encountered before. But they don't seem to be interefering with my understanding of the basic functions. Tom ought to be able to fly this ship right now if she were operational. The ancient Verunans were very logical, well-organized people." A sly smile touched her lips. "The Vulcans would like them."

"I know I sure do," Chakotay admitted. "Out with it, B'Elanna. I've known you too long."

She hesitated, then her words came out in a rush. "They're so close, Chakotay! They've <u>almost</u> got it! Nearly everything I'm seeing indicates that they were just a couple of generations away from figuring out cloaking, shielding, perhaps even a superior way to cross distances than warp drive."

Suddenly he knew what she was getting at and realized his hunch had been right. He *didn't* like it. He felt his stomach sink to his toes. But he had to make her say it, put it into words, so that he could coldly, calculatedly, shatter her hope. The uniform he wore, which felt right to him most of the time, now felt like it was smothering him. Duty was a damn heavy thing sometimes, never more than at this moment.

"If you'd just let me add a few things—put in some shielding capabilities—they'd be able to fight the Akerians on something resembling equal footing! Starfleet technology would do so much—"

"Come on, Torres, you know better than that." Chakotay's voice was harsh in his own ears, and each word seemed to cost him. "I can't do that."

She let out a frustrated, unhappy sound, somewhere between a whimper and a growl. "I wouldn't do much. Like I said, they're so damn close already—"

"Your job is to help *them* get *their* equipment up to speed, Lieutenant, not put in new technologies. That's a violation of the Prime Directive, and you can lie to yourself and bend it around all you want, but you know I'm right."

Her breast heaved with anger, but when she spoke, there was no trace of Klingon rage in her surprisingly soft voice. "Chakotay, they're good people. They deserve a fighting chance."

"Nobody knows that more than I do," he replied, his voice equally soft. "But we made promises, you and I, when we agreed to wear these uniforms. Sometimes the right choices aren't the easy ones." *Sometimes,* he thought bitterly, *the right choices aren't even very good.* "Don't waste your time thinking about what you can't do for these people. You're one of the most brilliant engineers I've ever seen. Use that brilliance to its best advantage within the limits you've been set. You can still make a difference but not if you spend your time being angry about the differences you can't make."

She averted her eyes, staring at nothing. Then with a speed that shocked even him, who ought to have known better, she slammed her fist angrily down on the floor of the vessel. Startled, Paris and Kaavi turned around. With a small shake of his head, Chakotay indicated that they should ignore the outburst. Paris nodded his understanding and began asking questions again, gently redirecting his liaison's attention.

Chakotay waited. One thing his culture and his life experiences had taught him was patience. He often thought that Torres had entered his life simply to be taught that lesson by him. That thought led him back to his animal spirit's strange advice: *You are a teacher. You are also a student. You teach the ways of your people. That is easy to do. What is harder to do is to be wise and teach the ways of people you do not know.*

But now Torres was looking directly at him, and he had to put his animal guide's words aside. "Permission to bring more hands down from the *Voyager*. This work will go faster if there's more than one person working on it."

"Agreed," he answered swiftly. That much, at least, he could do. Torres seemed calmer, at least a little, and eased herself up. She stood awkwardly, her muscles clearly stiff from being in the awkward position, and Chakotay extended a hand to help her. She twisted away from him, not meeting his gaze, and exited down the ramp.

He was not offended. They'd clashed before, he and she, and he knew this was how she handled what she regarded as a setback. He heard her speaking to Carey as he followed her off the *Conviction* and heard the anger in her voice mollify into renewed enthusiasm. She'd be all right.

Now it was time, past time, for him to start contributing. *Viha* Nata awaited him outside. She did not like the "closed place" as she called the caverns. Chakotay walked past a long line of computers, catching the eyes of the occasional Verunan engineer and smiling. The cavern narrowed and began to slope upward, gently at first and then steeply. Soon Chakotay was not walking, but climbing, seeking out finger- and toeholds as he made his way toward the surface.

There was a much larger exit, of course, otherwise the vessels like *Conviction* could not have been hidden underground. But Anahu had given him to understand that the exits were carefully camouflaged to escape detection from the Akerians. Under no circumstances was anyone, Verunan or human, to draw attention to those exits. Chakotay and the other visitors to Veruna Four would have to enter and leave the same way the natives did: climbing in and out.

But Verunan arms and legs were much stronger than human appendages, and their reach was far longer as well. Chakotay found himself pushing his body to its limits as he climbed, hauled, and scrambled his way toward the surface, but he didn't mind. He prided himself on staying in excellent physical shape. The workout also helped him release his own deeply controlled anxiety and frustration.

The Indian wanted to help the Verunans. Had he not taken an oath upon being promoted to first officer of the *Voyager* to uphold the Prime Directive, he'd have beaten B'Elanna in giving any aid he could to these beings who, in so many ways, reminded him of his own people. But he couldn't. He'd taken that oath, donned the uniform, accepted the responsibilities.

Chakotay began to smell the surface—the scent of rot and decay in place of freshness and growth. He grew even sadder as the smell grew stronger until at last, panting with the effort, he heaved himself out of the tunnel and onto the hard-packed earth.

Viha Nata was there, as she had promised, and wordlessly extended a clay gourd of water. He gulped it thirstily, knowing that it was pure and wholesome despite the odd taste and faint odor that clung to the liquid. When he had drained the gourd, he handed it back. She accepted it and gazed at him.

"And I assume you are hungry, friend Chakotay. I do not know of your people's needs, but here, we eat every few hours. Can you partake of our planet's hospitality—what little we have left to provide you—

or do you wish to procure sustenance from your ship?"

He thought for a moment as he caught his breath. No doubt, these people needed every portion of nourishing fare they could get. Probably, the trees and plants were starting to cease bearing edible produce. However, in many cultures, including his own, "breaking bread" was a powerful and honored ritual. The fact that *Viha* Nata had offered him food seemed to indicate that the Verunans followed that concept.

"If you would not mind me using my tricorder to determine if your food is harmful to my system, *Viha,* I would be honored to eat with you." He would take the offer this once. Later, he could get rations back on board *Voyager* and not use up any more of the Verunan supplies.

She nodded and led him over to what was clearly her own hut. Like all the others he had seen, it was mostly open to the elements. A rug of dried, braided rushes of some sort covered the floor. There were pillows, and Nata indicated that Chakotay should sit. He did so, settling himself in among the many surprisingly soft pillows, and waited in polite silence.

Nata seemed more quiet than usual. Something was on her mind, and though she moved briskly to furnish food for her honored guest, he could tell she was not fully concentrating on the task. No doubt young Paris would shake his head—*How can you tell? They don't look anything like us!*—but Chakotay knew even after such a relatively short time spent among the Verunans. The cock of the head, the movement of the tail, and above all, those large, soft, glowing eyes that revealed every shade of emotion their owners could possibly feel. He was not ascribing human traits to them, but he was learning to take them on their own terms, decipher their own complex array of ritual, gesture, and language.

At last she brought him a wooden plate piled high with an exotic assortment of what he took to be fruits and vegetables and other things he could not readily identify. He took out his tricorder and analyzed the food. Roots, tubers, grains, fruits—nothing dangerous there. The elder seated herself on cushions across from him, cocking her head expectantly.

"I thank you for this meal, *Viha,*" Chakotay said gravely. He reached for a long, thin purple item and bit into it. It was delicious—crunchy and sweet. He raised his eyebrows and nodded his approval.

"I am pleased you enjoy our fare," the *Viha* replied. She reached out a clawed, long-fingered hand and helped herself to something dark gray and lumpy. "I would you had come here earlier when the good earth gave forth better, sweeter food."

"You promised me that you would tell me the tales of your people, *Viha,*" said Chakotay, finishing the purple root and selecting a bright blue fruit.

Her eyes were unhappy as she chewed and swallowed. "I am the last remaining *Viha* of this section of our land. I have not had time to train another. The *Vihas* are the keepers of the tales, the keepers of our history. If I die before I can pass those tales along to another, they may die with me."

She toyed with the long, bulky pendant that hung from her sinuous throat. "I have told you that our history is oral. What we hear once, we remember for always."

The vocal equivalent of a photographic memory, Chakotay thought to himself, filing away the information for future reference. "Anahu mentioned that. He said you 'remembered' the forgotten technology. And you added that you had to find the truths cloaked in legend. Give me an example. Tell me how you remembered the caverns that housed the ships."

Nata smiled, and her eyes went misty. "One of the most inspirational of all our tales is that one. It is the story of the Soul's Journey to Truth. It is a long story—hours in the true telling—so I will summarize.

"As each one of us has a soul, so does everything else around us, in the earth, in the oceans, in the skies. And every soul must make a journey, till it reaches its final destination. Along that way, the soul finds allies: courage, faith, kindness, conviction, wisdom, and love. The tale tells how the soul finds each of its six Guardians and learns from them. With their help, the soul reaches its destination."

She watched him closely, seeing if he understood what she was so cryptically describing. For a moment, he didn't comprehend. The legend of the soul's journey was one he'd encountered in many alien cultures. It was not unique to humans. And it was usually an allegory. What was she driving at?

And then it hit him.

"Conviction," he breathed. "The ship *Conviction.* And the others are named *Courage, Faith, Kindness—*"

"*Wisdom* and *Love,*" completed Nata, obviously pleased that he had understood her.

Chakotay's skin prickled with foreknowledge. Almost, he could feel his animal spirit's warm presence here, in this little ceramic hut, nodding her approval. "And . . . the soul?" he ventured.

"Finish your meal," said Nata gravely. "And when you have done so, I shall take you to the very soul of our people."

Chakotay took with him a flask fashioned of the smooth, hardened mud. He'd filled it with water, an old-fashioned prevention against dehydration but still perhaps one of the best. After a few minutes of hiking in the hot, hazy environment, he was glad of it.

"I take this walk nearly every day," said Nata as she strode beside him, moderating her long stride so as not to overtax her guest. "Rain or shine. Viewing this place helps me to think, to remember. It was there that I recalled the legend of the soul's journey. I am hoping that perhaps you will be able to offer some insights."

"That is my hope as well," said Chakotay, puffing slightly in the thick air.

It was a sobering trip. Time after time, they would have to step over the bones of some creature or another. Trees festered, oozed, and occasionally there came a loud *boom* as one of them fell to the earth to facilitate its decomposition.

Once, the wind shifted, bringing with it so nauseating a scent that Chakotay's dark face went pale. He swallowed rapidly, trying to keep his meal in his stomach, where it belonged.

Beside him, Nata paused, and as he recovered himself, she did something that struck him as odd at first. She rose to her full height, extended her long neck, and began to sing.

I mourn, Sun who shall be no more;
I mourn, Stars who gleam in the night;
I mourn, Waters who breed death;
I mourn, Earth that cannot grow.
Sun-Eater has claimed you,
Sun-Eater has claimed me,
Sun-Eater has claimed us all.

Chakotay listened, then on impulse, he removed his comm badge and temporarily deactivated the translation device. Suddenly, *Viha* Nata's true voice, unencumbered by English words, came to his ears full force. The song was beautiful—lilting, sweet, pure. Her voice was a crooning, gentle sound that would put any child easily to sleep as though by a lullaby. She finished her song, bowed her head in silent mourning to all that was lost, that would be lost.

Chakotay hesitated, then, replacing his comm badge, he began to sing a Navajo chant called "Song of the Young War God."

I have been to the end of the earth.
I have been to the end of the waters.
I have been to the end of the sky.
I have been to the end of the mountains.
I have found none that were not my friends.

Startled, Nata whipped her head around to look at him. The beads in her long, soft, white hair bounced. She was utterly shocked but terribly pleased. An understanding silence passed between them as they continued walking.

The path took a sharp upward turn after about a half a kilometer. Chakotay began to pant with exertion, but his mind was not on his working muscles. He thought about the tales, about the song she'd just sung and his own response. And he thought about the Akerians.

"There is a legend among one branch of my people, the Cherokee," he said at length. "It tells of the Gentle People, the Nunnehi, who lived beneath the Earth's surface. One day, they appeared to the Cherokee and warned them that a great, terrible disaster was about to befall them."

Now realizing that Chakotay was telling a tale of his own, Nata turned to look at him, her mottled face alight with interest. "The Nunnehi offered to let the Cherokee come and live with them in the caverns beneath the Earth," Chakotay continued. "They rolled away a stone, and the place below was so beautiful, so kind and welcoming, that the Cherokee people were eager to dwell with the Nunnehi. But one group held back. The chief asked them why. The old people replied, 'This is our home. This is where we wish to die.' The young people replied, 'This is where we wish to bear our children. We want them to live as we did.' So the chief, knowing that the rest of his people would be safe with the Nunnehi, decided to stay with those who lingered behind."

"And did the disaster come?" asked Nata.

Chakotay nodded his dark head. "Another race of people came. They decided that the Cherokee could not live where they had lived since the world began.

These people marched the Cherokee, on foot, over a distance of hundreds of miles and relocated them far from their homes." His dark eyes were somber but not vengeful. He had forgiven, as most of his people had forgiven. But he could not—and knew that he should not—forget. *Those who fail to learn from history are condemned to repeat it,* he thought to himself, then he continued.

"Many people died on that long march. Women, children, the old, the sick. There was barely enough time to bury the dead. The Cherokee call it the Trail of Tears. My people have never forgotten it. So you see, *Viha* Nata, I share your pain. For though the Trail of Tears happened six hundred years ago and your people are suffering now, I do understand."

Viha Nata was silent, walking steadily with powerful movements of her clean, strong legs. At last, she asked, "What of the people who went with the Nunnehi?"

"They were never seen again. But we have no reason to think that they were unhappy."

"I think," said Nata slowly, putting the pieces together inside her large, complex brain, "that if what we are seeing now is your Trail of Tears, then what happened long, long ago was the other half of that tale. Then, we were not the Cherokee who stayed to suffer. Then, we were the Cherokee who escaped the terrible thing by the grace of the Nunnehi."

She stopped and regarded him. "What you are about to see is a thing of great holiness among my people. I do not show you this lightly."

He inclined his head. "I do not view it lightly," he said, his voice steady and serious.

"We call it the First Place. It is also the soul of our kind. Long, long ago, it sheltered us, saved us, until it was safe to leave it and partake of the bounties granted to us by this once most fruitful of planets. I come here often and sit up on that peak to which I now take you, and I wonder . . ." The old Verunan twisted her long, thin neck, regarded the stone outcropping. "I wonder if, perhaps now that our sun is dying, if that is not a sign that we should return to this place. It saved my people before, or so the tales would have us believe—and Chakotay, I *do* believe the tales—and I wonder, perhaps it might save us again."

She turned her attention to him again, and he realized, not for the first time, the latent power that was in her body and her spirit. Nata, as her people all seemed to be, was gentle. The Verunans fed on plants and roots, not flesh. There seemed to be no internal strife, no external strife, until the Akerians came to murder their sun and their entire system. But she was big and physically powerful, and the great and terrible beauty that manifested itself in her lambent eyes could not be denied.

"Ascend, Chakotay. Look upon the First Place, think on it, and tell me your thoughts."

Chakotay realized he hadn't felt this nervous since the early days of his youth, when he had gone with his father to the tropical rain forests of Earth in search of his tribe's origins. That world, those people, had been alien to him, the "contrary," who wanted to embrace the more orderly and contemporary universe offered by Starfleet. How ironic—or perhaps, how fitting— that that decision had brought him here, to that precipice up ahead which represented another step into another world, another challenge.

Challenge.

You are a teacher. You are also a student. You teach the ways of your people. That is easy to do. What is harder to do is to be wise and teach the ways of people you do not know.

But how do I teach what I do not know?

That is the challenge, is it not?

He could almost feel her, there, just out of reach, inside his mind as she always was, accessible at any moment but uncommandable. Chakotay's heart thudded inside his chest and not just from exertion.

At last he ascended and gazed down in the valley of the First Place.

The First Place was enormous. It was several kilometers long, stretching out its slim white arms in four directions. At each compass point sat a large bulge, each one easily twice the size of Nata's village. Its white metal gleamed in the sun,

Teach the ways of people you do not know.

Now he knew what she had meant. He could almost see the sleek animal spirit nodding her head as suddenly the pieces clicked together. Although he had never seen this structure before, he knew what it was, knew even better than *Viha* Nata, to whom it was a daily sight.

"Viha," he said softly, "it's a colony ship."

CHAPTER
10

THEY HAD REFUELED, REPAIRED THE *VICTORY*, COMMISsioned a second ship, and crewed her with those who, Linneas was convinced, would not falter in the conflict that was to come. In a few hours, they would be ready to depart for the Verunan system.

Garai, for his part, was relieved that he had been promoted to first warrior commander for the new Empirical Exploratory Unit vessel, *Destroyer*. That meant that he would no longer be Linneas's "trusted first hand." He would not have to watch Linneas rage at trivialities or punish innocent transgressions with a brutally heavy hand—or be an unwilling party to the lies Linneas was telling their empress.

True, lying to the emperor or empress had been practically tradition for centuries. A few rulers through the ages had been hard, or as Linneas might have put it, "wise," enough to be trusted with the secret—that the great glory of Blessing was obtained only by slave labor and killing a system's sun. But there had not been many. For the most part, the truth behind the harvesting of Blessing remained known only by the military. This fact, this odd tradition, did not make it any easier for Garai.

As Linneas and Garai headed toward their audience with Her Grace, here in the enormous, sprawling white metal palace that was both Akeras's seat of government and royal home, Garai, his commission already in hand, dared speak openly.

"With all honor, First Warrior," he began as they walked down the narrow, echoing corridors of the palace toward the receiving chamber, "I think it is time to tell the government the truth about Blessing—and about the new ship."

Linneas halted in midstride. Mentally, Garai cringed, but physically he did not retreat. Slowly, Linneas turned to Garai, his newly polished helmet gleaming in the harsh, artificial light of the corridor. The light threw the scores in his horns into sharp relief.

"Empress Riva is my kin, Lowborn, not yours," he hissed. "She is hardly of a temperament to handle this knowledge. This information has been kept within the military for centuries now. Why should we tell her or the government anything? The fewer people involved, the easier it is for us to operate efficiently."

Garai bobbed his horns in acknowledgment of the truthful insult but gathered his courage and continued. "The alien ship *Voyager* has entered into the scenario. They are players whose participation was never—could never have been—predicted. Do you not think that the government needs the facts—*all* the facts—in order to determine the proper course of action?"

A low rumble of angry impatience emanated from behind Linneas's mask. His gloved hands twitched. Garai's mouth went dry. Should Linneas charge him, Garai would be honor bound, due to his inferior bloodline, to submit without fighting. Dying by Linneas's hands was not something he would relish.

"Since when has the government ever needed the facts?" replied the first warrior. "They stay here and make laws, parcel out goods and food, playact their own little games. It is we who make the important decisions! Every Akerian would be dead by now—would have died long ago—had it not been for the courage of the warriors who dared venture beyond the sun, who dared enter the rift in space, who *dared* learn from those of other systems who have gone before!"

Keeping his helmet still so that Linneas would not see what he was doing, Garai couldn't help but glance about at the complexity of the palace. This was Akerian technology. This had not been stolen from a dead planet, paid for with the lives of creatures who had never offered a threat of any sort. This was all they really could call theirs, and for a wild, traitorous instance, Garai wondered if Blessing might not more aptly have been named Curse. The discovery of the planet within the concavity had given the Akerian military its power, had been the first step in building the empire into the fearful institution it was today.

Had there been no Blessing, had the Akerians been forced to rely on what they had to hand, what would have happened? Garai had always assumed that it would have been disastrous, as Linneas had just insisted. But would the Akerians really have died out? Or would they have learned to survive on their own without exploiting the technology of dead aliens and the labor of live ones?

Such questions, he knew, were dangerous. But Garai was growing older, and gradually, asking such things was becoming important to him.

Linneas was awaiting a response. Garai, defeated for the moment, gave it to him. "First Warrior is right, as usual," he said, keeping his voice dead serious. "We in the military act, as we have ever acted, for the benefit of our people. It was"—He did not want to say *wrong*, for such a word was loaded with meaning and could return to haunt him—"misguided of me to suggest otherwise."

Garai bowed low. He heard Linneas grunt, pleased.

"Clearly the encounter with the aliens has addled your brain, First Warrior. It has been a difficult time for all of us," he admitted with what he no doubt regarded as generosity. "Never before has our authority been so challenged. It is well that you have realized your misstatement."

And he walked on again, helmeted head held high, a shining armor-clad example of the best and the brightest the Akerian military had to offer.

Garai hesitated, then followed. His mind was made up. He would not question Linneas here and now. There was too much at stake, too many unresolved issues. He would command the *Destroyer* properly, with all Akerian honor, and bring it glory. But while aboard, he would watch his crew very carefully to see who, if any, might share his growing discontent and disillusionment with the military.

When they had returned, even if it meant his commission, even if it meant his neck, he would seek a private audience with the beautiful, gulled empress and reveal the mammoth deception that had been going on for centuries.

"Chakotay to Janeway."

"Janeway here."

"Captain, I've just discovered something very important about Verunan technology."

"I've heard about the six ships if that's what you're referring to. Lieutenant Paris gave me quite a run-down on them."

Chakotay smiled a little, never taking his eyes off the beautiful, giant colony ship that lay before him in the distance. "I'm sure he did. But this is something else. Captain . . ." He hesitated, reached for the words. "The Verunans are not native to this system. I'm looking at a mammoth colony ship, estimated two, maybe three square kilometers. From what I can piece together about Nata's people, I assume they came here centuries ago in that ship, escorted by the six Guardians."

"Excuse me?"

"Forgive me—the escort ships. Captain, I was right to come and speak with the *Viha*. According to her, all their stories, their mythos, are allegorical and refer to actual incidents and places."

Quickly, he summarized Nata's story of the soul's journey, mentioning the names of the six ships. "Nata herself has come to the conclusion that it is time to return to the ship, see if it has any answers for them. She thinks that, if worst came to worst, at least some Verunans could survive in there."

He did not voice his own thoughts, not with the *Viha* standing right next to him, hope—real hope—making her mottled, furred face glow. The colony ship might have served well enough to transport the Verunans, or whatever they had called themselves originally, through space to this planet. It might even, as Nata assured him, have housed them through violent planetary disturbances when they first landed. But protect these people from a dying sun? He doubted it. Still, Chakotay was not about to crush this kindly soul's hope, not when he didn't yet have all the facts in.

Janeway, exercising her own considerable wisdom, did not ask for Chakotay's thoughts. Instead, she asked, "Is *Viha* Nata prepared to take you inside?" Then, almost immediately, "Can you *get* inside?"

Chakotay glanced over at the *Viha,* raising his eyebrow in question. Nata nodded excitedly, her newfound hope straightening her spine, animating her body, and making her suddenly look much younger, though no less dependable.

"You have helped me find answers for questions that I never thought to ask, friend Chakotay. By all means, I will take you inside the First Place—the colony ship, as you call it."

He smiled at her. Excitement was also rising within him. Chakotay was blessed with an even temperament, had learned over years of hard lessons to keep a steady head, but he had never lost that sense of enthusiasm for the new, the unknown.

The captain continued. "Chakotay, we've found out a lot of things here, too—things that I think you should know."

He read between the lines. Had the information been for *Viha* Nata's ears as well as his own, Janeway simply would have told him. They'd found out something, something they weren't yet willing to share with the Verunans. Chakotay felt his initial enthusiasm ebb and prayed that it wasn't bad news.

"Understood, Captain. Do you want the away team to beam up now?"

"No, this can wait. Go ahead and see if you can get into the colony ship. I don't think it's necessary to instruct you to record everything. Our Mr. Kim would love to join you, but I've finally managed to convince him to get some sleep for the first time since this whole thing started. I'll send him down if there's something you need his expertise for, but otherwise I'd like him to get some rest."

"Agreed."

"One other thing. You've got five hours to learn what you can, then I want you and the other officers currently on Veruna Four back up here on the *Voyager*. From the information on the Akerian computers, we now know where their home world is and how fast their ships can travel. What we don't know is how badly disabled their ship was and how long it would take them to repair it. But I'd rather err on the side of caution. The minimum time for an Akerian ship to travel to and from Akeras has come and gone. We're on borrowed time. I'd like for us to get in and out of Sun-Eater before they show."

"Agreed," Chakotay replied. He felt anger stir within him. Didn't the Verunans have enough to deal with, with their murdered sun, their dying world, and their enslaved brethren, without having to worry about a renewed Akerian attack? "It would save time if you could have us beamed directly to the site."

"Very well." There was a pause, then her voice came again with a hint of mirth. "Happy hunting."

He gave her the coordinates, then signed off. "With your permission, Nata, we'd like to transport you to the site."

"Certainly," the *Viha* replied. "I have had more adventures in the last few days than I have all my life. If your people stay, Chakotay, they may well restore my youth."

A few moments later, they materialized fifty meters outside one of the bulbous ends of the ship. Up close, it was even more impressive than it had been from a few kilometers distant. This section alone was roughly the size of *Voyager*. It was more overgrown than it had appeared at a distance as well.

"Walk softly," were the first words out of *Viha* Nata's mouth. "For you tread upon holy ground."

Chakotay glanced down. Various items littered the brown grass: beads, necklaces, lamps fashioned of the hot muddy clay, trinkets of all sorts. For a brief instant he was confused and then realized that the gently swelling lumps of earth that covered the immediate area in front of the ship were not natural formations.

"It's a burial ground," he said softly, reverently.

Nata nodded. "We return to the First Place when we die—at least," she amended, "our bodies do."

Chakotay itched with curiosity about what the

Verunans thought regarding life after death. More than anything he could recall wanting in the recent past, he wanted to take Nata to meet his family back in his homeland. What stories, what rituals, what magic to ease the heart and spirit.

But there was no time for that, no time to be properly reverent to the dead Verunans who silently slept the eternal sleep all about him. There was only time to analyze the ship, to find a way in, to perhaps learn something from the Verunan past in order to ensure a Verunan future. Chakotay had been raised to revere the dead. It went against the grain for him to simply ignore them, but as Janeway had warned, time was growing short.

"I mean no disrespect . . . ," he began, but Nata held up a placating hand.

"There is no time to be respectful," she said, essentially reading his mind. "Our people are ever practical. Whatever spirits might linger here will understand the greatness of the need and forgive any violation. So," she said, straightening to regard the metallic orb that loomed in front of them, "what does your . . . tricorder, yes? . . . make of this?"

Chakotay opened his tricorder and analyzed the readings. "It appears to be fashioned from the same material that the six Guardians are," he said. "I had thought that the lack of wear and tear on the Guardians was due to the fact that they were at least somewhat sheltered from the elements, but this ship also appears in staggeringly good condition." A thought struck him. "Nata, the Akerians never targeted the ships because the materials in the soil hid them from their sensors. But I'm clearly picking up readings from this ship. Why didn't they attack this site?"

Puzzlement descended on her reptilian features. She cocked her head to one side, pondering. "Can you tell what is inside?" she asked.

Chakotay glanced back down at his tricorder. It efficiently showed him everything he could possibly want to know about the ship's exterior but revealed nothing of the ship's secrets. "No," he answered.

"Then perhaps they did not think it a pertinent target," said Nata. "Few come here, except to meditate, as I do, or to bury the dead. And recently"—her voice caught and her eyes shone with unshed tears—"may the Ancestors forgive me, but there has been no *time* to properly bury all those who have died . . ."

"And the overgrowth would continue to support the theory that this wasn't in use by your people, not now, at least," said Chakotay. Gently, he touched her arm, shook her out of her mourning, and together, treading softly as Nata had advised, they walked over the graves of countless Verunan dead and approached the ship.

The surface was smooth and white where it was not covered by centuries of growth. Nata reached out and laid her hand on the metal.

"Yes," she confirmed, "it feels just like the ships."

"Let's see if we can find an entrance of sorts," suggested Chakotay. "Keep searching with your hands beneath the growth. Look for cracks, unevenness, indentations—anything that might indicate a door."

Together, they set to work clearing a space. The heat wrapped Chakotay in its stifling embrace until he felt swathed in something tangible. He paused, took a few swallows from his water gourd, and wiped the sweat from his tattooed brow.

The vines were stubborn, and the work was hard. All they encountered for their efforts was the smooth, eggshell-like, gently curving surface of the ship's hull. The swollen sun climbed higher in the sky. Chakotay began to wonder if perhaps this was a dead end when the surface beneath his questing fingers suddenly changed.

"Nata, I've got something." Quickly the elder came to him and, with her superior strength, began ripping the vines off with renewed enthusiasm.

"It's a touch pad," he said softly. "For your people. Look." Indeed it was. There, the only blemish on the otherwise perfect surface of the hull, was the imprint of a Verunan hand—five fingers, each with long, wicked-looking claws. Nata stared at it, her already large eyes enormous with wonder.

"How long," she breathed, "how long has it been since one of us touched this?"

"I don't know, but I bet it will activate a door of some sort." Chakotay had to suppress his own excitement. "Be careful, Nata. We don't know what form this door will take. It might even open directly beneath us."

She glanced over at him, then back at the imprint. Slowly, she raised her own right arm. She hesitated, murmured a quick prayer, then gently laid her hand into the print. It fit perfectly.

There was a slight whir. The earth did not open beneath them. A door did not slide open with a frightening suddenness. Instead, directly in front of them, a circular portion of the hull dissolved, quietly and with no fuss at all. It simply wasn't there anymore. It was typically Verunan, thought Chakotay distractedly.

The dust of centuries slowly floated out, hung dancing in the sunlight. "What do your tales tell about what's inside the First Place?" asked Chakotay as he and Nata peered inside into the darkness. He was aware that his voice sounded hushed, reverent, befitting a holy place.

Nata's voice, too, was solemn. "That which is first is final," she answered him, extending her long, supple neck for a better view. She sniffed at the dusty air. "We begin with nothing but soul and end with nothing but soul. We buried our dead in the First Place's shadow. It appears that, before the knowledge of entry into this place was forgotten, we brought our dead to the heart of the First Place as well. Again, my friend, walk softly."

And then she moved inside, boldly, gracefully, walking with deference. The minute she stepped inside, a strip of lights illuminated the corridor. It proved to be wide, Chakotay guessed about fifty feet or so. And he now saw by the dim illumination what Nata had scented: Verunan dead lined the walls, each on a small pallet. Their bodies did not smell of rot. The climate inside the ship was dry and cool, a reprieve to the human's overtaxed system. The corpses had desiccated, not decayed. Most were skeletons now; some were merely piles of dust. A few appeared to be mummified. It was rather unsettling to Chakotay, whose people had a rich variety of theories regarding proper respect to dead bodies and dreadful results if such respects were not granted.

He swallowed hard. It was difficult to breathe, realizing that he was inhaling the dead, but, he mused with rueful amusement, there was no choice if he didn't want to join them. Chakotay took his cue from Nata, who seemed deeply moved by the sight of her dead ancestors but not in the least distressed.

Apparently, the Verunans had no ghosts.

He hastened to catch up with her. Quietly and unobtrusively, or so he thought, he drew his phaser.

"Is that a weapon?" asked Nata, dropping her head on its long neck to examine the phaser. The bulky pendant—the mark of her status as *Viha,* he had learned—slipped down her neck with the gesture.

Chakotay felt a blush, like a child who'd been caught with a toy in school. "Yes, Nata."

"I do not think you will have need of such things here," she answered, lifting her head and raising it to its natural position, nearly a meter above Chakotay's own. She continued walking with her steady, purposeful stride.

"I understand that your people are now very peaceful save in your own defense," the human began. "But you do not know the temperaments of your ancestors. Besides, if this place is a colony ship, as I am certain it is, it would be defended against attack from possible enemies to protect those it housed. It's only logical to be prepared. There might be traps."

Nata snorted, sounding very much like a horse. "I

recall all the tales, friend Chakotay. I remember nothing of a trap."

Chakotay frowned to himself. Granted, they hadn't been able to just walk in. The door was protected from outside violation by the handprint keypad. Chakotay was certain that, barring intensive use of phaser energy, he would never have been able to enter by himself. Perhaps that was all that the ancient Verunans had felt was necessary.

But that answer felt wrong to him. The Verunans, although unique in his experience in many respects, also seemed to have a great deal in common with Chakotay's people. And peaceful as some tribes were, the man in whose body flowed the blood of many chiefs knew instinctively that he and Nata were missing something.

A flash of inspiration occurred to Chakotay. "Perhaps a trap was not the right word. What do your tales say about . . . trials? Tests?"

At that, Nata's smooth stride faltered, stopped. She glanced down at Chakotay, her great yellow eyes revealing her surprise. "That . . . had not occurred to me."

At that precise moment, the corridor darkened suddenly. As one, Chakotay and Nata whirled around. Chakotay had his phaser at the ready.

Behind them, the door had disappeared. Quickly, the two companions ran down the short distance they had walked. Both Chakotay and Nata felt along the hull. The wall was utterly smooth. There was no indication of a handprint opening on this side of the wall. There was no way for them to get out.

The lighting changed yet again. The pale, weak

yellow light provided by the lighting strips that lined the corridors suddenly flushed into an eerie blue. They whirled at once.

Directly in front of them, a translucent blue shape floated two feet in the air. It was taller even than Nata, and it seemed more reptilian than she. It sported a ridge of spiny horns atop its head and partway down its long neck. Its eyes bored into them, and it hissed a challenge.

"Who are you, who trespass into the depths of the soul of the K'shikkaa? Speak, and speak truly, or die!"

Chakotay's mouth was suddenly as dry as the dead who lined the corridor walls. It seemed as if he'd been right. The ancestors of the Verunans, as he had thought, did indeed believe in tests and trials of those who entered this most sacred place.

But he'd been wrong, too.

Apparently, the Verunans *did* have ghosts.

CHAPTER

11

PARIS STOOD IN FRONT OF A LARGE DISPLAY CONSOLE, feeling absurdly like a Starfleet instructor teaching a bunch of raw cadets Starship Tactics 101. Except these cadets were all nearly twice his weight and he was in the strangest classroom ever.

He had in front of him an external diagram of the *Voyager*. To scale, beside it, were one of the ship's shuttlecraft and the six escort ships the Verunans would be flying. He gazed out at the eighteen eager pilots, some of whom he'd gotten to know slightly. There was Miweni, one of the older ones who had chosen to follow the call of technology. He had a personal reason: his mate was one of the enslaved Verunans. Another was named Takoda. He was larger than most but quiet, only tending to speak when necessary. One of the youngest was a lively young male named Rixtu, who tended to compensate for Takoda's silence.

Paris swallowed hard and began.

He explained the concept of the *Voyager*'s shields, pointing out where the Guardian ships would be positioned in relation to the craft. He discussed the methods by which Janeway planned to carry the six ships along, indicated where he, Paris, would be at all times. The graphic ships approached the graphic concavity, entered it, and encountered the graphic planet. Paris talked them through the three scenarios he'd been able to come up with, then called for questions.

There were a few: startlingly intelligent and on the mark. A few of them Paris didn't have ready answers for and was forced to admit he'd need to consult with others aboard the *Voyager*. At last the little lecture was over, and Paris turned back to the console, ending its program. He was surprised at how drained he was by the presentation.

"It seems you may have missed your calling," came Kaavi's voice at his shoulder.

Paris started. "What do . . . Oh, no. Believe me, this is not my usual line of work."

"I did not say that it was easy. I said that you were good at it." She peered past him at the image of *Voyager* that still blinked on the screen. "What a lovely ship. I cannot imagine anything so large. She must be hard to maneuver."

Paris thought about how easily, silkily almost, the *Voyager* responded to commands, how she turned and dipped and flew like a bird. Easier, smoother, than a bird. He felt a smile creep onto his face.

"Oh, no. No, she's a lady, all right. It's like . . . piloting that ship is like riding a tiger. She's all coiled muscle and power, poised and ready to go. And, Kaavi, oh, can she *go*. But she's smooth, see, and when I put my hands on the consoles and feel those keypads—those small, smooth, cool little pads—it just takes *this much* effort and—"

He broke off, suddenly embarrassed by his effusion. A blush began to creep onto his cheeks as he realized Kaavi was grinning. A thousand words came to his lips, but they crowded each other away, and so he remained silent.

Kaavi, reading his discomfort in his eyes, shook her head. "No, Paris, I know. I have only flown twice, and that was aboard the ill-fated scout ship before it went on its final mission. I have not yet known the joy of maneuvering *Conviction* or the other ships like her. But I cannot wait. It is a feeling like no other, like riding the wind and being a part of it as well. I understand your pleasure. Though you would deny it, we are more alike than you realize. I am sorry that you find me and the rest of our people so repulsive."

The words, spoken without a hint of rebuff, only regret, were like a slap in the face to Paris. He mentally shrank another ten centimeters. He wished, for the first time, that he was still in prison in New Zealand. It was more comfortable than standing here, in front of this being of such obvious intellect and integrity, and feeling like he was the biggest lout in the universe.

"Kaavi, I . . ." What could he say? She was right. He'd grown to respect the Verunans—their technology and culture, at least. But their serpentine movements, their strange, diamond-shaped heads . . . It was a deep-rooted revulsion. "It's nothing personal," he managed miserably.

"I understand," she replied amiably enough. "Your commander Chakotay explained that our people's physical appearance is evocative of certain creatures on your home world that make you uncomfortable. I was not rebuking you, Paris. I was merely wishing that you were not so ill at ease around us." She blinked, then brought her head down even with his. She peered, concerned, into his reddening face. "Is that a transgression of courtesy?"

For the first time, Paris forced himself to look evenly into Kaavi's golden eyes. He found nothing there to contradict her words—only genuine concern. He felt deeply ashamed and squared his shoulders.

"No, Kaavi, it most certainly is *not*. I'm the one who's transgressed, and I ask your forgiveness. It shouldn't matter what you look like—it should matter who you are."

The words were hard for him, and Kaavi seemed to know it. "Ah, but should and should not—they are words that can move mountains, destroy suns, reshape the universe. We *should* have a future here on Veruna Four. We *should not* be faced with the extinction of our race, the death of our very world." Her powerful jaw clenched, and her normally pleasant voice dropped to a growl.

"I *should* be able to fly through the skies with a mate and a child. I *should not* have to tinker with ancient ships in the desperate hope of being granted the right to die defending my planet. It is not right, Paris. It is not fair. The Akerians have stolen our children's future. *Viha* Nata preaches hope, but where is it? Veruna Four is dying by the hour! Where is the hope in that?"

Her great eyes were filled with tears. She was struggling very hard to keep them back, but they spilled out anyway, making dark furrows in the orange-brown fur of her cheeks.

"Kaavi . . ." Paris hated it when females cried, no matter what species they were. He never knew how to handle it. What did one say to a weeping female Verunan?

She's not just a female, Tom, she's a pilot, came the thought. *And she's not having a hissy fit, she's trying to come to grips with the death of her entire world, for pity's sake!*

"Kaavi"—the lieutenant steeled himself and put a hand on her arm, momentarily surprised to find it warm and pleasantly solid, not hard and scaly—"the hope is here." He gestured around, at the busy technicians, the gleaming *Conviction,* the active computers and display, and the Starfleet engineers in their black and gold uniforms.

"What you're doing is going to make a difference. I don't know how much of a difference, but it's *something.* Chakotay and Nata are off looking at your First Place. Maybe there'll be some answers. Maybe your enslaved people know something we don't— something they'll be able to share with us when we rescue—when *you* rescue them."

The Verunan pilot sniffled, wiping at her streaming eyes with a clawed hand. But she was now looking at him, and that dreadful combination of hatred and despair and premature defeat that had lain like a shadow over her reptilian face was gone. Paris felt his spirits rise a little.

"You're a pilot, Kaavi, a pilot in a world where until recently such a thing wasn't even *heard* of. You've got one of the prettiest little ships I've ever seen. And you're going to be taking her inside a thing out of legend to rescue innocent people from slavery. Some people live their whole lives never even having the chance to make a difference, to do a little good." *Like me, until not so long ago,* he thought. He reached up and wiped the tears from her cheeks. Her facial fur was very soft against his hand.

"And," he added, hoping he wasn't about to commit an egregious breach of etiquette, "the hope is *here.*" Gently, he laid his hand on her heart for an instant, then removed it. He punched her gently, playfully, in the shoulder. "Come on, sister, you don't have time to feel sorry for yourself. You've—we've—got a job to do."

Kaavi blinked, gulped, then smiled. He smiled back, unaware that for the first time since he'd laid eyes on a Verunan he truly thought of that gesture as a smile instead of a grimace.

"You are a very good person, Tom Paris. You have a greater heart than you would have others believe."

Paris didn't know what to say to this. Instead, he tugged gently on Kaavi's sleeve. "Let's get back to the *Conviction.* If we're going to be flightworthy in five hours like the captain wants us to be, we've still got a long way to go."

As they walked back toward the ship, Torres caught his eye. The chief engineer grinned. He'd have called it a smirk, but her eyes were too friendly for that. He desperately hoped word wouldn't get around that Tom Paris was soft on lizards.

"Paris?"

"Yes, Kaavi?"

"What is . . . a *tiger?*"

At once, Chakotay corrected his first startled assumption. Of course it was no ghost. It was a hologram, an ancient one to be sure, one whose hardware could use a tune-up to give it a full-color spectrum and get rid of that transparent quality. But it was far more dangerous than the spirit of one long dead, he realized a heartbeat later as tiny red lights flickered into life along the corridor. Those lights no doubt indicated a weapons system ready to fire if Nata did not give a satisfactory answer. And he couldn't take the risk that the passage of centuries had rendered the weapons system as faulty as the holographic system. Mentally, he wondered if he'd be able to fire his phaser at them before they had a chance to fire back. He might. He hoped he wouldn't have to.

Viha Nata was startled, but almost at once she drew herself up to her full, rather imposing height. When she began to speak, she used the formal words and clipped, precise gestures that Chakotay recognized as a full retelling—practically a ritual.

"Greetings, First Challenger of the Soul. I am no trespasser. My name is Nata, and I am *Viha* of my people, the People Who Live by the Standing Stone, the People Who . . ."

Nata continued with her formalized greeting. Chakotay only listened with half an ear. He was not a man who chose violence as a first alternative, but right now his fingers itched on his phaser. But Nata's response seemed to be working. The blue-tinged hologram settled back, adopting a listening pose. For a brief second Chakotay wondered at the fact that the hologram apparently spoke the same language as *Viha* Nata. Language was a living thing, mutating and developing over centuries. The hologram ought to have at least spoken with an accent that made its speech difficult for Nata to understand.

Almost at once he realized why. Nata's people kept their culture and history alive orally. Whole sagas were memorized verbatim. Though Chakotay knew that, for instance, he'd have had a hard time understanding Middle English, the Verunan—K'shikkaan?—language had not changed at all. He made a mental note of this.

Finally, Nata finished up, culminating with a deep bow. The hologram seemed satisfied.

"You are a true *Viha*. You bear the emblem of your status, and you have the Words to speak the truth. You may pass. This, the great ship *Soul*, is yours to command."

The hologram disappeared. With a low hum, the ship seemed to come to new life, as if the words that had been exchanged had woken a dormant life form. The red lights blipped out, but in their stead, new, hitherto unlit light of a warm, sunny hue came on. The corridor in which they stood was covered with fine dust—the crumbled remains, the Indian realized, of perhaps hundreds of dead Verunans. Their footprints, booted human and huge clawed Verunan, left clear trails in the inch-thick powder. The walls were bright white, clearly made of metal now that they were viewed in better lighting.

Chakotay motioned for Nata to follow him. Wordlessly, she complied as they retraced a few steps back to the area from which they had entered. When they were within ten centimeters of the wall, the door reappeared as mysteriously as it had vanished. Chakotay and Nata stepped outside. The door disappeared. Nata put her hand in the touch pad, and the door returned. Chakotay smiled up at her.

"You must have passed inspection," he said. "I wanted to make sure that we could come and go as we pleased now. No disrespect, but I have no desire to be trapped inside for the rest of my days."

"Nor do I," concurred Nata. "But come. If the . . . the protector of this place has granted me access, I wish to use it."

Chakotay nodded his close-cropped head in agreement, and together they reentered the ship and continued down the corridor. It was long, longer than Chakotay had even estimated. Ten, fifteen minutes passed, and Chakotay began to chafe at the time being thus eaten up. With a quick glance at the bodies that still filled the little alcoves to the sides of the corridor, he said, "Would it be disrespectful to run?"

"I was wondering that myself," confessed the *Viha* with a chuckle. "We have less than five of your hours. I would say, we should run."

At once Chakotay sprang forward. He was in excellent shape and could run in reality almost as smoothly as he could in imaginary excursions with his animal guide. He didn't pull his pace—Nata, with her powerful, long strides, was more than able to keep up despite her age. She ran swiftly beside him, her heavy feet *thump-thump*ing a rhythmic beat.

At last Chakotay glimpsed what seemed to be a dead end up ahead. He did not despair; having seen how the doors operated in the place, he was confident they would find that this was not truly a dead end. He slowed, panting only slightly as they reached it. Sure enough, when they got within ten centimeters, the wall dissolved into a curved entryway.

What lay beyond, greeting their astonished eyes as they stepped through, was beyond Nata's conception and even beyond Chakotay's highest hopes.

It was a huge, wide-open area. The overarching ceiling was at least five hundred meters above their heads. Balconies encircled the open section, hinting at more rooms beyond their immediate vision. *Private quarters? Mess halls? Holodecks?* Chakotay thought almost giddily to himself. But what held Nata transfixed and what so delighted the first officer of the *Voyager* was that straight ahead were groupings of hundreds of consoles, computers, and, over several hundred yards to the rear, what looked like inactive engines of a sort.

"Anahu and Kaavi must surely have had the right of it," Nata breathed at last, still taking in the staggering spectacle. "I had thought the simpler life was the right one, but obviously our ancestors—the K'shikkaa, as we must now properly call them—valued technology above all."

"Not true," interposed Chakotay swiftly, hearing a note of sorrow in his friend's voice. "You abandoned this ship because it was not meeting your needs. The

K'shikkaa chose Veruna because it was verdant and fertile. Technology and nature can peacefully coexist. I know."

Nata suddenly smiled. "'I understand that a sun can be a huge ball of burning hydrogen, yet have a spirit. I *think* like the Verunans. That can only be an asset,'" she quoted, capturing Chakotay's earlier words to the letter. "It has been an asset, friend Chakotay. Now, we must turn our attention to the task of learning all this technology." She shrugged helplessly. "Still, Kaavi or Anahu would have been a better companion on this particular soul exploration than I would, it seems. I do not know even where to start."

"Kaavi and Anahu would have been blasted to pieces by the Sentinel as trespassers," Chakotay reminded her. "You, as a *Viha,* knew the lore that deactivated the weapons and let us get this far. Well, I have some ideas as to where to start. Come on."

Forty-seven long, annoying, distressing minutes later, every single idea that Chakotay had thought of had been explored, found ineffective, and discarded. He knew a lot about engineering systems and computers—as a commander of a Maquis crew who kept constantly leaping from one jury-rigged, stolen vessel to another, he had been forced to wear just about every hat there was. But B'Elanna knew more about engines, and Kim knew more about operations. Chakotay was a jack-of-all-trades, and that availed little at the present moment.

There seemed to be no way to power up the equipment. No switch, no button—nothing. Chakotay had tried vocal commands. He'd even had Nata try everything he had, on the theory that the elusive command controls would respond to a Verunan touch where they had remained cold to that of a human.

He was ready to admit defeat, call in B'Elanna or Kim, and chalk up the hour or so they'd just squandered to experience. Sighing heavily, he straightened from his uncomfortable position beneath a console and turned to face the *Viha.*

He didn't have to speak. She was learning to read human gestures, as he was learning to read Verunan, and read his regret in his eyes. Her own gaze fell, and she closed her eyes. Automatically, her hand went to her *Viha* amulet, clasping it close as if the ritual metal talisman could offer comfort.

The light in the enormous chamber caught the metal, made it sparkle. Chakotay had seen Nata do this often before. He was sure she wasn't even aware of the gesture. But suddenly, this time, his heart leaped. The shape looked familiar, familiar in a different way than his repeated viewing of it around Nata's slim neck would indicate. His heart racing with excitement, he returned his attention to the console.

And there it was. Almost buried among other strange-shaped buttons, indentations, knobs, switches, and other gizmos was a fist-sized diamond impression in the white metal. Not a perfect diamond shape, no, there were notches and small, curvy holes as well— holes that Chakotay suspected would perfectly match Nata's "seal of office," as it were.

"Nata, come look at this," he said. She heard the tremor in his voice, and her whole body responded to the sound. Instantly alert, she was by his side in an instant.

"'You bear the emblem of your status,'" Chakotay quoted the Sentinel. "Your amulet—I'm not sure, but I think it might be the key that will power this thing up!"

The console at which they stood was pentagonal in shape. Each of the five sides was waist-high to Nata, almost chest-high to Chakotay. The working area of each side was at least three meters long. There was a flat space in the center, for what purpose, Chakotay couldn't even guess. The diamond-shaped indentation sat dead center in the console.

Trembling, Nata slipped the amulet over her head, snapping the leather thong easily. With a quick, hope-filled glance at her companion, she dropped the metal shape inside.

Nothing happened.

Chakotay tasted disappointment like bile in his mouth. But . . . it made sense. It had to work. *Had* to. It was in perfect harmony with everything he'd learned about how the K'shikkaa and their descendants thought.

"Nata, you are not the only *Viha* left, are you?"

"No. There are five of . . ." Her voice trailed off, and Chakotay knew that she was thinking what he was thinking: Five *Vihas*. Five panels on the console. Five amulets.

He didn't have to say anything. As one, they hurried to the next console, found the indentation, and inserted the amulet. Again, nothing happened. Undaunted, they moved to the third, then the fourth.

This time, the amulet did not catch on some hidden

obstruction. This time, there was a smooth, easy *click*. They waited perhaps two seconds—an apparent eternity.

Then, quietly and efficiently, as if the passage of millennia had been but a moment or two, the console at which Nata and Chakotay stood hummed into life. A dazzling display of colors and light intensity met their gazes. Lights twinkled and blinked. Grinning idiotically, Chakotay and Nata spontaneously hugged each other.

"Greetings, *Viha*. How may I be of service?" came a voice.

Startled, the two companions whirled to locate the sound. It came from the flat field in the center of the grouped consoles. Standing there, apparently solid, was the same Sentinel that had "greeted" them earlier. Only at this outlet, it would seem, the system worked perfectly. It seemed almost real; there was no hint of spectral insubstantiality about this one.

"Who are you?" Chakotay asked.

The hologram swiveled its delicately shaped head in his direction. "I answer only to the *Viha*. *Vihas* alone may command the computer."

"It's a manifestation of the computer," said Chakotay quietly. "Ask it something."

"Computer," began Nata, hesitantly at first and then with growing conviction, "it has been a long time since one of us spoke with you."

"Four thousand three hundred twenty-seven years, eight months, two weeks, and four days," agreed the computer.

"We have kept alive the tales," Nata assured it, "but

we have forgotten much as well. How . . . how did we come here? Why?"

The holographic K'shikkaa looked puzzled. "Full verbal downloading of information will take approximately two years, three months, three weeks, six days, and nine hours. Suggest narrowing question unless you wish the complete data."

"Very briefly, then," Nata continued, "why did the K'shikkaa come to Veruna Four?"

"The sun in the K'shikkaan system was dying. A supernova was inevitable. Various systems were determined to be suitable to sustaining K'shikkaan life. Veruna Four was the first planned colony. A colony ship called the *Soul* was dispatched here. Since you have reactivated the system, the colonization may be deemed successful."

"What about other colonies?" asked Nata.

"No information is available. They were scheduled to depart after the *Soul* departed for Veruna Four."

"A dying sun," mused Chakotay. "It seems your people have come full circle, Nata."

"What else should I ask?"

"Ask it . . . ask it how to operate this vessel."

Nata did so.

"Verbal downloading of information will take approximately seven months, one week, and two days. Suggest asking specific questions."

Nata clearly had no idea what to suggest and glanced pleadingly at Chakotay. "Ask them if they have detailed information about the Guardians and if they can provide an on-screen tutorial about their function."

Nata did so. The hologram froze, then nodded. "Such can be done. Please observe."

The hologram vanished. In its place there appeared a perfect miniature replica, only about two meters long, of the ship *Wisdom*. As Chakotay watched, hardly daring to believe, the ship was dismantled in front of his eyes. Other images appeared, explaining various functions. Chakotay thought of B'Elanna, complaining that Verunan technology was half child's play and half total mystery. Now, the mystery was about to be explained. There was even more to the vessels than Torres had guessed.

A slow smile spread across his face. "Come on. Let's get back to the others. We need to get the pilots and the engineers in here immediately. B'Elanna Torres is about to be made very happy indeed."

"But . . . I wonder something," said Nata thoughtfully. "How do I get it to stop?"

"Tell it to stop," said Chakotay. "Simple requests usually work best."

"Computer, stop," said Nata. Obediently, the program ceased, to be replaced by the hologram of the Sentinel. "I understand that with one amulet, I can operate the computer. What would happen if all five *Vihas* inserted their amulets?"

"Five keys are necessary to engage mobility," replied the computer.

"I don't understand," said Nata, though Chakotay thought she did. He could not believe what he was hearing.

"With five *Vihas* at the controls, the launching sequence may be engaged and the ultimate destination may be programmed."

"You mean," breathed Nata, "that with all five *Vihas,* with all five keys, this ship can *fly?*"

"Correct."

Of course, that was only in theory, Chakotay told himself in an effort to throw water on the hot hope that suddenly burned in his heart. Of course, the ship might be damaged beyond repair after so long a time. Of course, there would not be room for all the Verunans. Some would have to be left behind, even if the ship were still spaceworthy.

But his efforts to curb his joy evaporated like water in the hot Verunan sun when he looked at Nata's face. She looked like a prisoner who has just had a death sentence remanded. Because, of course, she was.

CHAPTER
12

CHAKOTAY, PARIS, TORRES, AND THE VERUNANS HAD PUT
the four remaining hours Janeway had given them to
good use. The computer system of the *Soul* had
proved to be, to use the twentieth-century term,
extremely "user-friendly." Its tutorials on the functions, controls, and technology of the Guardian ships
had been simple but thorough. After about an hour of
staring, engrossed, as the holographic tutorial played
itself out, Paris and Torres had grasped everything.
Another half an hour of interpreting it for the
Verunans, and Anahu knew enough about the ships
for the Verunans to be able to finish repairs on their
own.

Chakotay silently marveled at it. It seemed miracu-
lous to him. Then again, when one considered that the
minds of the Verunans had evolved so that they never

forgot the tiniest scrap of information once they'd learned it, it did not seem quite so startling. Now, it would stand the Verunans in good stead.

Torres and Anahu returned to the underground bays while Paris, the devil knew how, somehow managed to cajole the computer into constructing a flight simulation for the pilots.

Finally, Chakotay felt comfortable enough to leave them in order to make a report to the captain. He needed to step outside to do so. The material that prevented sensors from penetrating the ship also efficiently blocked communication. He'd barely stepped out into the hot, thick air when his comm badge chirped.

"Janeway to Chakotay."

"Chakotay here."

"You're overdue for your report, Commander. I was starting to worry."

He winced. He'd completely lost track of time. "Apologies, Captain, but we've found"—How to even phrase it?—"some wonderful things inside."

"I can hear that grin through the comm link, Chakotay. What have you got?"

"As I suspected, the Verunans aren't native to this planet. Their ancestors, the K'shikkaa, were fleeing—of all ironic things—a dying sun. The Verunan ship was the first colony venture. Thanks to Nata, we were able to activate the computer and get access to all the information we could possibly need. Torres is working with the engineers to incorporate this new information, and it's been invaluable for the pilots. I think if the Akerians decide to come be the bullies in this playground again, they may be in for a surprise."

Janeway's voice sounded as delighted as his own must have. "That's terrific news. Makes me feel a little better about what I plan to do."

"And that is?"

"What I want to discuss with all my senior officers," she replied, efficiently ducking the question. "We've been busy on this end, too. Mr. Kim has discovered some rather . . . well, *startling* might not be too strong a word to describe what he's found out about the Akerians. When can you all beam aboard?"

"You gave us five hours, Captain, and I'd like to use every minute of it. We'll be aboard *Voyager* at 17:00."

"Very well. Report to the conference room when you've beamed up. Janeway out."

Never had the recirculated air of the *Voyager* smelled so sweet to Chakotay as now, as he materialized aboard after spending nearly three full days on Veruna Four. He breathed deeply and, turning, saw that both Paris and Torres were doing the same thing. He caught their eyes and grinned.

"It's a nice little planet, but I wouldn't want to live there," quipped Paris, but his eyes didn't laugh. It had been a nice little planet, once. It was no longer, and Chakotay knew that he and his fellow crew members were glad to be back aboard, albeit temporarily.

The three of them headed for the turbolift. A yawn escaped Torres, who seemed irritated at this show of weakness.

"Must be the change in the oxygen content," offered Paris. His face showed no hint of teasing, but Chakotay still suspected him. One *always* suspected

that Paris was joking. Clearly Torres did, for she shot
him a rather nasty look.

"Must be," she agreed archly.

The turbolift doors opened, and Neelix and Kes
smiled out at them. "Welcome back, intrepid *Voyag-
ers!*" punned Neelix, stepping back to make room for
them. "Heading for the bridge as well, I assume?"

Chakotay nodded. The doors hissed closed, and the
turbolift smoothly continued its ascent.

"I wanted to let you know, Tom, the blood samples
that you took from Kaavi were very helpful," said Kes
to Paris in her soft, gentle voice. "If there's a battle,
and we need to get the Verunans medical supplies,
we'll know exactly what they'll require. That was very
wise of you."

"Shucks, ma'am, t'weren't nothin'," drawled Paris,
smiling down at the attractive young Ocampa.

"Speaking of Kaavi," put in Neelix, noting with
distress the proximity of his beloved to the man
Chakotay had heard him call That Walking Hormone,
"I hear that you and the Dragon Lady are quite . . .
friendly."

Chakotay closed his eyes briefly, waiting for Paris's
indignant outburst along the lines of *You think a
lizard and I would ever . . . You're sick!*

There was indeed an outburst. But the words were
the last thing Chakotay had expected to hear issuing
from the smart mouth of Lieutenant Tom Paris.

"Don't you *ever* call Kaavi or any of her kind
'Dragon Lady'! The Verunans are some of the nicest,
gutsiest people I've ever met, and you could learn a lot
about decency from them. I'll thank you to keep a
civil tongue in your head, *Talaxian!*"

Everyone turned to look at Paris, utterly startled. The same genes that had given Tom Paris his fair hair and blue eyes had also bequeathed him a fair complexion that blushed quite easily. Paris was red right up to his hairline at the moment, but he met the disbelieving gazes challengingly.

For once, Tom Paris wasn't joking.

Will wonders never cease, mused Chakotay. He caught Paris's eye and gave him a small, approving nod.

When they reached the bridge, Paris, clearly uncomfortable, shouldered his way out first and strode briskly over to the conference room. The others followed more slowly.

"Now what was *that* all about?" Neelix wondered aloud.

Kes smiled, one of her small, secret, wise smiles that made Chakotay recall just how little they knew about her race.

"I think," she said, pitching her voice very soft, "that Tom has met a female whom he likes, respects, cares about—and has no physical desire for." Her sweet smile deepened, became impish. "And I think he's finding it terribly confusing."

There was no literal clock ticking away the minutes, of course. But Janeway certainly felt as if there were.

There were just too many things that could go wrong for her to relax even for a moment. According to the information Kim had gathered from the Akerian ship, the vessels could obtain speeds comparable to *Voyager*'s warp factor nine. Conceivably, then, the *Victory* could cover the distance between Veruna Four and Akeras in a day.

Janeway had gambled that the disabled vessel wouldn't be able to travel at warp nine. Tuvok certainly agreed with her on this.

"Chances that the *Victory* will be able to reach and maintain maximum speed for the entire journey are approximately 2,358,489 to 1," he had rattled reassuringly right off the top of his curly dark Vulcan head.

So the *Victory* wouldn't be a problem for at least forty-eight hours. But how long after that did they have? How badly was the ship hurt, after all? According to the *Conquest*'s records, there was originally a total of eight light-speed vessels in the Akerian fleet. One had crashed on the planet, providing the Verunans with their first, badly needed glimpse into Akerian technology. That left seven. Janeway had disabled the *Conquest,* further diminishing the ranks of potential enemy vessels. But there were still six left.

The question was, Where were they? The *Victory* was, by everybody's best guess, heading home as quickly as possible to Akeras for repairs. From what she knew of the Akerian nature, Janeway felt certain it was coming back to continue the fight. Where were the other five being deployed? Were they back in orbit around Akeras? Off terrorizing other innocent solar systems?

Or were they inside the concavity, in the belly of the dreadful Sun-Eater, completely unaware of the turmoil directly outside the event horizon? And if they were inside the concavity, what was she going to do if they came out?

Every instinct was crying out to her that she should press her advantage while she had it. And certainly, *Voyager* and her crew were ready, willing, and able to enter Sun-Eater right this minute if she gave the order.

But then there was the question of the Verunans. Janeway herself had been the one to offer aid to their enslaved comrades, but that was before she'd realized just how backward the Verunan technology truly was, before she knew just how fast the Akerian ships could fly.

Now, she recalled her own words of three days ago, spoken here in this same conference room: *It would cost us nothing but a little time to escort them back out, see them safely back to Veruna Four, and reenter Sun-Eater. I'm willing to give them that time.*

She still was, deep in her heart. But she was playing a very risky game, with her own crew taking on a good part of that risk. The Akerians were a one-trick pony, certainly, and Janeway now knew how to avoid their only weapons and how to quickly and efficiently disable them. But still, but still . . .

The door hissed open. Janeway immediately donned what she privately called her "captain's card-playing face" and turned to face her officers.

Paris had obviously just been in some sort of verbal altercation with someone; his color was high. Judging from the hints of smiles on Chakotay's and B'Elanna's dark faces and the perplexed expression Neelix wore, she guessed they'd been privy to it. Kes, serenely lovely as ever, followed silently while Tuvok and Kim brought up the rear.

Janeway kept standing, watching her staff as they took seats. Good people, all of them. They'd done her proud. Silently, she resolved anew not to let them down.

"Before we begin our information exchange, let's have a quick status report," she said. She nodded to Tuvok, seated to her right.

"Tactical is prepared for any hypothesized eventuality. We have fully integrated the information provided by Mr. Kim into our systems. Every tactical crew member has been briefed and is familiar with the construction and weaknesses of the Akerian vessels. Phasers can be powered up upon your order, Captain."

Compete efficiency as usual. She nodded, then glanced at Kim. Kim tapped the PADD in front of him on the table. "I've spoken with every department, and they're up to speed. Everyone and everything is operating at peak efficiency. They're just waiting for the word, Captain—and of course to learn what the away team has discovered," he added hastily, glancing at Chakotay.

"Lieutenant Torres, how's Engineering?"

"Carey's been doing a fine job in my absence, Captain," said Torres with an unexpected graciousness. "All the damage has been repaired and everything's back on-line."

"In that case, then, I think it's time we learned just what the away team has been up to." She sat down, yielding the floor to Chakotay. The first officer did not rise, but he did lean forward.

"If we were on an ordinary exploratory mission,"

he began, "we'd be here for the next several months, helping the Verunans rediscover their technology. As it is, we can't do that. But they seem to be managing well on their own."

He paused, gathering his thoughts.

"The Verunans are descended from a race called the K'shikkaa. They sent out at least one colony ship, called the *Soul*." He pressed a touch pad, and an image of the ship appeared on the viewscreen.

Kim looked puzzled. "But that's—"

Janeway hushed him with a slight shake of her head. Chakotay, curious, looked at them both for a moment, then continued.

"Accompanied by the six escort ships, it landed on Veruna Four. There was everything in there to help the K'shikkaan colonists start a good life. The thing was, Veruna Four was so pleasant that over the years they forgot about the colony ship, stored the computer components and the escort ships in caverns to protect them, and returned to the land. The only ties they had to their past were cryptic stories, some of which Nata and I deciphered and which helped us learn about the ship."

He eased back into his chair, snapping off the image, and nodded to Torres, indicating that she could resume the thread.

"They are a very advanced people, Captain," said Torres eagerly. "I'd figured out most of how their ships worked, but there were some things I had no idea about. The information helped me and the Verunan crew working on the ships to effect repairs much more quickly. I wanted—" She broke off, horrified about what she was about to say.

Janeway could guess. "You wanted to put in some of our technology," she said softly.

Torres glanced down, her breast heaving with agitation, then looked her captain squarely in the face. "Yes," she said defiantly. "But I didn't."

"I know you didn't," replied Janeway, her voice still soft, still compassionate. "You're not Seska. You understand why we can't do that. Torres, if you think for a minute that any of us here wouldn't love to be able to just transport all the Verunans to safety, you're wrong. Wanting to break the rules out of compassion isn't a crime, B'Elanna. But a Starfleet officer knows that there are other ways to help."

Pleasure and pride spread over the engineer's face. "And we found them. The Verunans themselves—or the K'shikkaa, as I guess we ought to call them—provided what we needed. Anyway, I downloaded as much as I could, and Carey is at this moment transferring the information into our computer banks. Ironically, they may have information that could help *us.*"

"That would be a nice bonus," agreed Janeway, "but let's not count on it. But the ships are up to speed?"

"Yes, Captain."

"Paris, what about the pilots?"

There was a noise that might have been a muffled snicker from Neelix, but when she glanced angrily over at him, the Talaxian's face was open and guileless. Paris's mouth thinned, but his voice was calm when he spoke.

"They learn very quickly. They were able to follow everything I said in my presentation. We had hoped to have time to get in a few test flights of the repaired escort vessels, but . . ." He shrugged. "They should be just fine, Captain."

"There was a real sense of camaraderie down there," said Torres. Paris and Chakotay nodded agreement. "They're very grateful for our aid, that we've decided to take their side in this war."

Janeway stiffened in her chair. "It takes two to make war, Lieutenant. I'm not going to play that game—and neither is any member of my crew, is that understood?"

Torres's dark brows drew together in puzzlement. "With respect, Captain, the Akerians *did* declare war on us—right before they attacked!"

"It takes two to make war," repeated Janeway calmly but firmly, "and it takes two to make peace. I have reason to believe that I can get these two races talking to one another. Now *that* game," and she allowed herself a smile, "we might be players in."

"I'm not so sure about that, Captain," said Chakotay. "The K'shikkaa are peaceful by nature, but the Akerians have done some pretty terrible things. It's not likely that they will be forgiven their atrocities by the Verunans. And what makes you think that they'd even be interested in suing for peace? Everything we know about them indicates that they're warlike and hostile by nature."

Janeway smiled at Kim and Tuvok. Kim grinned back, but Tuvok merely nodded slightly. Did they have a surprise for the away team!

"Everything you know about them, perhaps, Chakotay. And you don't know everything—not yet. But before I have Mr. Kim share his findings with you, I have something to say." Her blue eyes scanned the table, looking at each officer in turn. "And I'm not saying this lightly. I've done a lot of hard thinking on this. If it turns out there is no wormhole in that concavity—and believe me, I hope there is—I propose closing Sun-Eater."

There was a stunned silence as the officers absorbed her pronouncement. She took advantage of the pause and continued.

"Both Ensign Kim and Lieutenant Tuvok share my opinion. This concavity was harmless until three hundred years ago. It should never have been tampered with. I believe very strongly that closing Sun-Eater is the right thing to do—and is not, in fact, as much of a violation of the Prime Directive as it may first appear."

"Captain—and I can't believe I'm saying this," began Torres, looking troubled, "but I'm afraid that I have to disagree."

"Ah, for crying out loud," exclaimed Paris, "it's like supplying them with phasers, keeping this concavity open! The Verunans have so little time—"

"Don't give me your opinions yet," interrupted Janeway. "I want you to have all the facts, just as I have, before we decide. Mr. Kim, please give our away team a recap of that enlightening presentation you gave me and Mr. Tuvok."

His grin threatening to split his face, Kim rose. Mentally, Janeway reminded herself that she needed to have a talk with young Harry about that. Officers needed to have a poker face. He could take a lesson or two from Tuvok about that. Diplomacy meant not giving everything away in the first five minutes of negotiations. Though, she mused sadly, it would be a shame to quash that boyish enthusiasm that seemed to be the epitome of Harry Kim. Maybe later. And maybe, her thoughts taking a darker turn, maybe one of these days he'd have that enthusiasm knocked right out of him. She desperately hoped not.

Kim launched into his presentation vigorously. He'd smoothed out a few things, and Janeway kept her eyes on her officers, watching their faces, their reactions.

Kim showed them where the Akerian system was in relation to the Verunans, summed up the planet's harsh environment and the eventual formation of the Akerian Empire. He discussed how the Akerians discovered the concavity, venturing inside it and learning from the dead civilization they found within. There was a murmur of mournful surprise at the complexity and beauty of the recreated culture. From time to time, Paris, Chakotay, and Torres asked questions, most of which had already been asked by Tuvok and Janeway herself in the earlier presentation.

She kept watching, wondering if anyone else would figure it out before Kim presented the pièce de résistance of his speech. She thought Chakotay might. And when Kim pulled up the detailed image of the Akerian vessel's weapons array, she saw comprehension beginning to dawn in Chakotay's earth-dark eyes. Quickly he glanced over at her, and she put a finger to her lips. She wasn't about to deny young Harry Kim his big finish.

Paris, Neelix, Kes, and Torres were still in the dark—just as she and Tuvok had been. Kim continued, showing the slave areas on the planet and explaining why the Akerians had brought in the Verunans.

He then turned to the image of the shrinking Sun-Eater and the video footage of the Akerians artificially "feeding" the concavity. Torres was impressed; Chakotay and Paris looked sick. Poor Kes looked as though she was about to cry at the scene.

Kim spoke about the log, the unguarded moment where Nelek had removed his helmet before turning the recording off. Everyone leaned forward eagerly, probably unaware that they were doing so.

Nelek removed his helmet.

Everyone gasped.

"They're . . . but they're . . . ," spluttered Paris.

"Exactly," grinned Janeway.

CHAPTER

13

"JUST LIKE OLD TIMES, EH?" GRINNED CHAKOTAY at Torres as they left the conference room.

The half-Klingon glanced up at him, smiling ferally. Her eyes gleamed with excitement. "You bet," she replied. "And everyone else is feeling it, too."

By "everyone else," the first officer knew B'Elanna meant those crew members who used to be—and perhaps still were, deep in their hearts—Maquis. It really *was* like the "old days," when everyone knew just what it was they were risking their lives for and knew, bone deep, that it was a good cause. Those people who used to be Chakotay's crew had some measure of that fighting spirit flowing in their blood, or else they would never have joined the Maquis. Starfleet might call them terrorists, but they knew who they were—they were Freedom Fighters, each and every one of them. At least, Chakotay's people were. They were men and women who had not been afraid to give up lives, homes, families, security, to fight and perhaps die to protest the encroachment of the calculating, cruel Cardassians.

While most of them had come to accept Janeway instead of him as their captain, he knew that sometimes they had problems seeing what they were fighting for. But now, word about the Verunan plight was common knowledge. Many of the crew had met them.

This time, on this mission, they knew exactly what they were fighting for. And Chakotay had to admit, it felt good.

"The difference is, this time the Federation's on our side," he said to Torres just before she stepped into the turbolift to descend to her station in Engineering.

B'Elanna turned. Her smile grew; her eyes sparkled. "I know," she replied. "And that's the best thing about it."

The doors closed. Chakotay stepped down, automatically heading toward his usual station at Janeway's left, then correcting himself and continuing down toward the conn. Paris wouldn't be maneuvering *Voyager* on this expedition. He was already in the shuttlecraft, waiting to rendezvous with the sleek little Verunan—K'shikkaan, Chakotay corrected himself for the umpteenth time—vessels.

Behind him, he heard Janeway's quick, light footfalls. Her hand rested briefly on his shoulder, a gentle reassurance for them both, then she stood behind him. Chakotay knew, without having to look around, what he would find: the heartening sight of his captain in combat mode, her hands on her slim hips, her chin slightly lifted, as if daring the unseen enemy to take a crack at it, and her blue eyes hard and sharp as steel.

Ready for anything, he thought. As were they all.

Here we go, thought Janeway. *Let's make this as smooth as we can.*

"Yellow alert," she snapped. "Janeway to Paris."

"Paris here," came the lieutenant's voice, sounding small and tinny.

"How is our little fleet doing?"

"Well, they're a little nervous, but all six liftoffs have gone perfectly. Okay . . . okay, here they come now."

"On screen." The planet appeared on the screen. "Magnify." Now, Janeway could see the six tiny little ships forming a perfect V, smoothly making their way toward the waiting shuttlecraft. Paris hadn't exaggerated. They were very attractive, well-designed crafts.

"I'm taking the lead," Paris continued, "and am bringing them in to our starboard side, parallel to the docking port." The shuttlecraft maneuvered into position, with the six Guardians falling gracefully in line.

"Looks good, Mr. Paris," Janeway approved. "We'll be ready to go to warp two in sixty seconds." She glanced back at Kim. He knew how important it was for everything to be timed correctly. He met her gaze evenly, nodded. She allowed herself a smile. "Everyone in place, Lieutenant?"

"Ready, Captain," Paris answered.

"Shields up," she ordered.

"Shields up, Captain," Tuvok confirmed. "All six ships and the shuttlecraft are safely inside the shields."

"Mr. Kim?"

Kim began the countdown. "Five . . . four . . . three . . . two . . . one."

"Engage," said the captain.

Voyager sprang into warp. "How are our friends, Mr. Paris?"

"We're fine, Captain. No one's having problems maintaining position."

"Put Sun-Eater on the screen," said Janeway. At once, the huge, gaping maw of the black, distorted space appeared. She gazed at it as it grew closer. At warp two, the fastest speed attainable by the shuttlecraft and the Verunan ships at this point (though Torres seemed to think that further investigation into the staggering Verunan archives would yield ways to increase speed in the vessels), they'd reach Sun-Eater in an hour.

Her body was taut. Janeway took a slow, steadying breath, forcing her muscles to relax. Intellectually, she knew they were not heading into a black hole. But it sure as hell looked like one.

"Mr. Tuvok, keep me appraised of the situation as we approach." She wanted to sit down, probably ought to sit down. It would send a message of reassurance to the bridge crew. But her legs were locked here, as if nailed to the floor, and she knew herself well enough to know that she could no more sit and feign ease at this moment than she could fly.

As the minutes crept by, Tuvok calmly rattled off

statistics, noting the gradual increase of the gravitational pull, the pressure being put on the shields, the percentage by which the ship's sensors were becoming inaccurate, the dimensions of the entrance into the mouth of Sun-Eater.

Suddenly he broke off in midsentence. Janeway's head whipped around.

"Captain, sensors indicate the approach of two Akerian vessels at warp seven." The Vulcan glanced up from his console. His brown eyes locked with hers. "Their heading is zero-four-six mark three-two."

"Directly for the concavity," breathed Janeway. She uttered an angry curse. "Red alert!" The bridge darkened and the bloodred pulse of the alert signal began. "Put them on screen."

There they were, two large, bulky vessels. Janeway recognized one of them as the *Victory*. Linneas was apparently not one to give up easily. It did not surprise her. The second was a new ship, which the computer translated as the *Destroyer*. The two moved in tandem, never varying from their obvious destination: Sun-Eater.

"Hail them, Mr. Kim."

She kept her eyes on the screen, hearing the soft sounds of the buttons Harry Kim was manipulating. "No response, Captain."

Janeway hadn't really expected one, but she had needed to make the gesture. "Keep trying, Ensign." She mentally ran through her options. They could not fire the ship's phasers while *Voyager* was in warp. She did not want to risk losing another photon torpedo out of their limited supply. Besides, knowing what she now knew about the Akerians, she did not wish to attack unless there was no alternative. And they hadn't fired upon her—not yet.

Voyager was still closer to the concavity. If only they could move faster, they could beat the two Akerian ships inside. But that would mean losing the shuttlecraft and the six Guardian ships nestled beneath *Voyager*'s protective shields, and that was unacceptable.

Damn, but they had been quick in repairing the ship. For all her words of caution to the away team, for all her nagging worries and doubts and what-ifs, she hadn't honestly expected to see the Akerians for at least another day. Apparently, though, Sun-Eater and the treasure trove of information it housed was of paramount importance to the Akerians. They were not attacking; they were racing to get inside, to do what they could to defend what was . . . inside? On the other side? Soon Janeway would know the mystery of what exactly lay within the concavity. And soon, her ship and the six small ships she protected would be confronting the Akerians.

She watched, cursing softly and angrily, as the two ships sped away and disappeared into the darkness of the concavity. "Cease hailing attempts, Mr. Kim." They were inside now, waiting . . . for her.

But that doesn't make sense, part of her brain whispered. *Everything I've learned about this aberration tells me they* can't *fire on us once we're inside! If they were going to defend that ruined planet, they'd attack now, while we're outside.*

Suddenly she knew why the two Akerian ships had not engaged the *Voyager,* and her mouth went dry. Outwardly, she did not react save to turn to Tuvok and bark out her swift, certain knowledge in a voice that was utterly steady. "Phasers on-line, Tuvok. They're going in there to get reinforcements."

Scarcely had the words left her mouth than the *Victory* and the *Destroyer* reemerged from the gaping mouth of the concavity. And, just as Janeway had predicted, hard on their heels came another ship.

And another.

And a third.

Five of the remaining six Akerian war vessels were assembled here, fanning out in a semicircle and approaching the *Voyager* at warp speed.

"They're trying to encircle us," said Chakotay.

"I can see that, Commander," his captain replied, still not moving from her standing position. "Janeway to Paris. Watch your people, Tom. Keep them close—it's going to get bumpy."

"Aye, Captain," replied Paris.

"Chakotay, take evasive action—and I mean evasive. These people don't waste much time."

Immediately *Voyager* dove like a dolphin. Everyone was pitched forward slightly. Janeway stumbled, catching herself on Chakotay's chair.

"Neither do you, apparently," she hissed with a flicker of grim humor to her first officer. Chakotay didn't reply; she doubted he had even heard her. His dark, intense gaze was fastened on the viewscreen, and his fingers flew over the controls. The maneuver worked. Chakotay had taken them directly under the approaching line of Akerian ships, and with another abrupt movement, the ship veered upward. Janeway decided she was better off in her chair. She sank down in it, keeping her own gaze on the screen.

"Rear view," she snapped.

The Akerians were behind them now, wasting precious moments in circling back around to continue the hunt. But their would-be prey was heading back toward Sun-Eater with a vengeance. Janeway allowed herself a tiny, satisfied smile. Paris's touch on the conn might have more finesse, but Chakotay certainly got the desired results.

But *Voyager* could only travel at warp two, and the Akerian hounds on their heels had the luxurious advantage of speed. They took it, coming back with a terrible acceleration. This time, three of the ships, one of them the *Victory*, pulled directly in front of them, the other two hanging back to port and starboard. It was almost, Janeway thought, as if they were acting as an escort.

And that thought made her think of the small Verunan vessels clustered together with Paris's shuttlecraft. The perfect target.

She had just turned around to face Kim, her mouth open to voice her suspicions, when the young Asian man interrupted her.

"Captain, the ship on our starboard bow has just launched its pods at us!"

Her mind's eye filling with the last, disastrous time those shiny black pods had approached her ship. "Get us out of here, Chako—"

He executed another sharp zig-zag, this one upward and to port, before she'd even finished her order. "On screen!" Janeway cried.

Chakotay, fast as he'd been, hadn't been fast enough. The gleaming black circles were spiraling toward them, already forming their dreadful hexagon.

The ship that had fired had lined itself up astonishingly well and daringly close to compensate for the *Voyager*'s speed. Even that brilliant calculation, though, would have failed them had the Starfleet vessel been able to move as she had been made to move—swiftly and efficiently. The Verunan ships were slowing the vessel down, and now, it seemed as though the Verunan ships would be made to pay the price.

"They've attached themselves to our shields," said Kim. Unsaid was, *just like the first time.*

"Paris to Janeway," came Paris's strained voice.

"Go ahead," she replied, though she knew what he was about to say and wasn't at all sure she wanted to hear it.

"We're only about fifty meters away from where the Akerian pods are opening a hole." His voice revealed his distress, though he was clearly fighting to stay calm.

Janeway thinned her lips. There was no alternative. They'd have to stay and fight their way into the concavity.

"Paris, advise your group to slow to impulse, and keep this channel open. I want you to know what's going on up here. We'll be slowing down ourselves on the count of five. Ready, Chakotay?"

"Aye, Captain."

She nodded to Kim. He began the countdown. Janeway kept her eyes on the six Verunan ships as they dropped out of warp. Paris had been right about the pilots: they kept perfectly in synch with the starship. Her mind raced. The last time they'd fired phasers on those pod ships, they'd ended up further damaging the shields and the ship. And right now, that was the last thing they needed. The shields would have to hold flawlessly in order for *Voyager* to safely navigate the gravity well.

She was about to suggest tractor beams when a flurry of movement on screen caught her eye. One of the Verunan ships had broken formation. It had swiftly flown out of the expanding hole in the shields—a hole barely big enough for it to get out—and was headed straight for the big Akerian vessel that was controlling the pods.

Dear heaven, thought Janeway, *it's a suicide run.*

At that precise moment, Tom Paris's voice reached her ears. It was tense, almost strangled.

"Captain, that's the *Conviction.* That's Kaavi's ship."

For a heartbeat, Paris watched in frozen horror as his friend and her two comrades aboard the *Conviction* sped toward their certain doom.

He flicked open a channel. "Paris to the Verunan fleet," he cried, "everybody *stay put!* Keep up with the *Voyager!*" Then he sprang into action. He didn't bother to contact the *Voyager;* Janeway could hear him through the open channel. He slammed his shuttlecraft hard to port, circled back behind the remaining five Guardian ships, and fled through the hole in *Voyager*'s shields after Kaavi.

The complete and total unexpectedness of the *Conviction*'s maneuver had caught the Akerians utterly off guard. For a long moment, nothing happened. The *Conviction,* dipping and dodging like a crazed hummingbird as she approached her target, fired twice on one of the glowing red generators.

Paris's eyes dropped to the sensor readings on his console. As had been the case the last time they approached the concavity, the sensors were going crazy. Even so, they were able to pick up that the two directed energy weapons fired by the *Conviction* had damaged the shields of the larger ship.

Suddenly the *Conviction* zagged wildly to starboard. Trusting Kaavi's piloting sense, Paris immediately imitated the movement. He was glad he had, for the space around the area where he had just been shivered and distorted. The Akerians had fired their gravity wave at him and the *Conviction.*

"Tom Paris, what the hell do you think you're doing?" Janeway's voice was tense, hinting at anger.

"What does it look like, Captain? I'm being the good shepherd and going after a wandering lamb."

The comment was flip, automatic, but nothing about Paris's expression or his emotions was humorous. He was grim, intent. That was his friend out there, about to plaster herself, her companions, and her ship against the front end of the giant Akerian warship in a not-very-vain attempt to destroy its control. "If you can keep the wolves off our tail," he continued, "I should be able to bring it back to the fold."

Kaavi's plan had been a good one. Tuvok would have approved of its logic. The small black pods were mechanical, operated by the Akerians from the larger ships. Without the big ship to control them, the pods would probably cease to function and drift off, nothing more dangerous than space debris.

The problem was, it would take the destruction of the *Conviction* and the three Verunan pilots aboard her to do it. And Paris was not about to let that happen.

"Captain, I'm going to try to get a transporter fix on two of them and beam them out of there. Can you get the third?"

"We can't drop our shields now!"

"You don't have to," replied Paris, speaking quickly. "You've already *got* a hole in your shields. It's narrow, but a transporter beam—"

"It just might work. We'll try. But the spatial distortion around that Akerian ship won't make it easy to lock onto them. Good luck, Tom."

Red suddenly flashed off the metal of his console. Paris knew that Janeway was carrying on her own fight aboard the *Voyager* and had fired at the Akerian vessels.

"Paris to *Conviction*," said Tom, keeping his eyes on the vessel before him. "Prepare to be beamed out."

"Paris, you can't!" came Kaavi's voice. "We must be permitted to destroy the generators aboard that ship! Your own ship is in danger unless—"

"*Voyager* will find another way out of this mess," replied Paris. Out of the corner of his eye he saw a movement. "Watch out, bearing two-four-six mark zero-seven!"

Kavvi heard and dove, narrowly missing another gravity wave attack from a second Akerian vessel that had come to the rescue of its fellow. Paris swallowed hard, aware that his forehead was dappled with per-spiration. *Conviction* had no shields. One square hit from that weapon—

"Get a running start, Kaavi, and I'll try to beam two of you out. The third I'm leaving to *Voyager.* Ready . . . go!"

The little ship turned around and headed directly for the bow of the first Akerian vessel. Paris swore softly under his breath, working the controls. With the sensors being so untrustworthy, Paris would be unable to distinguish who he would be able to beam aboard. That was, if he could get *anyone.* He couldn't get a lock on them. It was like trying to sculpt an object out of mercury. Every time he had them, there would be an energy surge from somewhere or the sensors would fail, and their coordinates became confused. Finally, for an instant, he had them.

He immediately hit the controls. "Paris to *Voyager.* I've got a lock on two of them. Have you got the third?"

"Transporter room is having a lot of problems, Tom," came Janeway's voice, revealing her tension. "And we're pretty busy up here as well." The truth of her words came an instant later in another flash of red that bathed the interior of the shuttlecraft in warm crimson.

"Captain, we don't have much time . . ." Paris's blue eyes were fastened on the terrible sight of the tiny *Conviction* speeding toward her doom. "Kaavi, I'm bringing two of you over *now!"* He said a quick prayer and lowered his shields.

"Paris, no, not yet—" Kaavi's imploring voice was

cut off. Behind him, Paris heard the hum that indicated the transport was in progress. He couldn't spare a moment to turn around, not yet. He touched the pad that reinstated the shields. Not a moment too soon, for half a heartbeat later, the empty (he hoped it was empty, oh, God, he hoped) *Conviction* crashed headlong into the Akerian vessel.

There was a flash of blue as the warship's shields protested, then gave way beneath the attack. A blinding explosion forced Paris to avert his gaze, and the shuttlecraft shook with the resonance of the explosion. He locked his legs around the base of the chair, forcing himself to stay in his seat.

Paris blinked, refocused, then grinned happily as he saw that the crash had done exactly what *Conviction*'s pilots had intended. The huge, clear dome that served as window for the Akerian bridge had been crunched inward. The four orange-red "eyes" that marked the generators had gone dark. Slowly, the warship tumbled backward from the impact. And out of the corner of Paris's eye, he saw the six little black balls that had once posed such a threat to *Voyager* and the six ships she shielded floating off harmlessly into space.

"We didn't get the third one, Tom. I'm sorry." Janeway's voice was filled with genuine regret. "Did . . . Is your friend aboard safely?"

Something cold squeezed Tom Paris's heart. Behind him, he knew, were two Verunans. One of their number didn't make it, had faced death with quiet courage as his . . . her? . . . ship completed its suicidal mission.

Who had it been?

A large, sharp-clawed Verunan hand closed on his shoulder. Steeling himself, he glanced up to see who it was.

She smiled down at him with mingled sorrow and gratitude, her enormous mouth curved and her great, lambent eyes brimming with tears.

"Kaavi!" he whispered, telling himself that surely it was just the tension of the moment that closed his throat and clouded his eyes.

"We lost Rixtu," Kaavi said, her own voice thick. Paris's joy was suddenly, harshly, undercut by the three words. Rixtu, little, lively Rixtu, the youngest of the eighteen pilots. The one who always had "just one more question, Paris!" The chatterbox of the group whom you couldn't get angry with because he was so genuinely upbeat and friendly. Rixtu was gone, that cheerful voice forever silenced.

"Oh, Kaavi," he began, but there were no words.

The second Verunan, the large, quiet male called Takoda, also reached to clasp Paris's shoulder in a gesture of gratitude, but kept his eyes on the screen.

"You had better hurry, Par-is," he commented. "That second warship is heading straight for us."

CHAPTER

14

TAKODA WAS RIGHT. A SECOND SHIP WAS NOW BARRELING down on them at staggering speed.

"Hold on to your hats," warned Paris, slamming the shuttlecraft into a sharp turn. Kaavi tumbled into the seat on Paris's left, while Takoda immediately sat down and anchored himself as best he could.

"But Paris, we have no hats," reprimanded Kaavi. Paris ignored her, his mind utterly on evading that behemoth that was now seemingly just a few kilometers away. Paris had completely reversed direction now and was heading at top speed toward the hole in *Voyager*'s shields. It seemed dreadfully small, but he'd gotten through it once . . .

"Paris to bridge. I'm heading back toward the hole in the shields. Captain, I know you're trying to dodge these people as much as I am, but please, try to hold a steady course. This is not going to be easy."

"Holding steady. But make it fast, Paris," came Janeway's cool voice, "make it damn fast."

"Aye-aye, Captain," the lieutenant replied. He glanced down at his sensors, getting his bearings. The hole in the shields, while certainly physical, was not visible. He'd have to rely on the not-very-reliable sensors to navigate.

Kaavi dipped her sinuous neck, staring down at the controls and watching him like a hawk. Her large, clawed fingers splayed over the console, poised. After what he'd learned of her race's remarkable ability to absorb information quickly—and to remember everything they learned letter-perfectly—Paris had complete confidence in her ability to help him maneuver if he needed it. When she deemed it time to bring those wicked-looking claws down on the instrumentation, she'd be as well versed in its use as nearly anyone aboard *Voyager*.

Takoda, meanwhile, had craned his own long neck to see out the windows. Paris heard him gasp. "Par-is, they've fired—"

The gravity wave shook the little vessel wildly. Paris was nearly flung out of his chair. Scrambling back into his seat, he checked the shields. Down sixteen percent but still holding. The gravity weapon so beloved of the Akerians might do nothing to *Voyager*, but Paris now knew that his smaller craft was vulnerable.

"Keep an eye on them for me, Takoda," he instructed the pilot. *Voyager* was only a few hundred kilometers away. Paris slowed to full impulse, feeling

Kaavi's eyes watching every move he made. He didn't mind.

Suddenly he swore as the bigger vessel dodged to starboard, away from them. *Voyager* fired, apparently only a few meters over the top of the shuttlecraft. An explosion flashed briefly somewhere to the shuttlecraft's stern.

He opened his mouth to ask Takoda what had happened, but the Verunan beat him to it. "Your ship has just destroyed the Akerian vessel's pods."

"Too close for comfort," muttered Paris, then aloud to the comm link, "Captain, I'm beginning to think you don't like me."

"We don't," quipped Chakotay's voice, "but we'll hold our position here for a few seconds. Hurry, Lieutenant."

Paris glanced again at his sensors, found the hole, and headed for it. "This is it," he told his passengers. Closer, closer. Gently the lieutenant maneuvered, dipping to port. He'd just reached to complete the move when the shuttlecraft suddenly balanced out for him. A quick, startled glance to his left reassured him. Kaavi was on it, doing a fine copiloting job. Even at this tense moment, Paris found he could spare a grin for her.

"We've cleared the hole," Paris told his captain. "I'm again taking position at the head of the fleet."

"Welcome back, Tom," said Janeway, warmth and relief in her voice.

The Verunan suicide run, which had cost the life of garrulous young Rixtu, had indeed bought *Voyager* some time. But Janeway was just as glad that her crewman and his two Verunan friends were safely back beside the Starfleet vessel.

"Bridge to Engineering. Paris and his passengers are back inside the shields. Torres, get to work on repairing—"

"I'm on it, Captain." Torres's voice was cool and efficient. "The damage is relatively minor. We should have shields up to full efficiency in a few minutes."

"You've got them," Janeway assured her chief engineer, silently marveling at her crew's competence.

"Captain." Tuvok's voice interrupted her brief moment of pride. "One of the Akerian vessels has veered away, bearing four-three-two mark zero-five."

"It's heading back to complete the mission we interrupted three days ago," said Chakotay grimly. "It's going back to destroy Veruna Four."

Janeway's lips thinned. She leaned forward in her chair. "Pursue it, Commander. Mr. Tuvok, lock onto the ship's engines. We've got to disable it before it reaches the planet."

Smoothly *Voyager* veered away from the concavity, dipping to avoid the remaining three Akerian vessels. The last one they passed—the ship whose pods they had just disabled—fired its weapons at them, a gesture of impotent anger—or fear. *Voyager* rocked slightly, but the shields were undamaged.

Mentally, Janeway assessed their situation. There had been five fully armed ships at the outset. The *Conviction*'s suicide run had destroyed one. *Voyager* had destroyed the pods of a second, though, as it had just demonstrated, it could still fire its weapon, and if

Voyager got another hole in her shields, it could still be as deadly as its fully accoutred companions.

That left three: the one now racing for the Verunan system, the *Victory,* and the *Destroyer.* Chasing the first ship would cause a dangerous delay, but Janeway was not about to let the Verunans be obliterated. Her eyes hardened as she watched the ship veer away from *Voyager*'s pursuit. A few more minutes, and it would be of range. In the background, she could hear Tom Paris through the comm link, instructing his little fleet to stick close and hang on.

If they got out of this, she'd give him a commendation—officially, for his heroic rescue and his level-headed command; unofficially, for opening his mind and affections to an alien race against whom he had been prejudiced.

If they got out of this.

"Lock phasers on the engines," she ordered.

"Phasers locked," replied Tuvok.

Her eyes narrowed. "Fire."

Red energy screamed across space. "Direct hit," reported Tuvok. "Their shields are down by twenty-four percent."

"Repeat firing until we've damaged those engines," Janeway ordered grimly.

Tuvok obeyed. Twice more phasers landed squarely on target even though the Akerian vessel tried to evade them. The third time Janeway saw one of the four mammoth engines explode, then sputter dimly before its orange light died.

"Get all four of them." She felt vaguely like a bully, hitting a smaller child when he was down, but rejected that. It wasn't an accurate image. That "child" was bent on destroying an entire civilization, and knocking out the engines completely was the most efficient and most merciful means of rendering them unable to complete their mission of genocide.

At last the ship hung limply in space, its engines dark but other lights and its gravity wave generators still active and glowing. Even as Janeway watched, the ship in a final act of defiance launched its six black chitinous pods. Janeway didn't even have to order Tuvok to fire on them. The phasers hit their target, and the potentially deadly pods exploded harmlessly, one by one, a good several hundred kilometers away.

"Reverse course. Let's get back to that concavity," she said. Awaiting them, as she knew they would be, were the two remaining ships: the *Destroyer* and Commander Linneas's vessel, the *Victory.* "Janeway to Engineering. Lieutenant Torres, how are those shields coming?"

"We're back up to ninety-six percent," replied Torres.

"Not good enough. We can't enter that concavity until we're back up to full strength. Let me know the *instant* we get there, understood?"

"Aye, Captain."

Janeway settled back in her chair. Her hands reached to grasp either arm in an unconscious bracing gesture.

"Mr. Kim, let's try again to hail Commander Linneas and the *Destroyer.*" They were facing the two ships now. The *Victory* drifted to port, the *Destroyer* to starboard, as if trying to corner her between them. *Oh, no, you don't,* she thought darkly.

"No response," replied Kim a moment later.

Janeway sighed. She hadn't expected one, but she kept hoping. "Chakotay, you know where we're vulnerable. Watch out for any pods or weapons fired in that direction."

"Aye, Captain," the commander replied.

As long as neither ship made a hostile move, she was reluctant to attack first. She waited, tense, as the *Voyager* steadily moved back toward Sun-Eater. The ships to their port and starboard continued to make no antagonistic moves. As before, they were almost behaving like escorts.

What are you up to, Linneas?

Harry Kim broke the silence. "I almost wish they'd attack," he said awkwardly. "At least do *something*."

"I'm right with you, Ensign," Janeway replied. "When you wear this uniform long enough, you get to be a pretty good judge of character. Sometimes you even get a sixth sense about people. And my sixth sense is telling me right now that Linneas has got a trick or two up his armored sleeve, and I'm willing to bet real money that we're not going to like them."

Tuvok lifted an eyebrow. "One should not attribute to some mysterious 'sixth sense' what is easily explicable by logical deductive reasoning. Commander Linneas has been actively hostile to us and to the inhabitants of Veruna Four every time we have encountered him. It is therefore reasonable to assume that when he does decide to engage in an action, it will be an antagonistic one."

Janeway, her blue eyes never leaving the ships on the screen, allowed herself a slight smile. "Lieutenant, you take all the fun out of it."

"I would not consider waiting to be attacked 'fun' under any circumstances," replied the Vulcan almost haughtily.

Janeway was about to reply when the *Victory* suddenly veered off and headed straight for the concavity.

"Heads up," snapped Chakotay.

"There he goes," said Janeway simultaneously. She sat erect in her chair, longing to stand, but not wanting to be tossed about should *Voyager* have to engage in sudden maneuvering.

"He's going right inside . . ." Her voice trailed off. Her first thought, the most logical assumption as Tuvok would have put it, was that Linneas would go into the concavity and try to prevent them from rescuing the Verunan slaves or going through the wormhole, if there was indeed one inside. Instead, the Akerian vessel sailed through the whirling dust and particles that comprised the accretion disk and positioned itself at the very entrance to the concavity.

Sun-Eater was large. But a goodly portion of its entrance was taken up by the furiously moving stream of hydrogen and star matter that it was devouring. There was a relatively small area through which *Voyager* could travel safely, and right now, *Victory* was effectively blocking the entrance.

Destroyer had not moved. It merely waited—for, Janeway assumed, further orders.

"Mr. Kim, open a frequency." She waited until he nodded for her to proceed. Janeway rose, planted her hands on her hips, and strode forward until she was standing almost directly behind Chakotay.

"This is Kathryn Janeway, of the Federation *Star-*

ship Voyager. It is our intention to enter this concavity, Commander Linneas. I suggest you move and let us do so. We will not retreat."

There was no response. Janeway waited, feeling the tension on the bridge, then continued.

"Commander Linneas, I know you can hear me whether or not you care to respond. I repeat, we are coming in."

Silence. The seconds ticked by. Then Janeway heard Paris talking to himself or perhaps to one of his Verunan companions. He said a word that would have been humorous in its incongruity had not the situation been so dire.

"Chicken," said Paris softly.

"I didn't get that, Mr. Paris," said Janeway. "Please repeat."

There was a pause, then Paris cleared his throat. "Um, I said, 'Chicken,' Captain."

"Explain."

"Um . . . well, it's a game that the cadets back at the Academy used to play. Two ships make a standoff, then approach each other at full impulse. The one that veers off at the last moment is a chicken. Linneas is playing a game of chicken with you, Captain. He's counting that you'll back off." A pause. "Not, of course, that *I* ever played such a dangerous, foolhardy game, Captain."

"I'm sure you didn't," lied Janeway, "and I'm thinking you're right." She took a deep breath and turned to her crew. "Suggestions."

"Linneas does not strike me as a person of great logic," said Tuvok. "Hostility and aggression, certainly. But not logic. We have superior weaponry, and he has never yet seen us retreat from a conflict, though we have taken great pains not to provoke any. Therefore, it is not logical to assume we would back away now. He seems to wish to protect the planet inside; yet a collision this close to the mouth of the concavity would certainly collapse it. Therefore, I think he is, as you would say, bluffing."

"I don't think Linneas is a stable personality," put in Chakotay. "Many of his orders are contradictory, some dangerously so, some merely foolhardy. We can't count on him backing off."

"Torres to Janeway."

"Go ahead, Lieutenant."

"The shields are up to one hundred percent."

A smile spread across Janeway's face. "Wonderful news, Torres. We're going to need those shields any moment now." She rubbed her chin. On the viewscreen, the immobile *Victory,* its very name a taunt, waited.

"I've seen a lot of bullies in my day," she said slowly, reaching her decision. "A lot of loud talk and underhanded tricks and dirty fighting. But I've never yet seen a bully that would stand up and die for something like this. Bullies are cowards, gentlemen. And I'm going to bet that First Warrior Linneas is a prime example of a bullying coward. Ensign, open that frequency again."

"Ready, Captain."

"This is Captain Janeway for the final time. We are going into the concavity. I suggest you move aside"— suddenly she recalled Linneas's taunting threat from days earlier and added—"or face the consequences."

She gestured to Kim, who abruptly terminated the channel.

"Mr. Paris, did you hear that?"

"Aye, Captain. We're all ready down here."

"Excellent." She returned to her chair and sat down. Her heart was hammering with slow, hard strokes. "Take her in, Commander Chakotay. Full impulse. Let's find out just who it is who's chicken."

CHAPTER
15

THE GLEAMING STARSHIP MOVED FORWARD PURPOSEfully. Unconsciously, Janeway's hands tightened on the arms of her chair. If she had guessed wrong about this, had misjudged Linneas in any way—

But I'm not wrong, her deep, inner voice assured her. *Linneas isn't exactly what one would call stable, but I don't think he's insane. He wouldn't destroy everything for this.*

"What's the *Destroyer* doing?" she asked Tuvok.

"Nothing at the present time," reported the lieutenant.

"Keep an eye on that ship," ordered Janeway.

Closer they came. The *Victory* sat sullenly, stubbornly, a gun metal blue lump of obdurate ugliness in a milieu of dangerous but beautiful cosmic activity. Behind it loomed the mystery of Sun-Eater, and around it whirled the colorful, luminous accretion disk.

"Phasers on-line," ordered the captain.

"I would remind you that once we enter the gravity well, our phasers will become extremely volatile and dangerous," warned Tuvok.

"I'm well aware of that," Janeway answered. "But I want to be able to fire on an instant's notice in case the *Victory* or the *Destroyer* tries anything."

"Aye, Captain," agreed Tuvok, making the necessary motions. "Phasers on-line."

Janeway took a deep, steadying breath and felt the profound calmness that nearly always descended when she was in a life-or-death situation. Later, she would react. She was human; she'd have to. But now, and for as long as this crisis continued, she was utterly calm, her thinking startlingly clear. She and her crew were at peak efficiency. She was ready for anything Linnea or his cronies might dish out.

The *Victory* grew larger, began to fill the screen. "No indications of movement from either the *Victory* or the *Destroyer*," Tuvok reported calmly.

"Keep going, Chakotay," said Janeway.

Closer it grew and closer. Still no sign of movement. "One hundred kilometers and closing," reported Kim. Still the *Voyager* moved inexorably forward. "Fifty kilometers . . . thirty . . ."

"Move," Janeway whispered softly, for her own ears alone. She wasn't wrong. Linnea would move. He had to.

"Twenty . . . ten . . . five . . . *two* . . ."

Suddenly the *Victory* roared into life, surging hard to port. At the same moment, it released its six pods.

The crew knew what to do. Before Janeway could even inhale to snap out the orders, they responded. Almost instantaneously, Tuvok, reacting faster than any human, fired his phasers on the deadly little orbs. If they managed to attach themselves to the shields now, it would mean disaster.

Chakotay, not far behind Tuvok in his speedy efficiency, brought *Voyager* hard to her own port and dove like mad. The ship bucked like a fish for a moment, and more than one bridge member lost his seat, including the single female who was on the bridge. Quickly Janeway scrambled back into her chair.

"Did we get them?" she cried, meaning the pods.

"Affirmative," Tuvok replied, "and the *Victory* took some damage as well. The only problem I can foresee—"

But the problem was upon them before he could finish his sentence. Light, orange and red and yellow and as beautiful as it was dangerous, suddenly engulfed the ship. Grunting a little in pain, Janeway instinctively threw her arm up to her face, shielding her eyes.

She knew what had happened. In his desperate and ultimately successful attempt to avoid the pods, Chakotay had brought *Voyager* directly into the stream of burning hydrogen that flowed in a luminous, flooding tide into the hungry maw of Sun-Eater. *Voyager* bobbed and weaved, and Janeway was reminded of a small toy boat caught in a rampaging white-water river.

Chakotay was fighting like mad to keep the ship level. "Kim, the shields!" demanded the captain.

"Holding, Captain," came the reassuring response from the ensign.

"Paris, report!"

"We're all still here, Captain," came Paris's voice, unsteady with the motion of his craft.

"Chakotay, get us out of this hydrogen stream. Engineering, do you copy?"

"Here, Captain." B'Elanna sounded calm. Silently Janeway thanked her for that.

"In a few seconds we'll be entering the gravity well," said Janeway, speaking rapidly. "I want you to transfer all available power to the shields. As we go in, I want the strength at different areas—fore, center, and aft. We need the most resistance at the point where the gravity is greatest. Do you understand?"

"Aye, Captain. If Ensign Kim will—"

"I'm on it, Maquis," replied Kim, hitting touch pads rapidly. "All nonessential energy is being diverted to Engineering."

At that moment, with a mighty surge, *Voyager* pulled free of the river of light.

"We're going in . . . *now!*" cried Janeway. "Tuvok, monitor the shields along with me."

Quickly Janeway hit a few commands on her own console to her left. Damn, but the pressure was extraordinary. But true to her word, Torres was transferring the most power to the shields as the pressure descended. Satisfied that her plan was working, Janeway turned her eyes toward the screen.

They were inside Sun-Eater.

Garai was fearful for First Warrior Linneas's sanity. Garai was a true Akerian. He loved his planet and his people deeply. He had been in the Akerian military for a long time now, and he was military to the bone. He had absorbed the discipline, the unbreakable determination, the willingness to die for what was right, that is, what advanced the Akerian way of life.

He was willing to kill. He was willing to die. And had this been all Linneas had demonstrated, Garai would have found nothing amiss.

But Linneas seemed to have lost the ability to reason. He jumped from one decision to another. Already, Garai knew, one crew member of the *Victory* was dead, choked by the first warrior himself, for having questioned Linneas's decision to block the path of the sleek, pretty, dangerous ship called *Voyager*.

Such behavior was not appropriate. Again, Garai rejoiced that he was no longer directly under Linneas's heavy hand. But commanding his own vessel was proving to be almost as stressful.

Repeatedly, Linneas had refused to talk to the captain of *Voyager,* Kathryn Janeway, even though Linneas, indeed none of the Akerians, knew just exactly what it was that she wanted inside the concavity. Linneas thought he knew—"They will try to steal what has taken us centuries to harvest!" he had snarled—and had issued an order that none of the Akerian warships was to respond to Janeway's hail.

Back and forth he had gone. "We need to continue harvesting the planet, therefore, we need to have slaves!" he would proclaim in one breath. In the next, he would announce, "We must destroy the Verunans utterly!" How, Garai wondered cynically, can you use slaves if you kill them all?

And how vital was protecting the concavity if Linneas was prepared to destroy it?

And most confusingly, most unforgivably to Garai's way of thinking, why did Linneas, having once taken a stand in front of the mouth of the concavity, *back down and show his cowardice?* Had any other Akerian done such a shameful thing, Linneas would have been on him at once, ripping his throat out with his own hands.

Now, Linneas was hailing Garai, speaking frantically, disjointedly. His helmeted face was on the screen.

"They have gone in, and *Victory* is damaged. Our shields will have to be repaired before we can follow. Pursue, *Destroyer,* and stop the intruder."

A low growl of frustration and irritation began in the back of Garai's throat, but he kept it soft.

"How do you wish me to do this thing, First Warrior?" he snapped, not quite keeping the sarcasm from his voice. "To fire the gravity weapon would be to destroy the concavity. To ram the ship would be to destroy the concavity. To attempt to board them using our transporting beam would be to—"

"Silence!" roared Linneas, and he actually leaped toward the screen.

Startled, Garai instinctively jerked back. There was utter quiet aboard the bridge of the *Destroyer.* Linneas appeared to gather himself with an effort.

"I leave how best to stop Janeway and her ship up to your wisdom, First Warrior Garai. But you are never, never, to take such a tone of voice with me again."

"Understood, First Warrior Linneas." Garai kept his voice serious. "I shall proceed per your orders."

He ended the transmission, turned his attention to his crew. "Shields at full strength. Prepare to enter the concavity. Let us find this Janeway and do what we can."

Garai leaned back in his command chair as far as the bulky armor that was like a second skin would let him and thought thoughts he did not dare—not yet—share with another soul.

A few days ago, Paris had made a quip about Alice falling through the rabbit hole. Now, Janeway had an inkling as to how that fictitious little girl might have felt. Even through her tension, even through the apprehension that lurked in the back of her mind, she felt herself responding with awe and wonder to the magnificence of the scene that unfolded before her.

Light for vision was not a problem; the glowing matter from the dying sun provided plenty of illumination. The most gravitational pressure they would face they had already endured in entering the mouth. As they moved forward into—what? Janeway wondered—the pressure eased until it was only somewhat stronger than that exerted by normal space. They were entering what looked to be a tunnel or pocket.

Vision, as she knew it would be, was distorted. The planet ahead, which they were rapidly approaching, was twisted in appearance as if she were looking at it through a fish-eye lens. She knew that the closer they got to it, the less dramatic the distortion would be. The ships landing on the surface would see no distortion at all.

"It appears to be some sort of pocket," she said softly. "The hydrogen—it's being drawn by the gravity to the . . . I guess the best word is walls . . . of this space. Mr. Kim, are we still picking up verteron emanations?"

"Yes, Captain, we certainly are. There's a lot of activity around here." He hit a few controls, a frown furrowing his forehead. "I'm trying to locate where it's coming *from.*"

Janeway sighed. "Remember to compensate for the sensor distortion. Tuvok, any sign of company?"

"Negative, Captain. All the ships appear to have been deployed to the outside to combat us there. There are a few vessels on the planet but nothing approaching the size of—Correction. One of the ships from the outside has just entered the concavity. It is the *Destroyer.*"

"Damn!" Janeway swore. "Let's get those ships down to the planet, then we'll try to decoy the *Destroyer.*"

"Aye-aye, Captain," Chakotay replied. Smoothly, he brought the vessel into orbit around the dead planet. This close, the distortion was minimal. For an instant, Janeway allowed herself a hint of compassion. Who had they been? What had happened to them? How had they gotten trapped in this aberration, this bizarre hybrid of black hole and wormhole?

Some answers, she'd never know. But the last one, she suspected she would find out—somehow.

"Janeway to Paris. We'll be lowering our shields

momentarily. They won't be down long, not with *Destroyer* in here with us, but we'll give the five ships enough time to get clear."

"Understood, Captain." She heard Paris intake a breath; there was more. "Captain, request permission to join the scout ships in this mission."

"Request denied, Lieutenant," Janeway replied at once. "We promised we'd get them in here and get them out. The rest is up to them."

"With all due respect, Captain, they're down to five ships now. There won't be enough room on them to take all the slaves. I don't know about you, but I don't think I want to tell four innocent people that they're not going home when their fellows are."

Damn. He was right. She did not want to engage in any action that could be interpreted as antagonistic, not when her final goal was peace, not war, between the Verunans and Akerians. But she had to agree with Paris. She couldn't just abandon a random few while saving the rest.

And what about Tom Paris himself? She'd sent him on this mission because he was the natural choice—he was indeed, as he so often bragged, the best pilot *Voyager* had. But she'd also wanted him to befriend the Verunans, to overcome his initial repugnance and learn to see beyond appearances. Well, he'd obeyed that second, unspoken order only too well. He'd made friends. She could not urge him to trust, to let down his guard among a race of beings, and then ask him to turn his back on them.

She recalled the sleepless night she'd been fighting when this whole thing began. Sleeping at nights was never easy for her, not anymore. If she turned away from the Verunan slaves now and ordered Paris to do likewise, she doubted she could ever have a night free from nightmares again.

"In for a penny, in for a pound," she sighed to herself, dredging up an old Earth phrase. "Very well, Lieutenant. You've done a good job leading them this far, you might as well take it all the way. But be careful, Tom. No heroics. Get in, get the Verunans, and get the hell out, understood?"

"Aye, Captain." His voice held a pleased grin.

Tom Paris would never have thought he'd be pleased about going into possible combat. But, he mused with a hint of dark humor, fighting his way past Akerian guards was preferable than continuing to sit next to Kaavi with that heartbroken expression on her mercurial, reptilian face.

When he beamed her and Takoda aboard, they had been wearing what served the Verunans as envirosuits. Except, of course, the helmet. No need to put that on until the last minute. Now, safely aboard the shuttlecraft, the two pilots were alive, but without their helmets they might as well have been wearing nothing at all. There was no way that a human helmet could fit the long, sinuous Verunan head and neck.

So not only did they not have a ship in which to transport their fellow Verunans, Kaavi and Takoda were unable to even go to their rescue. Kaavi had been so distressed about this and so pleased when Paris suggested going in their stead that he knew he'd made the right decision. He was glad he'd been able to talk Janeway into letting him go. Kaavi would have understood his not being able to disobey a direct command from his superior, but she still would have had that dreadful, miserable look on her face. And that, Paris was discovering, could not be borne. It made him feel far too guilty.

She took the controls while he stepped quickly into his own envirosuit, keeping up perfectly with *Voyager* as the bigger ship slipped into orbit around the dead planet and yielding the controls to him when he sat back down. He took over with a nod of thanks, then hit the comm link.

"Paris to the Verunan fleet," he said. "*Voyager* will shortly be lifting her shields. We'll have a brief window and we'll have to move fast. Then everyone is to follow me. I have been put in charge of this part of the mission, but otherwise everything will go exactly as we discussed. Sit tight, everyone. I'll let you know when we go."

He kept one eye on the five ships, patiently waiting for his go-ahead, and the other on the empty space. A few seconds later, there came a brief flash of blue. "Okay, the shields are down. Everyone, follow me!"

The shuttlecraft leaped forward, gliding down toward the dead planet. "How are they doing?" he asked Kaavi.

"Everyone is in perfect formation. They are all keeping close."

"Good." There was another flash of blue and Paris knew that the shields were back up. "Paris to the Verunan fleet. *Voyager* is going to attempt to distract the Akerian ship so we can complete our mission. It will be another few moments before we can land. I advise everyone to call up the map of the area and go over our orders. If anyone has any questions, feel free to ask them now. I don't want any confusion about our mission."

There was silence as they drew closer to the planet. Paris knew that on the five remaining Guardian vessels fifteen Verunan heads were poised over the map, mentally reviewing their instructions. There were no questions. He wished that these people were in the Alpha Quadrant. They'd be shoo-ins for Federation membership—and therefore Federation protection. For that matter, he thought darkly, he wished *he* were in the Alpha Quadrant.

The distortion faded as they approached. They were close enough now to see the scarred rubble that had once been a thriving, advanced civilization. Everything was gray. There were no oceans, no clearly recognizable buildings, nothing save gray powder, craters, worn-away rocks, and debris.

Paris checked the atmosphere. They would all still need their envirosuits—there was no breathable air. But the gravity on the planet surface was only about two *g*. They would be able to maneuver almost as easily as in regular atmosphere. Well, that was one good thing.

The Verunans had their own version of handheld directed energy weaponry. Paris would be toting a phaser rifle; here on the planet surface, with its almost normal gravity, energy fire was not nearly as dangerous as it was in open space. Each ship's pilot had a tricorder, which they had promised to return after the mission was completed. There had been discussion about "contamination," but Paris had reasoned that the Verunans had already seen tricorders in action. And when there were lives at stake, being able to pinpoint the Verunans was an advantage he would just as soon they all had.

Mentally, Paris went over the mission himself as they drew closer to what was clearly a landing pad of sorts. They had a complete map and timetable, downloaded from the Akerian vessel. They were coming right as a shift was ending, which meant that the odds were good that most of the prisoners would still be in their envirosuits, ready to run for the scout ships and the shuttlecraft without delay. They knew exactly where the prisoners were kept. Ideally, this mission shouldn't take more than twenty minutes start to finish. But Paris had an idea that the Akerian guards would do their best to keep the mission from proceeding perfectly.

Paris quickly put on his helmet, sealed it shut, and checked to make sure the ETCs, the emergency transport carriers—"living body bags," he'd once quipped—were easily accessible. These were large sacks whose environmental controls could be activated the moment the individual was safely inside. That person would then have to be carried, of course, but at least he or she would be alive for the trip. Conditions were harsh on this still, dead planet. The slaves were not treated well, and there was a good chance that some of them might not be able to walk out under their own power.

He took a deep breath, glanced over at Kaavi, and flashed her a grin. She responded.

"Okay, people," he said to the listening Verunan ships. "We're coming in for our landing. Gravity is tolerable, so we ought to be able to move pretty much as usual."

A sudden movement caught his eye. Below him, the wide, flat, sunken landing field beckoned. A short distance away was the building that, Paris knew, housed the slaves and the guards. Other buildings, where the scientists and researchers did their work, dotted the barren landscape. They were functional, but little more, and in that respect mirrored the Akerian vessels; they were hardly more than large, metal domes.

But Paris cared more about what had caused that movement, and in another moment, it was repeated. He knew it. The guards were on to them and had taken up strategic defensive positions behind boulders and large mining equipment.

"Attention, Verunan fleet," he said, keeping his voice calm. "It looks like we've got ourselves a welcoming committee."

CHAPTER 16

"BE CAREFUL, PARIS!" KAAVI IMPLORED. "OH, HOW I wish I were going with you . . ." The last thing Paris saw before the shuttlecraft's airlock closed was her worried face. He tried to give her a reassuring grin but wasn't sure if he succeeded.

He double-checked his phaser rifle, then pulled out his tricorder. A few light touches, then the instrument clearly displayed where the guards were, where the Verunans were clustered, and where their would-be rescuers were.

Here goes nothing, Paris thought and stepped into the fray.

Red energy fire whizzed past him. He barely managed to duck in time, overcompensating for the heaviness of the suit, and stumbled. That misstep saved his life, as another shot blasted the rock where he had just stood. Paris whipped the phaser rifle into position and fired in the direction of the shots. But the guard who had attacked him, clad in a less-ornate version of Linneas's armor, slipped behind a boulder. Paris's phaser blast impacted harmlessly.

Other shots were being fired. Paris risked a look around. The five Verunan ships had landed safely. Ten pilots were tumbling out; five stayed behind, one on each ship, to protect them. One Verunan, whom Paris did not immediately recognize, went down almost at once. His fellows seized him and hauled him back into the safety of his vessel. He caught a glimpse of one of them through the faceplate. It was the oldest pilot among them—Miweni, if Paris recalled his name correctly. He looked scared but determined. Paris imagined that the rest of the Verunans bore variations of the same expression.

Paris waved them forward, and they came, scurrying up as best they could on big long legs that were not used to moving in this dense gravity, carrying weapons they had never before fired at living, moving targets. But despite their understandable fear and inexperience, they were not about to let Paris—and through him, their imprisoned friends—down.

They moved in formation as they had rehearsed, and one of them even managed to get a square shot off a guard who popped up unexpectedly. The guard lay where he fell, ignored by his fellows. Bitterly, Paris thought that that was the quintessential difference between Verunans and Akerians.

Counting quickly, Paris determined that there were four guards, one of which was down. But he was not here for a showdown. He was here to keep his group moving and to get to the prisoners. When another blast came screaming past him, kicking up the lifeless dust of the dead planet not half a meter from his booted feet, Paris didn't return fire. Ahead of him, only a few meters away, was the bunker, and that was where his duty lay. He ran forward as fast as the envirosuit and the dense gravity of the planet would permit. Nine of the Verunans followed.

The door, a huge black slab of metal at the mouth of this utilitarian building, loomed ahead. Paris pulled out the tricorder and called up the entry code Harry Kim had gotten from the Akerian ship computers. Panting a little, he reached the door, looking around for a touch pad. He glanced back at the ships—the three remaining guards were laying siege to the small vessels. The Verunans were doing a pretty good job of keeping them back, though, and the numbers favored them. As long as the Akerian fire didn't make the vessels unspaceworthy, all would be well.

Quickly, Paris punched in the code and waited breathlessly for a long second.

Nothing happened.

Sweat dappled his brow beneath his helmet. He tried it again, making certain that each was the correct symbol. This time, he got a response: the thing began to beep angrily.

Paris swore loudly. Miweni glanced at him. "What is wrong, Par-is?"

"They've changed the damn code. You keep the guards at bay if they come back at us. I'm going to see if I can't break it with the tricorder."

He could always simply blast his way in, but he knew from the blueprints Kim had shown him that this first door was the entry to an airlock. Without the protection from the planet's atmosphere, anybody inside not already in an envirosuit would die almost immediately. And that certainly was not the game plan.

Frantically Paris made the necessary adjustments to the tricorder, aimed it at the lock, and said a short prayer as it went through its paces.

The alien symbols that served as numbers and letters rolled past, faster than the human eye could see but not fast enough for Paris.

"Come on, come on," he hissed to the inanimate object, resisting the completely illogical temptation to shake it in order to make it behave better. It went as fast as it was able to, and that would just have to be fast enough. Thus far, it had determined two of the seven numbers required to open the door.

He huddled back against the metal door, taking his eyes off the spinning numbers and letters long enough to see what was happening back on the landing pad. His heart sank. As he had guessed, the guards had figured out that the little band of intruders had been delayed and were redirecting their fire from the shuttlecraft and the Verunan escorts to the ten figures that crouched at the door. As Paris watched, one of his friends went down. The pilot next to him whirled with astonishing swiftness and fired upon the guard who had injured his comrade.

"How is he?" called Paris through the comm link.

The pilot didn't spare him a glance but kept firing in the direction of the guards. "Not good. He is still alive, but we will have to get him treated soon."

Not for the first time since this mission began, Paris

cursed the fact that there was no beaming anybody back up to safety. *Voyager* wasn't even in the vicinity, wouldn't be for several long, dangerous more minutes. He and the inexperienced Verunans were truly on their own.

He made a decision. "When we open this airlock, get him inside and stay with him. The rest of us will go get the slaves. We'll pick you both up on the way back. Understood?"

"Yes, Par-is," replied the Verunan, still not looking in his direction and still spitting fire upon the enemy.

The lieutenant glanced again at the tricorder. Five of the seven numbers had been found. Paris tried to block out the grim sound of battle behind him. Six numbers.

Seven.

There came a slight click, and the door began to open.

"Okay, everyone inside, let's go, let's go!" he cried, waving one arm vigorously and keeping a firm hold on the phaser rifle with the other. Seven rushed forward, one or two of them hanging back to get in one final shot. The Verunan who had been protecting his friend now hoisted the injured party and carried him inside.

Once everyone was safely inside the airlock, Paris reactivated the controls. One of the guards rushed the door, firing. Without even thinking, Paris dropped to his belly and fired through the rapidly closing crack between door and floor. He didn't know if he got the guard, but at least the Akerian didn't make it inside. The door slammed shut.

Almost at once Paris heard the *click-click* of the guard attempting to reopen the gate. Of course. There had to be a manual override, something to block an exterior "attack." He looked around and saw a huge metal bar. He pulled on it with all his might, but it did not budge. Paris didn't even have to open his mouth before two Verunans were there, lending their powerful muscles. The override mechanism clunked into place almost as the guard entered the last number. Paris waited an instant, then, satisfied that they had effectively blocked the attack from the outside, for the moment at least, turned his attention to the second gate.

He didn't bother to check to see if the Akerians had changed the code on this door, too. He knew they had and immediately set to work using the tricorder.

As the symbols flipped past, Paris turn to his companions. "This is an airlock," he explained. "The atmosphere in here is adjusting right now to accommodate us. When this second door opens, the inside environment will be comparable to the environment on Veruna Four. Movement's going to be a lot easier. But I'm sure there are going to be more guards on the other side of this door, so, everyone, be ready."

Paris couldn't feel the environment changing; his envirosuit protected against that as well as more hostile changes. He glanced over at the Verunans.

"Flatten yourselves again the sides and have your weapons at hand. Miweni, while my tricorder's unlocking this gate, I want you to locate the slaves."

Miweni nodded, activating his tricorder. "Found them. They are just where we thought they would be. Down this long corridor, past the first two rooms on the left and right, right at the first intersection of corridors. They are in that first room on the left."

Paris nodded, his blue eyes still watching the symbols. Six. "Good. Everybody, here we go." Seven.

The door began to open, and Paris quickly exchanged his tricorder for his phaser rifle. He flattened himself against the wall just as he had instructed the Verunans.

The door clanged against the ceiling. There was no sign of any guards. Paris didn't like this, not one bit. True, the Akerians had not had much advance warning. After the battle during which *Voyager* had disabled the *Conquest, Victory* had left for Akeras. The first time anyone inside the concavity had heard about *Voyager* was just a little over an hour ago, when *Victory* and *Destroyer* had gone into Sun-Eater and returned with three other ships.

He thought over what he knew about the Akerian mentality and couldn't conceive of such arrogance as Linneas had displayed having thought for an instant that *Voyager* would get past their defenses and enter Sun-Eater. Even if Linneas had warned the people on the planet—and Paris was willing to bet that he hadn't—there would have been no time to beef up the guards on the planet.

Paris thought that the first warning anybody on this empty, dead shell of a planet had had that *Voyager* and her little band of Verunan rescuers was on its way was when the six small ships had penetrated the atmosphere.

Time enough to position guards outside on the landing pad, as they had seen. And certainly time enough to change the code on the off chance that the intruders could break in. But not time enough to stage complicated traps.

Most likely, the Akerians were waiting in ambush in those two rooms Miweni had mentioned. He voiced his concern to the others, who nodded their comprehension. Then, taking a deep breath, Paris stepped forward into the corridor.

It was a lot easier to move now, for which he was grateful, but the guards inside had the advantage of not wearing cumbersome, unfamiliar envirosuits. His phaser rifle in his arms, Paris glanced about. There had been several buildings, dotting the scarred surface of the planet. Many of these were science stations, where the data and artifacts gathered by the laboring Verunans were analyzed and notated. These were of no concern to Paris and his friends. The only building that was of interest to him was the one in which they were—the single building that housed all the slaves and their guards.

It was large, gray, and brutally efficient looking. The corridor was long and wide. Naked beams of metal, the skeleton of the building, arched overhead. No attempt to hide or beautify them had been made. To the right and left, Paris noticed large windows. For a moment he wondered why such a pragmatic building had windows, but a quick glance outside showed him the reason. He could see large, heavy equipment, now quietly at rest. Their function was to move huge chunks of rock and debris. When active, these monstrous machines could be extremely dangerous. Just as well, Paris thought darkly, to have someone watching from inside as well as outside, just in case the Verunans tried to murder one of their captors using the machines as weapons.

What the Akerians didn't understand was that the

Verunans—desperate, sick, angry, brutalized as they might be—would never even think of doing such a barbaric thing. It simply would never occur to them.

He moved slowly down the corridor, his eyes on the large rooms that loomed just ahead. That was where the ambush would come, if it came—and he was certain it would. He gestured to his companions, and they fanned out, tense, weapons at the ready. Paris's own heart thundered in his ears.

They edged up to the rooms. The entrances had no doors, and Paris flattened himself against the wall and motioned to the others to do likewise. He raised his right hand, the left one cradling the rifle, and his fingers counted down: *Three . . . two . . . one.*

Paris leaped into action. He jumped in front of the doors and began firing. The phaser was on heavy stun—determined to be the most effective means of rendering the guards helpless for the duration without actually hurting them and the same frequency at which it had been set from the moment Paris had landed. The Verunan weapons were similarly programmed.

He'd been right. They had been waiting in ambush, six of them in each room. He could not see their faces, but he suspected that they were surprised at the fact that their ambush was ambushed. Quickly Paris dropped three of them and then staggered back, pain shooting up his left arm. One of them had found its target. The envirosuit had been engineered to immediately seal if ruptured, but the damage had been done. Paris's left arm was now in agony and, worse, utterly useless. A second shot screamed, and Paris threw himself to the hard floor and rolled, barely avoiding being hit.

At once he heard another sound, deeper, more resonant than the Akerian weapons, shriller than a phaser. His Verunan friends were coming to his rescue, their weapons blasting away and dropping the remaining three guards. Then a strong, gentle hand was under Paris's right arm, lifting him up as though he weighed next to nothing.

As he scrambled to his feet, he heard the sounds of combat up ahead. The guards who had been stationed in the second room had heard the noises and had taken the offensive. Two more Verunans went down, one with a minor injury and one, Paris couldn't tell who, with a gaping hole in his—her?—chest. The Akerians were not using weapons set on stun. His stomach twisted in pained horror, but he grimly kept going. Whoever it was, the Verunan would not wish to have died in vain.

His left hand hanging limply at his side, Paris managed the phaser rifle with his right and fired. There were only two guards, both of whom fell before the Verunan weapons. Miweni had his tricorder out and cried, "They're just up ahead! Turn right, turn right!"

"No, wait!" screamed Paris, but he was too late. The first group of Verunans, the ones who had gone ahead and not hung back to help Paris, had already rounded the corner.

He did not see the fight, but he could hear it. With a burst of energy, Paris pulled away from his assisting friend and caught up, phaser at the ready. The

Verunans had held their own, though, and where Paris had feared to find corpses, he found the Verunans standing over two inert guards. Even as he rejoiced that the pilots were uninjured, some quieter, less-heated part of his spirit mourned their effectiveness—their ability to so quickly learn how to attack.

"They're in here," Miweni said excitedly. "But how to open the door? Should we fire upon it?"

Paris glanced at the door, recognizing the symbol on the keypad with a jolt. He shook his head. "The guard," he panted, "the key. It should be a chunk of metal that will fit right in the door."

One of the pilots knelt beside the fallen body of the guard, his long fingers in their protective gloves patting him down quickly and efficiently. He located the key and with a flourish of triumph showed it to Paris for a nod of confirmation before inserting it into the door.

There was a click, and a light flashed on. The Verunans put their shoulders to the door and pushed. The door swung open.

Seventeen Verunans, most still in their envirosuits, stared back at them with suspicious eyes that grew even wider when they caught sight of Paris. They gasped and huddled back, no doubt thinking that this was some new variety of Akerian, come to exact dreadful retribution for some nonexistent trespass. Then one of them recognized Miweni.

"Miweni! My mate!" And the female Verunan, weeping freely, ran into the arms of her beloved. Excited chatter broke out, but Paris cut it short.

"We have ships waiting for you," he explained,

"but we've got to get going. Those of you still in your envirosuits, stay in them. The rest of you, I've got emergency transport. How many of you can walk?"

Fourteen Verunans, all in their suits, indicated that they could move unassisted.

"Then go. The three of you"—he gestured to Miweni and two others—"go with them. Keep an eye out for more guards; we don't know who's been alerted to our arrival. You two, give me a hand with the injured. Don't forget to pick up the rest of the pilots; some are injured back there." It was an unnecessary statement, and he knew it, but he had to say it just to make sure.

The seventeen former slaves and their escorts took off. A few moments later Paris heard firing. "Damn," he swore. He didn't know if the sound was from the guards outside coming in or new arrivals. He hoped it was the former.

He placed his phaser rifle down and began searching for the ETCs he carried, hampered by his dead hand. The pilots had gone to their ill and injured friends, offering reassuring words. Paris felt his heart twist in sympathy. The Akerians were not good masters. The Verunans were thin, their long ribs showing clearly through their soft, furry pelts. The three not in their envirosuits were clearly unfit for work: one had an injured leg that had at least been treated. The others were sick, their usually clear and lovely amber eyes rheumy and tired. Their breathing was labored, and one of them lay on the floor, barely breathing. Only its eyes, wide and alive, showed that it was cognizant of its surroundings.

"These are emergency transport carriers," Paris

explained, grappling awkwardly with his one good hand. One of the three pilots who still remained quickly moved to his side to assist him. Paris smiled his thanks. "They're sort of emergency envirosuits. Place the injured in these, seal them up, and the bag acts as a protective environment."

He talked his friends through it, and the injured Verunans did what they could to assist. Mostly, though, the best they could do was sit and be passively lifted into the ETCs. Paris saw the curiosity, the gratitude, and the still-lingering traces of fear on their faces as the bags were sealed. They did not know him, had never even seen his species before. It was a huge gesture of trust.

At last the three of them were safely in the ETCs. The pain in Paris's arm was not subsiding, and it threatened to break his concentration. He willed the agony back, forced his head to clear. He had no doubt but that the Verunans would be able to carry out the mission without him—indeed, that was the way it had been planned in the first place—but he sure didn't want them to have to.

They looked to him to give the signal to return. He waited—silence. Then came a sound that was music to his ears.

"Par-is," called Miweni from somewhere down the main corridor, "the others are all on board. Most of the guards are down . . ." His voice was coming closer, and now he rounded the corner and finished his sentence. "And the few who are left have retreated!"

Paris felt a sudden surge of apprehension at the last comment but willed it aside. *Gift horse, mouth, and all that,* he told himself and aloud, "Then let's get the hell out of here and back to the ships!"

They clattered down the hall, empty now save for the fallen, unconscious Akerian guards. The fallen Verunans, dead and injured, had been spirited away by their friends. Even encumbered by the ETCs, the long Verunan legs devoured the distance as they ran down the corridor. Miweni and another pilot hung back to keep pace with Paris. The gesture was deeply moving and inspired the lieutenant to his own best efforts.

Miweni had been right; the coast was completely clear. He headed for the shuttlecraft and leaped inside. The door closed at once and pressure returned.

Gasping, he looked around. There were four Verunans, one presently being helped out of the ETC, sharing the airlock with him. Then Kaavi exploded out of nowhere, hastening to help Paris remove his helmet and then giving him a mammoth hug.

She hurt his injured arm, and white lightning exploded through his brain, but somehow it didn't matter. He grinned fiercely at her, then stumbled forward to the cockpit and slid into his seat.

"Everybody aboard safely?" he asked the Verunan ships. A chorus of "ayes" met his ears. "Then let's get off of this planet!"

A few practiced tappings on the console, and the shuttlecraft lifted off. A quick glance confirmed that the five Verunan vessels had done likewise. In a few moments, the little fleet of rescuers and rescued were in the comfortable blackness of space.

Tom Paris let out a heavy sigh and leaned back into his chair. He closed his eyes. They were ahead of schedule. As long as no one on the planet pursued them, they'd wait right here for *Voyager*. With any luck, she'd have some good news.

His arm hurt. Badly. He couldn't wait to get to sickbay.

"Paris?"

His eyes still closed, Paris replied, "Yes, Kaavi?"

"I think we may have trouble."

His eyes snapped open. Adrenaline shot through Paris, and his heart began to slam against his ribs.

Kaavi was right. Directly ahead and moving toward them with speedy purpose was the *Destroyer*.

CHAPTER
17

JANEWAY HAD JOINED STARFLEET BECAUSE WHEN SHE WAS a young woman, she had fallen in love. Science was her great and lasting passion; and the mysteries it posed still intrigued, and the curiosity it aroused in her still burned hot after some twenty-odd years of romance.

Now, though, she and science were having a lover's quarrel. Or maybe it would better be called a knock-down-drag-out fight. Sun-Eater hid its answers coyly, teasing her with facts that contradicted and did not enlighten. The last time she'd been this annoyed with anything was when Molly Malone, jealous of Janeway's affection toward Mark, had soiled Mark's rug.

Trying to figure out where the wormhole was—and incidentally the nature of the concavity itself—would have been trying enough. But she also had to deal with the Akerian ship that dogged her like a silent shadow and the fact that at least one member of her crew was on the planet and in grave danger.

At least, she thought to herself, the decoy had worked. The *Destroyer* had followed her, seemingly uninterested in what transpired on the planet's surface. It would appear that the commander, whomever he or she might be, did not think that six small vessels posed any kind of real threat to the dead planet the Akerians called Blessing.

Janeway hoped that the commander was wrong. In fact, she was gambling Paris's life on it.

Questions within questions, and what she and her crew had learned did not enlighten. They were presently hugging what Janeway had taken to calling the wall, for want of a better term. From what they could tell, the concavity was shaped like a balloon, with a comparatively small entrance and a large, spherical shape inside. The gravity here was stronger, and it drew the lighted particles of the dying Verunan sun to the wall.

"Any luck on narrowing down the origin of those verteron particles, Ensign Kim?"

"Negative, Captain. They seem to be coming from everywhere." A sudden thought occurred to the young man. "Captain . . . could Sun-Eater *itself* be a wormhole?" he queried excitedly.

"I hate to dash your hopes, Mr. Kim," replied his commander, "but I've already thought of that. We've seen the entrance—an entrance far too large for a black hole—but we've yet to find an exit."

"Captain," said Tuvok, straightening to face her. "I am reminded of the incident involving a Vulcan science vessel some dozen years ago. It experienced a breach of the warp core while exploring a small wormhole that had appeared in the vicinity of Garus Prime and was instantly destroyed. The resulting explosion collapsed the wormhole but not immediately. One end collapsed first. The second followed but not until many moments later."

Janeway's breath caught in her throat. "Are you suggesting that this was once a wormhole and that there was an explosion here?" It made sense. It matched the facts. But what had exploded? And why was the planet trapped in here? More theories, more questions, more dead ends.

"Precisely, Captain. It is the only theory that appears to fit all the facts."

"Kim, get someone researching that incident. I want all the details. In the meantime—"

"Captain!" Kim's startled exclamation was almost a yelp of sheer surprise. "We're being hailed by the *Destroyer!*"

"Mr. Tuvok," ordered Janeway, "ready whatever defenses won't blow us to kingdom come in here. Mr. Kim, put the commander on screen."

The eerie orange glow of the illuminated pocket in space disappeared, replaced by the head and shoulders of a helmeted Akerian. His—her?—armor was in every way identical to that worn by First Warrior Linneas, but there were fewer notches on the horns that curved gracefully up from the helmet.

"I am Garai, first warrior of the Empirical Exploratory Unit, commander of the Akerian vessel *Destroyer*. In the name of the great and glorious empress Riva, I demand to know your business here in our territory."

Hope that she might be able to reason with First Warrior Garai warred with her knowledge of Linneas's behavior in Janeway's heart. "I am Captain Kathryn Janeway, captain of the Federation *Starship Voyager*. Our business here is exploration. We bear you no hostility, First Warrior Garai."

"Then why have you sent six of your vessels to the planet surface?" replied Garai. "Was their purpose purely exploratory as well?"

His voice held a challenge, but it did not tremble with the suppressed anger and arrogance that had characterized Linneas's conversation. It was calm, cool . . . rational.

Janeway decided to take a risk. "Only one of those was our ship," she said honestly. "The rest are Verunan vessels."

Garai was silent. Not for the first time, Janeway wished she could see the facial reactions of her peer in the other ship. She imagined, though, that her revelation stunned him.

But he seemed to recover. When he next spoke, his voice was as steady as before. "The Verunans do not have the technology. You are lying to me, Captain Janeway."

"I am not. The Verunans may not be as primitive as you think them to be. They have come to rescue their enslaved kin, nothing more."

"Then we shall destroy them," replied Garai coolly.

"Those puny ships are no match for us. They seemed to need you to even penetrate inside the concavity in order to reach Blessing. Will you fight on their behalf, or are you too cowardly?"

But Janeway was not about to be baited so easily. "It is not cowardice, First Warrior, but rather a desire to let the empire and Veruna Four solve their own problems. But here's a suggestion for you. You might better be employed in removing your scientists from the planet rather than sending more guards after those six ships." She spoke in the same cool tones Garai had used.

Again, Garai was silent before speaking. "I repeat my earlier question. What is your purpose here? Your last words sounded more like a threat—something one would hardly expect from an *exploratory* vessel."

"It was not a threat. It was a gesture of friendship. I would not wish to be responsible for the lives of people who have done nothing on that planet but honorable research for their empire."

Garai sat up straighter. Janeway hid a smile. *I've got you now,* she thought. She waited a second longer, then, to save the warrior face in front of his crew, explained her statement.

"We are travelers who are not native to this part of the galaxy. We are searching for a way home. Your concavity seemed to us to house a wormhole—a shortcut, if you will, back to our part of the galaxy. Our search has availed us nothing. If there is a wormhole, First Warrior, I ask you to tell us of it."

Garai snorted. "If I knew of such a thing, why should I tell you of it?"

"I'll tell you why." Janeway's voice was deceptively soft. She tilted her chin slightly higher, and her eyes snapped blue flame. "Because if there is no wormhole in here, no way for us to get home, then I intend to fire a photon torpedo at the mouth of your precious concavity. It ought to have collapsed long ago. You're feeding this abomination with the sun of a people who have done you no wrong. And I think . . . I hope . . . that somehow you know that it's wrong."

She paused, letting her words sink in. "So what's it going to be, First Warrior? Is there a wormhole that we've somehow missed?"

He was silent for a long time. Only the tense clenching and unclenching of his fingers in their protective gloves betrayed his inner turmoil. Finally, he spoke.

"I am no liar. There is no wormhole within the confines of the spatial concavity. But I ask you, Captain Janeway—as one commander of a proud people to, I think, another—please reconsider your decision to destroy everything we have wrought here."

There was a slight tremor to his voice. Janeway could guess how much the statement had cost him. She felt a twinge of sympathy for his plight but no more.

"I appreciate your honesty, and I reiterate: it is time now to save lives, not destroy them. Evacuate your people, First Warrior."

He did not reply. With a savage grunt, Garai brought his fist slamming down, and abruptly, the communication ended. Janeway found herself staring at the whirling miasma of star matter once again.

But not for very long. Almost at once, the *Destroyer* leaped into motion. It reversed with a surprising speed and headed directly for the dead planet.

I hope I got through to him, Janeway thought grimly. Aloud, she said, "Follow him. Full impulse."

Paris's injured left arm throbbed with distracting pain, but there was no time for it. He was on the comm link at once to his fleet, his eyes fastened on the huge ship that was approaching with steady purpose.

"Everybody, follow me!" It was their only option. Directed energy fire might collapse the concavity. He could only hope that the Akerian ship knew it, too. It was a curious position: staring straight at your enemy and being unable to fire. He thought about hailing the ship but decided against it. Paris tried to move his left arm, found it still dead, and swore as he made the right do the work of two.

Quickly, expertly, the shuttlecraft veered sharply starboard. The five other ships followed, keeping their remarkably perfect formation. Paris set the screen to rear view and kept an eye on the Akerian ship.

It did not pursue. It continued on its path, which, Paris now saw, was not toward them, but toward the planet itself. Even as he watched, a bay door opened in the side of the mammoth ship. Four small vessels emerged and headed straight for the surface.

"If they're trying to get the Verunans, they're going to find them gone," Paris murmured to himself. "If not . . ." He had no idea why the *Destroyer* would suddenly appear and send shuttlecraft down to the planet.

Relief overwhelmed him when, hard on the heels of the *Destroyer,* the *Voyager* appeared.

"Was your mission successful, Lieutenant?" Paris thought he'd never heard a sweeter sound than his captain's crisp, cool voice.

"Aye, Captain. We lost a few and there are several injured. Better alert the doctor that he's got some"— he was about to say *dragons* but stopped himself just in time—"patients waiting for him," he amended.

"Understood. I'd like to get out here myself as soon as—"

Her voice stopped in midsentence, and Paris understood why. From the mouth of Sun-Eater, escorted by dancing chunks of dead, burning star matter, loomed the repaired *Victory.*

"Traitor!" screamed Linneas, his deep voice seeming to penetrate to the bone. Garai was glad that he could not see Linneas's face at this moment. It might have shaken his resolve. Even as it was, Garai felt his conviction start to trickle away.

"Captain Janeway plans to destroy the concavity with a torpedo," Garai announced coolly, fighting to keep his hands still on the arms of his command chair. "She advised us to evacuate our scientists. The slaves have already been removed by the Verunan ships. We can renew the attack on her vessel once we are outside, but I deemed it a sensible precaution to—"

"You would be dead by my own hands, vile betrayer, were not the vastness of space between us!" Linneas continued to rage. "How did you even come to know this when your orders were no communication whatsoever?"

"First Warrior, I am your equal now, at least in command," Garai replied, keeping his voice steady with effort. "I was the only ship in the area. It was my right to decide what to do."

Filth spewed from Linneas's mouth. Oddly, it did not intimidate Garai anymore. It merely confirmed his worst fear: that Linneas was cracking under the strain. That only made him sorrowful, not angry. Once, Linneas had been a great commander. Garai had admired and learned from him. Out of respect for the leader that Linneas once was, Garai silently grieved.

But he did not yield. He waited until Linneas ran out of curses, then calmly continued.

"I have begun the evacuation."

"You took an oath!"

"We took an oath, First Warrior!" Garai let the heat of his own anger infuse his retort. "We took an oath to protect our people! That is the job of the military in this concavity. Those scientists on Blessing took no oath to die at the whim of a first warrior, but *we* swore to protect *them*. And sacrificing them on the altar of pride is something that is not in the honor code of a first warrior!"

Linneas did not reply. Garai found himself staring at the planet again instead of at his comrade. *So be it,* he thought grimly, more convinced than before that his course of action was the right one.

"Shall we stop the evacuation?" asked his first hand. Garai shook his horned helmet.

"We continue. Then . . . we leave Blessing behind. First Warrior Linneas is on his own."

Voyager lowered its shields, and quickly the six ships hastened to the safety the larger vessel provided. Once they were in place, Janeway ordered the shields back up.

"Let's get out of here," she said tiredly. She believed First Warrior Garai when he had said there was no wormhole. Their own research had come, reluctantly, to the same conclusion. The entire concavity might once have been a wormhole, or perhaps there were billions of microscopic wormholes littering the "wall" of Sun-Eater, thus providing the dead star matter an exit of sorts. Or both. Kim was working on a theory, but that would have to wait until everyone, the Verunans included, was safely out of this perplexing, bitterly depressing concavity.

"Mr. Kim, try to raise the *Victory*," Janeway ordered.

A moment, then, "No response, Captain."

"What a surprise," said Janeway sarcastically. "Well, then, prepare to broadcast this message on all possible frequencies. This is Captain Kathryn Janeway. I urge all Akerian vessels to vacate the concavity immediately. This concavity will be destroyed shortly. I repeat, evacuate all your people and remove all vessels from this area. The concavity is going to be destroyed." She nodded to Kim, who began to broadcast the announcement.

"Bridge to Engineering. We're getting ready to head out again, Torres. You got us in beautifully. Let's go out the same way."

"Aye, Captain," Torres replied.

"Are your friends prepared, Mr. Paris?" she asked of the lieutenant heading the Verunan fleet.

"Aye, Captain. We couldn't be more eager to be out of this place."

A slight smile touched Janeway's lips. "I hear that, Lieutenant. We'll be out of it soon, and then . . ." And then, what? "Then we'll sort things out. It seems as though First Warrior Garai understands what's at stake here. Let's hope Linneas does, too."

Traitor!

The word burned through Linneas's mind like a red-hot brand. Oh, he'd been taken in, all right, he'd been as gullible as a Verunan. Garai had been all obedience, subservience, everything one could want in a first hand. It had been the greatest mistake of Linneas's life to promote him to a first warrior. He saw that now, now that it was too late, now that everything Linneas had fought, lied, and killed for was about to be destroyed at the whim of some arrogant alien who prattled on about justice and balance and other such nonsense.

He was breathing heavily, his talons clenching and unclenching. Oh, he'd get the traitor, all right. He'd get them *all*. And he would do it as a first warrior should: by battle prowess and a willingness to sacrifice.

Ahead, the *Voyager* hastened toward the mouth of the concavity, the six cowardly little ships clustered beneath her, relying on the bigger ship to protect them. The *Destroyer,* an ill-named vessel as it turned out, had finished its ignoble task of collecting the frightened scientists and was following close on *Voyager*'s heels.

"First Warrior," came the voice of his first hand, "the *Voyager* is hailing us."

"Ignore it."

The first hand did so but an instant later was bothering his commander again. "Apologies, First Warrior, but the captain of the *Voyager* is broadcasting a message on all frequencies."

Linneas nodded. This, he would listen to, as he had all the other open messages the captain named Janeway had sent.

"This is Captain Kathryn Janeway. I urge all Akerian vessels to vacate the concacivity immediately. This concacivity will be destroyed shortly. I repeat, evacuate all your people and remove all vessels from this area. The concacivity is going to be destroyed."

Linneas breathed deeply, slowly. Pleasure began to grow, hot in the pit of his stomach. He permitted himself a smile beneath his concealing helmet.

"Prepare to fire the gravity wave," he announced.

"First Warrior?" The title was a question as pronounced by Linneas's first hand.

"You heard me," he replied, swiveling in his chair to fix his baleful gaze upon the uncertain officer. "This so-called captain plans to destroy the concacivity. There is nothing I can do to stop her nor the traitorous Garai. But, for honor's sake, open a frequency to the *Destroyer*. I must at least inform my former first hand of my plans."

When Garai's visage appeared on the screen, Linneas spoke. "You have yet one chance to redeem yourself, First Warrior Garai. If Janeway is determined to destroy everything we have worked for, then destroyed it must be." He leaned forward. "But I will take her and everyone else with me."

"Linneas . . . you are insane!" gasped Garai, all composure shocked out of him.

"No. Only true to my people. You can yet be true to them, Garai. Stop the ship from leaving! You are closer than I. Fire upon the *Voyager,* and we will all die together!" He felt spittle clinging to his mouth. It trickled down his chin, tickling, but with his helmet on he could not wipe it away.

He waited, his heart slamming against his chest, for First Warrior Garai's response.

It was totally unexpected. "I pity you, Linneas, and all the innocents who will die with you. I shall inform your widows."

And then his image disappeared. Just like that. For a long second, Linneas simply sat, utterly stunned. Then he let out an enraged, affronted, abandoned roar, a sound deep and primal and bestial.

"Follow them!" he cried.

"Captain, the *Destroyer* is hailing us," said Kim.

"On screen."

The image of Garai appeared. He began speaking at once.

"Captain, we are far from allies. And once we are both safely out of here, do not think we will bare our throats for your sword. But honor compels me to warn you that you are in grave danger. Linneas is insane. He plans to destroy the concavity before any of us can escape. Can your vessel move any faster?"

"We're at top speed now," Janeway replied.

"Then keep it up." Garai blipped out.

The tension on the bridge escalated, but Janeway kept calm. "Keep her steady, Chakotay."

The commander only nodded, his brown eyes fastened on the screen and his hands moving on the controls.

"Where are the *Victory* and the *Destroyer?*"

"Directly behind us, Captain," answered Tuvok. "They have halted, with the *Destroyer* between us and the *Victory*. I believe our reluctant ally First Warrior Garai is trying to buy us some time."

Janeway hoped that the time needed for *Voyager* to escape wouldn't have to be bought with the blood of Garai and everyone aboard his ship. Smoothly, though slowly, the Starfleet vessel moved toward the entrance. As before, Torres strengthened the shields as the ship progressed—fore, mid, aft. They kept well away from the river of light this time, though as they moved through the aperture, Janeway saw it glowing orange and yellow on their starboard side. Ahead, she could see the starfield of normal space drawing closer until, finally, they were free.

"Paris, get ready to go into warp one on the count of three. Three, two, one—engage!"

Voyager and her small fleet streaked away from the deadly trap. Janeway watched the screen and saw another ship emerge from the mouth of Sun-Eater. It was the *Destroyer*.

"Tuvok, ready photon torpedo," she snapped. "Fire on my command—and not an instant before. Shields at maximum." She was going to give Linnea a chance to emerge to discuss things rationally.

But he did not take that chance. Even as the crew of

the *Voyager* watched *Destroyer* barely escaping, there came a sudden explosion of light from the mouth of Sun-Eater. The burning hydrogen and star matter burst forth in a shower of orange, red, and yellow, like fireworks of old. For just an instant, the dark depths of Sun-Eater lurked behind the radiant shower, then all at once it was gone—vanished as if it had never been. The explosion caused by Linneas's suicidal, fruitless attack had restored the fabric of space to its norm.

The mighty *Destroyer,* though it had escaped certain destruction, was caught helplessly in the shock wave. Janeway saw the force take it and toss it like a piece of driftwood on a raging river. A volley of huge asteroids, all that was left of the ill-named *Blessing,* were spewed out from the collapsing concavity.

"Brace for impa—" But the wave hit *Voyager* before she could even get the words out. She dug her fingers into the arms of her chair and just barely stayed seated. Lights flickered, died, went to emergency backup. She heard cries of pain as others, less fortunate than she, hit the unforgiving metal of the *Voyager* as the ship was buffeted about.

At last, the vessel stabilized. "Report!" she snapped.

Kim had a vicious bruise on his handsome face, and his right eye was swollen shut. No pain colored his voice, however.

"Injury reports coming in from all over the ship. Our shields are down fifty-six percent. One of the Verunan ships was severely damaged but no casualties." He glanced up at her. "We seem to be okay for the moment."

She nodded acknowledgment. "Where's the *Destroyer?*"

It appeared on the screen. It had been closer to the concavity at the moment of explosion and had fared far worse than the *Voyager.* "Its shields are gone, Captain, and it's taken a lot of damage," said Kim.

"Open a frequency. Offer assistance. I've got a hunch that this may have knocked the fight out of First Warrior Garai."

While Kim did so, Janeway gazed at where Sun-Eater had been. It was a huge cluster of swirling asteroids and still-glowing chunks of star matter. In time, it would become a planetary nebula. Even now, the inhabitants of Veruna Four would be able to look up and instead of seeing a great bruise against their sky, they would see a swirling, colorful assembly.

The sun was no longer immediately endangered. The river of light that had flowed toward the concavity slowed, ceased, began to turn back on itself.

The great Sun-Eater was no more.

CHAPTER

18

Captain's Log, Stardate 43897.1: As I had predicted, with most of the Akerian fleet disabled, First Warrior Garai was willing to cooperate. I have found him to be intelligent and thoughtful, and my brief conversations with him give me hope that what I plan to do will be successful.

Though the Destroyer is disabled, life-support systems are still functional. We have transported all the remaining Akerians from the various damaged vessels on board and have locked a tractor beam onto the ship. More survived the encounters than I had thought, which is also encouraging if peace is to be achieved.

After a brief stopover on Veruna Four, we are heading for the Akerian star system. We should reach Akeras in approximately forty-seven minutes. On board with us is Viha Nata and a small entourage. Let this record show that the destruction of the concavity, which the Verunans call Sun-Eater, has bought the inhabitants of Veruna Four time. The planet will be habitable for more than a century now instead of a brief twenty-five years.

Janeway paused, wondering if she should enter the news about Kaavi and Anahu. It pleased her, and she knew it had pleased and touched Tom Paris, though he wasn't one to show it. But she'd seen his reaction when Nata had told him, though he claimed loudly that he'd "gotten something in my eye."

But perhaps the formal log wasn't an appropriate place to record it. She decided that in her personal log, she'd state that, with a real future ahead of them, Kaavi and Anahu had chosen to become lifemates, that they had gone to the hatching pit, that a youngster had hatched and imprinted on them within less than three hours, and that they had named the large-eyed, inquisitive male child Tom Paris.

Smiling, she continued her entry.

Let the record show that Lieutenant Tom Paris has displayed great initiative and leadership abilities as well as compassion and adaptability. Let the record also show that Ensign Harry Kim has performed exceptionally under trying circumstances. His research and integration of information from a variety of alien sources—and several intense bouts of discussion with a captain who was a former science officer—has made a significant contribution toward understanding what transpired in this sector centuries ago. And that understanding may well be the cornerstone of a lasting peace between the Verunans and the Akerians.

But Ensign Kim has declined the offer to present the information he has worked so hard to gather. After some discussion with First Officer Chakotay, he and I decided to jointly present our findings to Viha *Nata and the empress Riva—in a very unusual fashion.*

I believe that the strange feeling in my stomach just might be stage fright.

An hour after completing her entry, Janeway stood with *Viha* Nata and First Warrior Garai in the empty holodeck. When not in use, the holodeck was a bleak, peculiar-looking room—cold black with yellow grids interweaving in a precise pattern.

Nata stood, shifting her weight from foot to foot. She was painted, after the manner of her people in a highly formal situation, with bright colors and symbols, though her body bore only a few token scraps of colorful cloth. Bright blue encircled her large, wise eyes, and jagged yellow and red symbols turned her mottled coat into an array of decoration. The *Viha* held her head high and proud, but tension was in the normally fluid lines of her body.

For his part, Garai stood solid and almost unmoving. He was a formidable sight in his head-to-toe armor. He had offered to remove his helmet for the peace negotiation—a gesture, Janeway knew, of great goodwill—but she had asked him to keep the helmet on until the empress herself arrived.

The three stood in anticipatory silence. There was at present too much blood and anger between the Verunan and Akerian representatives for small talk, but Janeway hoped that, once Empress Riva arrived and the presentation had concluded, the empty room would echo with questions.

The door hissed open. Janeway tensed. Chakotay stood there, a half smile on his lips, his eyes glowing with suppressed . . . could it be mirth?

"Captain Janeway, *Viha* Nata, First Warrior Garai, I present to you Her Excellency, the empress Riva, ruler of Akeras and the Akerian Empire, queen of the Valley of Suns, mistress of the Tikkari Isles, lady of the Faith and keeper of the Word."

He stepped aside, and the empress entered. *Viha* Nata gasped, shocked. Even Janeway raised an eyebrow.

The empress had large, lambent yellow eyes, which were cool and yet betrayed a hint of apprehension in their depths. Her pale fur was fawn-colored, her long snout with its strong, white teeth a darker hue. Long white hair—almost a mane—was braided with jewels and bright strands of metal. More metal, gleaming brightly, encircled her long, sinuous, draconian throat. Her slight body was modestly draped with an ornate, carefully tatted lace overtunic and shawl. Even her white tail, which belied her outward composure with its restless swishing, was decorated with the same care as her mane.

So much, Janeway had known to expect. What the captain of the *Voyager* had not expected was the empress's youth. The great lady of the Akerian Empire stood only a little over a meter and half high. She was a mere child—the equivalent of a human ten-year-old.

Empress Riva caught sight of *Viha* Nata, and her eyes widened with the same shock that clearly galvanized the Verunan. When she spoke, forcing words past a throat closed with amazement, her voice was soft and dulcet.

"You . . . but you are no monsters!"

Viha Nata found her own voice. "Neither are you."

It was a profound revelation for both of them. Garai lifted an instrument to his throat, activated it, and removed his helmet. He shook his own sweat-dampened white mane, dropped to one knee, and his face was somber when he spoke to his empress.

"Great Empress, forgive your humble servant. You ought to have been told a long time ago the truth of what happened on Blessing. The Verunans are no mindless monsters. I knew this. I had resolved to tell you when I returned after defeating Janeway and her crew."

Utterly confused, Riva looked from Garai to Janeway and then let her gaze linger on Nata. "We were told . . . that you were monsters. Good only for labor. We have never seen you before."

"That was the reason for the ceremonial masks," continued Garai. "The Verunans would not know that they were being enslaved by a people similar to themselves."

"You . . . First Warrior, do you mean to tell us that our kinsman has been lying? To his empress, indeed to all of Akeras?" Shock was beginning to give way to a righteous anger on the small Akerian's face.

Garai nodded miserably. "I am telling you precisely that. We—the warriors—have known since the beginning, hundreds of years ago. We deliberately misled Akeras. The military was reluctant to give up the power we obtained from Blessing. It was wrong. I knew it. I am sorrier than I can say."

"You . . . you betrayed us! Betrayed your people!"

"That is in a sense truer than you know, Your Grace," interjected Chakotay. "The Akerians and the Verunans are the same race."

"Impossible!" cried *Viha* Nata, clearly offended.

"Not impossible. The evidence is almost incontrovertible. Empress, your people have lived for millennia on a desert planet. You have, over that time, developed protective, cooler, lighter-hued fur for that environment. *Viha,* your people are jungle dwellers. Hence, your mottled fur and your duller teeth, better suited for eating plants. There are many other differences, but without question, you are the same race."

"But . . . ," began Nata, then stopped. "The colony ship . . . Was Akeras then another colony?"

"Colony?" repeated Riva, bristling. "We are the founders of the empire, not mere *colonists!*"

Janeway held up a placating hand. "This must be very unsettling for you both, I understand. But we've been working hard to put together the pieces of your history and the history of the concavity. Commander Chakotay tells me that your people, *Viha* Nata, keep history in the form of storytelling. I believe this is true also for the Akerians, isn't it, Empress?"

The little empress, her composure returning slowly, nodded regally. "We are the lady of the Faith and the keeper of the Word," she replied, reminding Janeway of two of her titles. "But all of our people know the great tales."

"Then Chakotay and I would like to present our

findings to you in that manner—as a tale," said Janeway. She was pleased to see the looks of interest that crossed the aliens' faces—faces so similar, yet so different. "This room is a holodeck. We can use holographic images to help illustrate our story. Is this an acceptable means of communication for you?"

Nata glanced over at the empress. The younger female nodded, and Nata, more reluctantly, nodded as well.

"Then," said Janeway, feeling the butterflies in her stomach, "let's begin. Computer, begin program Kim Seven."

At once the room was plunged into darkness. Janeway heard the swift intake of breath from the young empress, heard the quick, heavy steps of Garai as he moved protectively nearer his liege. She hoped she was doing the right thing.

As they had rehearsed, Chakotay began first. His deep, rich voice filled the silent room.

"Long ago, before even your recorded time, the K'shikkaa dwelt on their planet, a world far away from this place."

A form began to materialize. Janeway knew it was a copy of the holographic Sentinal from the colony ship Chakotay and Nata had explored on Veruna Four. The figure had a combination of both races in its features, though it was much taller than even Garai and had a more reptilian cast to its visage. A ridge of spiny horns crowded atop its head and ran partway down its back. It was obvious to Janeway that this was the common ancestor.

"But all things must end, and so too did the world

of the K'shikkaa," Chakotay continued. A sphere manifested about four feet above Nata's head. A few feet away glowed a large red star. As the attention of the spectators was drawn to the star and planet, the life-sized image of the K'shikkaa faded away.

"The K'shikkaa knew that their sun would soon die. They set about preparing for the eventuality. In their wisdom, they sent colony ships to every habitable planet they could reach." The "planet" launched ships, and as they moved past the viewers, Janeway heard both Nata and Empress Riva gasp in recognition.

"The First Place!" exclaimed Nata.

At the same moment, Riva whispered, "The Great Palace!"

Janeway had seen both the "soul" of the Verunans and the palace that served as the seat of government on Akeras. Both were colony ships of the K'shikkaa.

"One ship landed on Veruna Four, the primary colony. Veruna Four was rich, bountiful—a paradise for the K'shikkaa. Over time, the stories, which had been kept alive through a strong oral tradition, became regarded as myth, not factual history. The Verunans, content and nourished by the planet, moved out from the colony ship, forgetting from whence they had come.

"A second ship was sent to Akeras, which was not so hospitable, but which supported life. They, too, forgot their origins with the passage of time. And it is possible, though we cannot confirm this, that a third colony ship went through this portal."

A wormhole, a pulsing, shimmering corridor, appeared between the planet and the sun. "Nata, Riva, you may have cousins in a part of the universe you have never even heard of." Stepping back, Chakotay nodded his dark head, indicating that Janeway should continue.

"With their people safe," began the captain, "the K'shikkaa waited for the end. And it came."

The sun swelled further, pulsed, and then went nova with a powerful explosion that dazzled the eyes of the attentive assembly. Janeway didn't need to narrate; the drama played itself out. As the sun went nova, the force of the explosion slammed into the entrance of the wormhole. The corridor in space sucked in the explosion. It was a bizarre spectacle, and Janeway, her great passion for science stirring, wished that they could have witnessed this event and not just recreated it. She knew that it was probably unique. The universe would, in all likelihood, never see anything like this again.

Janeway began speaking again, suiting word to action.

"The wormhole engulfed the explosion and was distorted, expanded, by the force. It reached out to swallow part of the galaxy at its far end, and one of the things it devoured was an innocent planet."

She fell silent, watching as the holodeck enacted the scene. This hapless planet would be called Blessing by the Akerians. What happened, though, was no blessing to the inhabitants. Janeway couldn't imagine this part of it; the terror as suddenly, with no warning at all, the populace of the planet was swallowed by a mutating wormhole and instantly obliterated.

"The far end of the wormhole collapsed. It became a pocket in space, with the planet the Akerians called Blessing enclosed within it. The centuries crawled by, and the concavity began to stabilize and finally began shrinking. Had this procedure been permitted to continue, Blessing would have been crushed by the immense gravitational torrent, and its remains ejected in a nebular cloud. The normal fabric of space would have been restored. But it was not permitted to continue."

Chakotay again began to speak. "The Akerians," he said, and another planet in another corner of the room came to life, "had developed early sublight-speed by this point. Because of the harsh nature of Akeras, it was vital that they expand their empire. They had begun to investigate this sector, and they discovered the concavity."

A ship launched from the miniature Akeras found its way to the concavity. It was far simpler and more primitive than the present Akerian vessels; much of their technology, she knew now, would come from what they discovered within the concavity.

"At some point, the Akerians took a courageous step. They ventured into the concavity, unaware of what might lie inside. That bravery was rewarded. They discovered the ruins of that long-dead civilization inside and called it Blessing. And so it was. The Akerians learned from that lost civilization, developed new technologies such as the gravity wave and faster-than-light travel. Blessing became the heart of their empire."

Chakotay's voice grew harder as he continued.

"But they also discovered the Verunans—gentle, peaceful, physically strong, but their weapons long since disregarded. Blessing made the Akerians arrogant. They had a long history of taking what they wished, and so they took the Verunans."

Garai had the grace to look ashamed. The young empress looked as though she might cry. Janeway felt sorry for her. All this was news to the child. All her life, she had believed in the glory of the empire and its willing, happy subjects. She did not know that the "glory" had come from exploiting innocents.

It was again Janeway's turn to continue the narrative. "But about three hundred years ago, the Akerians discovered that the pocket in space that housed Blessing was shrinking at an accelerated rate. They had used the Verunan people for their purposes up to now. Now, they used the Verunan sun."

The next scene that played itself out was a three-dimensional recreation of the incident that Harry Kim had shown her and Tuvok earlier. Once again, the propaganda was trumpeted, and the Akerian ships, linking their generators, siphoned the hydrogen of the Verunan sun into the gaping maw of the concavity.

"It worked, all right," said Janeway. "The concavity stopped shrinking. But the cost was deadly."

"It became Sun-Eater," said *Viha* Nata, pain making her voice catch. "Now we know. Now we know that the Akerians deliberately murdered our sun for their own purposes!"

Even in the dim lighting, Janeway saw the

empress's eyes flash angrily. She forestalled the angry retort. "This is the past," Janeway reminded them both sternly. "It cannot be changed. Only the future can be, and if you wish to change it for the better, you must listen and learn—and forgive, both one another and yourselves. Commander?"

"This is where the past merges with the present," continued her first officer. "The Verunans rediscovered their past, learned from it, resolved to fight. You all know what happened from this point. But Captain Janeway is right. You, *Viha* Nata, are one of the leaders of your people. Empress Riva, the populations of whole planets listen when you speak. Sun-Eater is no more, Nata; but Empress, neither is Blessing.

"But both of you and your people *are* left," he emphasized. Janeway watched him, watched how the K'shikkaan descendants all responded to him. He knew how to speak to them.

"Nata, the colony ship *Soul* is ready to be reactivated. Riva, you have the technologies to help the Verunans in their quest for a new home. The death of the Verunan sun is still inevitable, but the death of Veruna Four has been postponed a full century. You come from the same race. You were never, ever, meant to be enemies, but allies—even sisters."

The two leaders, old and young, looked at one another uncomfortably. "But . . . it is difficult, letting go of hate," admitted Nata.

Riva hesitated, then offered quietly, "It is more difficult to ask for forgiveness."

Those words hit Janeway almost like a physical blow. Hope made her eyes sting. They were wise, both of these leaders. And that might mean their people—all of them—would survive.

"We, myself and my crew, are members of the United Federation of Planets," said Janeway. "Many worlds, many peoples, gather together. We have difficulties. Some of us," and here she glanced slyly over at Chakotay, who smiled slightly, "were even on opposite sides for a time. And take it from me, you don't know what difficult is until you've tried to get multiple races, with no common background save a history of fighting one another, to sit down and hammer out a peace, much less work together side by side."

"But it can be done," said Chakotay, moving to step closer to Janeway. "We're one crew now. And we've faced a lot of difficulties. You at least have the benefit of being of the same race with the same heritage."

"I am," said Nata, "reminded of the tale of the starving man. He wanders from house to house, begging for food."

"And only the poorest man fed him, giving him the last *yisski* fruit he had," chimed in Riva—the keeper of the Word, Janeway recalled, feeling goose-flesh rise on her skin beneath her uniform. "But from the seeds that remained after the two had shared the fruit, a glorious orchard grew that fed the whole city."

They stared at one another, surprise and pleasure on their oh-so-similar reptilian features. Janeway and Chakotay shared a glance of their own. She was no Betazoid, but Janeway figured she didn't have to be able to read minds to know what was going on between the two leaders. She caught Garai's gaze, and the big warrior, calm finally sitting on his anguished spirit, nodded and smiled.

They were back on course to the Alpha Quadrant. Janeway had permitted herself a cup of hot herbal tea from her rations. It sat, untouched and steaming, as Janeway stared out her large viewing window into space as the stars streaked by.

The door buzzed. Janeway was mildly surprised. It was late; she'd allegedly retired to bed over two hours ago. Wrapping herself in a robe, she called, "Come."

Chakotay entered. "I hope I'm not disturbing you," he apologized.

"Of course you're not," she teased gently. "You know me well enough to know I'm a night owl." She indicated a chair, and he took it.

"I wasn't able to sleep myself," he admitted. "It was quite the encounter, wasn't it?"

She nodded, brushing her hair back from her neck. "That it was indeed. I think," she added softly, "especially for you."

His dark eyes held hers, then he nodded. "I understand them. They might almost have come from the same traditions as myself."

"They're a touch furrier than your people, though," she joked.

He grinned, the expression lighting his handsome face. Then the smile faded a little. "But they've been through almost as much. Both Akerians and

Verunans. I'm amazed that they seemed to be so willing to work together, to cooperate."

"We did," Janeway pointed out.

"Ah, but we had to."

"So do they."

"Not really. In one sense, yes, in another . . . They could have gone their separate ways. It would not have been the best answer, but they could have. But I think that Nata and Riva recognized something of themselves in each other. And that . . . well, I didn't even dare hope for that."

"Chakotay . . ." Janeway stared down at her hands, then continued. "Do you . . . blame us still? Blame me?"

"For what?" He seemed honestly confused.

"For making peace with the Cardassians. For, even farther back, taking your land away from you on old Earth. We'd have been enemies back then, you know."

He thought a moment, then shook his dark head. "No. That's ancient history. Even the Maquis part of it. Someday, it might be important again, but here, now . . . Things unfold the way they do, that's all. It's the present and the future that matters. Now we're friends, not enemies. And I hope," he added, gazing at her intently, "that whatever comes, Captain, you and I will be friends."

She thought of all she'd learned from the rock-steady Indian in the time they'd been together on this strange, unplanned journey in the Delta Quadrant. She remembered how she'd always trusted him and how he'd never let her down. She thought of the beautiful world of the animal guides he'd introduced her to, the new way of thinking he'd taught her. Without him, she could have taken some serious, dangerous missteps in handling the Verunans. Instead, Chakotay had subtly shown her how to deal with this strange, wonderful new race in a manner both respectful and effective. If Tuvok was in truth her oldest friend on the *Voyager*, Chakotay was her newest oldest friend, for it felt like she'd known him all her life.

"Yes, Chakotay," she promised him. "I don't see how we could be anything but friends. Even," she added intently, "if we should be enemies."

He studied her for a long moment, his eyes searching, seeking out the words she did not say. At last he nodded. He understood.

Rising, he said, "Well, I'd better let you get back to your insomnia. You shouldn't be drinking a stimulant this late at night, you know."

"Mother hen," she chided. "It's herbal tea. No caffeine."

He nodded his approval. "Ah, that's all right then. Good night, Captain."

"Good night, Commander."

The door hissed closed behind him. Janeway returned her attention to the stars, but she also took a sip of the hot rosehip tea. The conversation had comforted her somehow, helped her sort out her own thoughts. She sat a few moments longer, downing the beverage, then instructed the computer to dim the lights. As she slipped between the cool sheets, she felt a warm drowsiness steal over her. She had done the right thing, had helped build a bridge between two peoples who ought never have been so divided. She could sleep.

In a few moments, the captain of the *Starship Voyager* was sound asleep. And elsewhere on the ship, alone with his dreams, her first officer raced with a laughing-eyed animal spirit in a landscape that never was.

Christie Golden spent her math classes in high school writing Star Trek scripts, so she is delighted, fifteen years later, to be an official part of the Star Trek universe.

Golden has been all over the map in her writing. She's written gothic horror/fantasy (*Vampire of the Mists, Dance of the Dead* and *The Enemy Within*), several short stories, and an epic fantasy novel, *Instrument of Fate,* due out in April from Ace Books. *The Murdered Sun* is her first foray into science fiction, and she has found that she likes it.

She lives in Colorado with her husband, Michael, and two cats.